THIS SALTED SOIL

The Battle for Tunisia, 1942-1943

Jamie Kirkpatrick

A PEACE CORPS WRITERS BOOK
2023
OAKLAND, CALIFORNIA

For all those who served in Tunisia. *Yahia*!

"Imagine a Carthage sown with salt, and all the sowers gone, and the seeds lain however long in the earth, till there rose finally in vegetable profusion leaves and trees of rime and brine. What flowering would there be in such a garden?"

Marilynne Robinson, <u>Housekeeping</u>

"You are the salt of the earth; but if the salt loses its flavor, how shall it be seasoned? It is then good for nothing but to be thrown out and trampled underfoot by men. "

Matthew 5:13

OPERATION TORCH

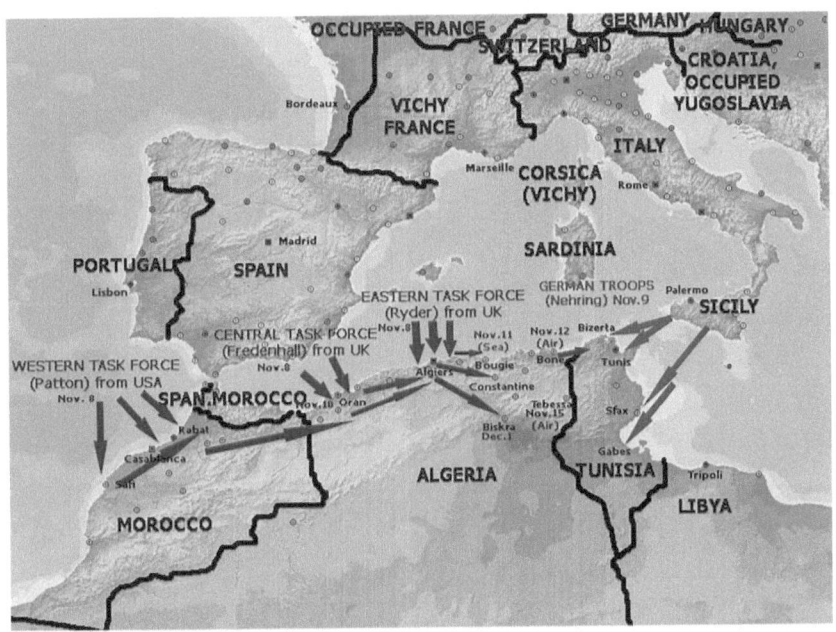

THE RACE FOR TUNIS

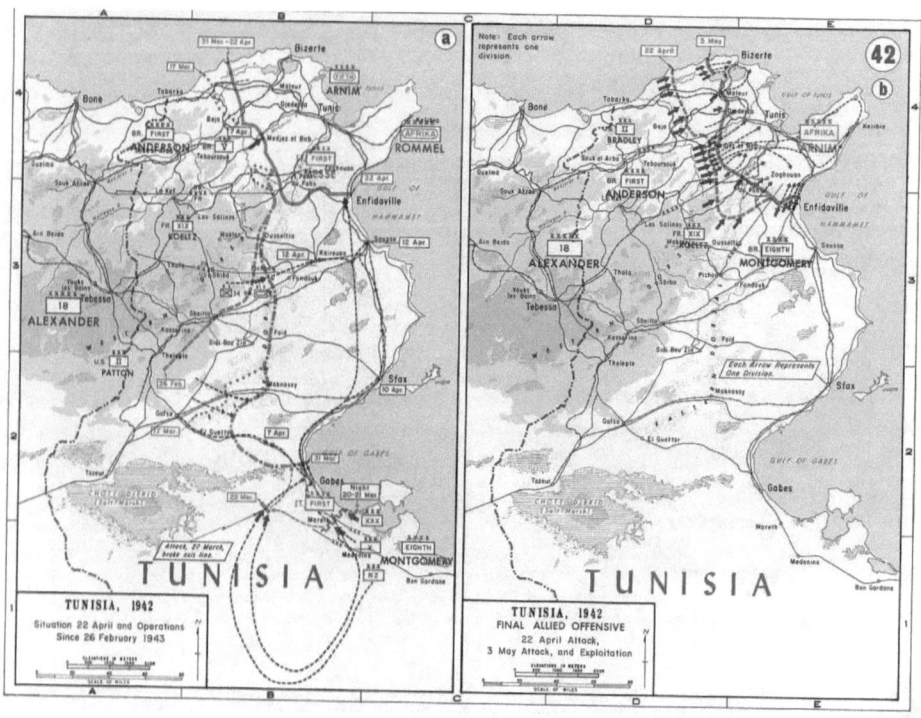

A NOTE TO READERS:

I arrived in Tunisia in September, 1970, one of a group of about twenty-five Peace Corps Volunteers newly assigned to that country. Our group had already been in training for six weeks: we were given daily doses of language training in French and Arabic along with what Peace Corps liked to call 'cross-cultural' lessons. Now we would begin six more weeks of intensive 'in-country' language training before being assigned to our posts where, for the next two years, the females among us would be training their Tunisian counterparts who were preschool and kindergarten teachers, and the males would be serving as physical education teachers and coaches helping Tunisia prepare for the 1972 Olympic Games—the ill-fated Munich Games.

That first morning, I rose early and walked out onto a small balcony at the dormitory where we were housed. At that moment, the balcony shook and I looked out on a gently roiling world. It was a small earthquake, probably one that hardly registered on the Richter Scale, but it certainly caught my attention. My Tunisian journey had begun.

Near the end of the in-country portion of our training program, we all boarded a bus for a week-long tour of the country's southern region which borders the Sahara Desert. Tunisia is a lemon wedge of a country lodged, for better or for worse, between two giant neighbors—Algeria and Libya—and looks somewhat like a larger version of New Jersey; it's only about 63,000 square miles, smaller than New England, so it's possible to visit much of the country in a relatively short period of time. Near of the end of our tour, our bus headed back to Tunis, Tunisia's capital, through a region of the country where narrow roads wound among and through small towns nestled in the narrow passes at the eastern end of the Atlas Mountains. At one point, we stopped for fuel in a small town named Kasserine. I looked out the bus window and knew in a flash this was where I wanted to live. I told that to one of the officials assigned to our group who looked at me as though I had gone insane.

"But we are going to assign you to Sousse!" he said. Sousse is a large and very tourist-centric city on Tunisia's Mediterranean coast, by any measure a "plum" assignment. But I wasn't looking for plums; I wanted a more authentic Arab experience. I held my ground and by the time the bus reached Tunis four hours later, I had been reassigned to Kasserine where I would live and work for the next two years.

At the time, I was completely unaware of the role Tunisia had played in World War II and totally ignorant of what had occurred at the Kasserine Pass. It didn't take long to learn. It was not uncommon to encounter American or British veterans of the North African campaign, particularly ones who had survived the battle of Kasserine Pass, who had returned to revisit that haunted place. Moreover, my own landlord in town had been a small boy in 1943 and had been one of the urchins who had flitted through the German and Allied lines, trading eggs for chocolate or cigarettes. His limited English was constructed mainly on curses directed at him by Allied soldiers.

What follows is not military history. If you are inclined to that type of literature, there are many excellent sources available. In writing this book, I drew heavily on several fine volumes including Rick Atkinson's *Army at Dawn*, Charles Whiting's *First Blood*, William Breuer's *Operation Torch*, and Orr Kelly's *Meeting the Fox*. All are worth your time and attention. I also availed myself of the copious resources available on the Internet, but wherever possible, I attempted to verify source information. Still, this is a work of fiction, one that uses the backdrop of the war in North Africa to tell a more human story centered around a place and people I have come to admire and love.

One final note: I believe language is a gateway to culture and so, throughout these pages, I have incorporated words and phrases transliterated from dialectic Arabic to give the story a bit more authentic Tunisian flavor. Like English, Arabic comes in many forms. Classical Arabic, the language of the Quran, is equivalent to the language of the King James Bible or to the Middle English used by Chaucer in

The Canterbury Tales. Modern Standard Arabic might be most likened to the English one would hear on the BBC, formal and precise, but not the language most people speak on the street. Dialectic Arabic varies from country-to-country and its Tunisian forms are what I have attempted to render here. Its specialized vocabulary, syntax, and even use of slang are peculiar to Tunisia, and rather than render it in more formalized transliterate ways, I've used my own aural method: I've chosen to spell Arabic words as they might most logically sound in English. Experts in Phonology will cringe, but if I were to use more commonly recognized means of transliteration, what is already difficult to pronounce would become impossible for the reader to "hear."

I spent two years in Kasserine, then two more years in Tunis working on the Peace Corps staff. But all that was a long time ago. Many changes have occurred, most notably, the drama of what has come to be known as the 'Arab Spring.' The spark of that political revolution that has gripped the Arab world since December 2010 was figuratively and literally lit when Mohammed Bouazizi, a street vendor in a small Tunisian village not far from Kasserine, set himself on fire to protest the seizure of his vegetable cart by local police because he had failed to obtain a government permit. The final chapters of that critically important story about human dignity and the plight of the dispossessed are still unwritten.

JWK

PRELUDE

Gide

1 November, 1942; Sidi Bou Said, Tunisia. It is All Soul's Day; the Day of the Dead. The old man leans back on a bench in a corner of the *Café des Nattes*, wrapped in a burnished russet burnoose, sipping a glass of mint tea. He can still hear the rain. The afternoon light is growing thin and smoke from a few argilah pipes gives the dim interior of the café a dusty air of forgetfulness. André Gide is balding, with thick glasses; he exudes an air of faint disdain, and therefore no one bothers or even pays any attention to him. He is not recognized here except perhaps by a few French ex-patriots who are riding out the war in Europe by teaching at the University of Tunis or at the elite Lycée Carnot. They will begrudge him his Nobel Prize five years hence and condemn the Roman Catholic Church for banning his books four years later when the tide has turned again. But all that is to come. Now he is here in Tunisia for one thing and one thing only: escape. And maybe anonymity. At seventy-two years of age, he needs no more adulation or even recognition. Maybe he craved it once but no longer. He wants nothing more than a few last moments of peace and quiet and maybe just a soupçon of intellectual honesty. He would be perfectly happy if the world would just go away and fuck itself, but, alas, it won't and probably never will.

Gide drains his tea, swallowing the pine nuts at the bottom of the glass. The waiter brings him another glass on a silver tray, but Gide politely waves him off. He'll go home to his manuscript and a glass of decent red wine. The rain is stopping now; the setting sun is slipping below a layer of cumulus clouds, casting golden light on the whitewashed walls of the village and illuminating the twin peaks of *Bou Cornine*—the Father of the Devil—on the far-off eastern shore of the Bay of Tunis. As Gide descends the steep stairs that lead to the cobbled street below, he passes a young couple, a sight not often seen in such a male-dominated environment. They are in their early twenties by his estimation. She is exquisite, she is Botticelli's Venus: a cascade of thick amber curls, green eyes, the complexion of warm *café au lait*, the perfect combination of not just two people but two distinct races. The man on the other hand—more of a boy, really—has all the attributes of a Parisian boulevardier: thin hips, lank black hair (unwashed and uncombed), a sallow complexion surrounding compressed lips and a sharp nose. He is wearing artificially casual clothes and an over-abundance of arrogance. He seems out of place with her but she doesn't seem to care. Perhaps she is too young or too shy to appreciate her glory, how transient it is. He appears content to bathe in her light, or perhaps he merely assumes it compliments his own.

The little village seems far too quiet, too empty. On his way down the steep steps, Gide meets the girl's eyes, nods politely. She smiles. He stops for a moment to admire a blood-red bougainvillea that trails along the wall of one of the shuttered houses on the opposite side of the street. It is lovely to observe but its thorns are dangerous to the touch. The young man and woman continue making their way up the steps to the café. Inside, she will be the only woman among all the men but she understands the culture; she is instinctively modest. At the arched doorway, she pauses to pull a scarf over her hair and keeps her eyes down and her voice quiet; her companion snaps his fingers to summon the waiter.

CHAPTER ONE

Ike

2 November, 1942; London. By the time America woke up on that Sunday morning the previous December, Europe had already been at war for more than two years. Poland and Czechoslovakia were gone; England might well be next. A million men were already dead in Russia. The Third Reich was poised to rule the continent for the next thousand years.

America was in danger of losing the war in the Pacific. In Europe, the Americans were full of ideas but not much else. For the past few months, *a* relatively unknown but highly respected staff officer named Dwight David Eisenhower had occupied offices at 20 Grosvenor Square, not far from the American Embassy. "Ike" was from Kansas, wide, flat, see-to-the-horizon Kansas. Thin, plain-spoken, and ramrod straight, he was in London because President Roosevelt and his Chief of Staff, General George C. Marshall, had plucked him from a desk job in the Pentagon and charged him with the task of turning the war around in Europe. Of beating Hitler.

Whole sections of London had been flattened by German bombs. The last-minute evacuation at Dunkirk barely saved a badly wounded army. Thanks to Prime Minister Winston Churchill, the British people were enduring valiantly, but the situation was grim. German armies occupied France and most of Europe; they were massed thirty miles away across the English Channel patiently awaiting an opportune moment to exploit their advantage and move in for the kill. The Russians were also reeling, desperate to stop the Nazi's massive assault on Stalingrad.

The Allies needed a victory badly; they could not afford to lose another battle.

At West Point, Ike had excelled at boxing and he understood what it meant to punch and counterpunch. He also understood winning and losing. War was like boxing in that coming in second equalled losing.

Upon graduating from the Academy in 1915, Ike sought to go to the Philippines but his request for assignment was denied. When World War I broke out, he again requested an overseas assignment and again was denied. He spent the first years of the Great War at Fort Leavenworth in Kansas and Fort Meade in Maryland. He eventually commanded a unit that trained tank crews for combat but he never left Camp Colt in Pennsylvania. He finally received orders to go to France but a week later, the armistice was signed and he never left the United States. Now, another war later, Ike was in London, Supreme Commander of the Allied Expeditionary Forces in Europe. He had never lead troops into battle, never even been fired on. He was a good student of war but he had never fought in one. His baptism would come soon enough.

Joseph Stalin, leader of the Communist Party and Premier of the Soviet Union, was pleading with his British counterpart, Winston Churchill, to open a second front. The two men detested each other as much as they needed each other in the battle against Hitler. According to Stalin, without an active second front, the Soviet Union would fall. When that happened, Hitler would be able to concentrate his forces along the Western Front and the invasion of England would be just a matter of time. The war would, for all intents and purposes, be over.

The Americans had yet to fight a single battle in Europe. Some in the chain of command were arguing for a cross-Channel invasion of France but the British thought that would be suicide. Much as that might please Stalin, Churchill knew his American allies weren't yet ready for slaughter. There would have to be another option.

The war in the North African desert had been going on for more than two years. The British Eighth Army had bent at El Alamein but German Field Marshall Erwin Rommel and his *Afrika Korps* had not been able to break it. By the summer of 1942, British forces under Lieutenant General Bernard Montgomery had begun to make headway against the Desert Fox, clawing their way westward away from Suez,

Britain's lifeline to its empire in India. It was a seesaw battle: ground gained, ground lost, ground regained, but by early summer, Rommel was beginning to run short of fuel and supplies. He begged Hitler for supplies and reinforcements, but the Führer needed all available men, fuel, and supplies to finish off the Russians. Rommel would have to stand and fight. Ike sensed an opportunity.

French Northwest Africa—Morocco, Algeria, and Tunisia—was guarded by 125,000 Vichy French troops, nominally allied with Germany but of questionable loyalty. Ike and his staff wondered that if the Allies could manage to neutralize or win over the Vichy French and invade Northwest Africa, maybe they could then move eastward unopposed and trap Rommel and his beleaguered army in Tunisia. That might eventually make it possible to invade Europe from the south. Operation Torch was born.

Ike didn't want to have to fight the Vichy French with one hand and the Germans with the other. If a plan as audacious as Operation Torch—America's first hostile intervention in the European Theater of war—were to succeed, it might well depend on what the French decided to do. It was a gamble Eisenhower and the Allied forces would have to take.

Months of planning for an invasion of North Africa had nearly exhausted Eisenhower and his staff; they had been working twenty-hour days for months. The plan called for an amphibious landing of more than 107,000 raw American troops sailing into battle on 500 transport vessels protected by 350 warships. It was a monumental undertaking and it all had to be done in utmost secrecy. Every last detail of the invasion was painstakingly considered, right down to the number of vehicles, ammunition, fuel supplies, food, and even toilet tissue that would have to be offloaded once the troops were onto African soil. American forces had never undertaken an operation of this scale and to make matters worse, their British allies were not convinced the Johnny-come-lately Yanks could pull it off. True: British forces were finally making headway against Rommel in the Libyan desert but the ultimate success of the entire North African campaign depended on trapping and killing the Germany army in Tunisia. Unless the Americans could successfully land troops in Morocco and Algeria and advance eastward to confront the German army, the costly war in the desert would be in vain. Maybe the war, too.

As meticulous as the planning of Operation Torch had to be, so, too, was the secrecy surrounding it. Intelligence was of paramount importance to both the Allies and Axis war efforts and therefore, so was disinformation—anything to put Hitler and his general staff off the scent of an invasion of North Africa. One of Ike's staff officers went so far as to leave a winter parka and a pair of snow boots in a visible spot in his office so some nosy reporter would print that something was about to happen in Norway. And an OSS agent named Murphy stationed at the American Consulate in Casablanca advanced his career one night by pretending to get drunk at a hotel bar and spouting off about an imminent American invasion aimed at Dakar in Senegal in West Africa, thousands of miles away from the actual landing target.

Operational plans changed day-by-day, hour-by-hour. By late September, only weeks before the planned D-Day of November 8, everything was still in flux. In theory, Operation Torch called for three great task forces of more than 30,000 men each: the Western task Force would sail—in secret!—from the naval base at Hampton Roads in Virginia, cross the Atlantic undetected by German U-boats, and land on three different beaches near Casablanca in Morocco. It would be under the command of General George Patton, one of America's most colorful commanding officers and a pal of Eisenhower's from West Point days. The assault force, the Central Task Force, would be under the command of Major General Lloyd Fredendall; it would depart from England and sail southward along the coasts of Spain and Portugal before turning east through the Straits of Gibraltar to come ashore near Oran in Algeria. The Eastern Task Force, commanded by Lieutenant General Charles Ryder, would land near Algiers and immediately turn eastward on a run to capture Tunis, more than 500 miles away.

These amphibious landings would not be the only first engagements for American forces in the European theater. The beach landings were to be supported by a massive airborne assault behind enemy lines, the first time American soldiers would be parachuted into battle.

Like most plans, this one, as comprehensive and detailed as it was, was not without risks. Would an armada of Allied ships sailing past Spain draw Franco into the war on Germany's side in order to seize Gibraltar? What would the Vichy French troops in North Africa do? Would they resist the invasion or cooperate with the Allied forces? Perhaps most importantly was the question of American readiness. This was a massive undertaking and Eisenhower—and Roosevelt and Churchill, too—prayed their forces would be up to the challenge. Roosevelt, in fact, did more than just pray. When General George Marshall and a few other senior officers advised against Operation Torch, Roosevelt gave a direct order to support it as soon as possible. It was only one of two direct Presidential orders ever given in World War II.

Still, Eisenhower had serious doubts about Torch. Training exercises under controlled conditions on the Maryland shore of the Chesapeake Bay and in Scottish lochs had been disastrous. What would happen when the untested American troops came under live fire or met fierce resistance from a battle-hardened army under the command of a general as talented as Erwin Rommel? These were questions without precise answers and they kept Ike and his staff working and worrying late into the night.

But of all the unknowns affecting Operation Torch, probably the greatest was the disposition of the Vichy French forces in North Africa. Ike went to great lengths to enlist their support or at least ensure their neutrality. In late August, two months before the operation would begin, he dispatched his trusted chief of staff, General Mark Clark, on a secret mission. Clark flew to Gibraltar, then boarded a submarine for the trip across the Mediterranean. His objective was to rendezvous with General Charles Emmanuel Mast, the Commander-in-Chief of Vichy Forces in Algiers and win him over to the Allied cause. Everything went smoothly enough until the police unexpectedly arrived at the meeting place; Clark barely escaped, losing his pants in the process.

There were bitter dregs in the French cup. Fifteen months earlier, British warships, Task Force H, had shelled and sunk a French fleet riding at anchor at Mers el-Kébir in Algeria to keep it from falling into German hands; more than 1,200 French sailors had been killed. It was a chasmic breach of trust between the two former allies. To make Vichy cooperation with the Allies more palatable, Ike decided the operation would be portrayed as an entirely American one. It was not. Some of the British warships participating in Torch would fly American flags.

Churchill even considered having the British troops wear American uniforms so that the Vichy French who distrusted the British would be more inclined to come over to the Allied cause. The idea was eventually scrapped but worry over Vichy intentions kept Ike and his generals worried and sleepless.

As D-Day neared, Operation Torch had a momentum all its own. Ike knew most of that was political. With the war in the Pacific not going well and Hitler in control of almost all of Western Europe and well on his way to Moscow, the Allies desperately needed to land a counterpunch. Even though Torch posed all manner of military complications, in the end, it would be the civilian politicians and their considerations that drove the effort—for better or for worse.

CHAPTER TWO

Declan and Punch

3 *November, 1942; Tunis.* Most Europeans wouldn't think of living in the Tunis *medina*, the traditional Arab quarter of the city, but Declan Shaw wouldn't have it any other way. Built around the ancient Zitouna mosque, it was more than a thousand years old—a thousand years of human habitation, commerce, and history crammed into a medieval warren of winding streets and shops. Declan loved the medina—it was a haphazard place with no apparent plan to it, just neighborhoods and souks; chaos, noise, smells, and color. Exciting by day but peaceful at night when the shops were all closed and shuttered and the narrow winding streets lay deserted and silent. Tonight, the only sound Declan could hear was the fading clip-clop of a donkey carrying an old man up the steep hill behind the jewelers souk.

"Declan, darling, come back to bed. I'm cold."

"In a minute."

"What are you doing?"

"Just finishing up this story. I have to file it first thing in the morning. Won't take long." But these things always took longer than expected and by the time Declan returned to the bedroom, his "*petite amie*" was already asleep, snoring faintly.

She was still snoring—a little less faintly—when Declan popped one eye open to look at his watch the next morning. Shit; already a little after seven. He thought briefly about rolling his naked friend over to see if her peaches were as ripe as he remembered from the night before but he knew all-too-well where that would lead and he couldn't afford

7

another bureau chief tirade about deadline delinquency. So he slipped out of bed, lit the kerosene space heater and a cigarette, dressed quietly, grabbed his worn leather postman's bag, the one he used as a briefcase, and headed downstairs.

The street was already wide awake; how could it not be with all the noise of another new opportunity to make a little *flous?* Metal doors screeched up, all the merchants hawking and spitting, the coffee sellers—the *kahawajis*—extolling the virtues of their particular brews. Declan liked his thick, medium-sweet, and flavored with cardamom. He gave the first coffee-seller he saw five millimes and drank the little glass down to the dregs in three quick sips. A donkey nudged past him— maybe the one from last night—but loaded this morning with tin pots and pans. It was being led by a boy of no more than ten, heading down the narrow street toward the *Bab el Bahar*, the Sea Gate, that was the line of demarcation between the original fortified Arab town and the new French city that had grown up around it with its wide central boulevard lined with plane trees and outdoor cafés.

By the time he reached the Guardian office on the second floor of a nondescript building on the Rue d'Espagne, Declan was already on sensory overload. He handed his story to a copy editor and made for the office of the bureau chief. It was already filled with smoke from one of Punch's pungent Gauloises. "Anything out of Chartwell yet?"

"Not Chartwell, you bloody Papist; it's bloody Chequers these days. All quiet on that sodden front," Punch said without looking up. "Maybe we'll hear from the great man after his poached eggs and second breakfast whisky."

"Where's the Desert Fox today?"

"You're the journalist—in theory anyway—you tell me."

"Don't know why, but I have a funny feeling we're about to get pinched like a Mayfair girl's bottom. There was an odd report on the wire yesterday about a huge flotilla of ships heading into the Mediterranean probably to resupply Monty or maybe relieve Malta. I just hope they're not heading this way. Tunisia is perfect battle terrain."

"Flotilla? Was that the word?" Punch arched his black, bushy eyebrows. He was a florid, ham-fisted man from Dundee. Rumor had it he had been the boxing champion of the first battalion of The Queen's

8

Own Cameron Highlanders. Also, he had fought in—and somehow survived—the Battle of the Somme. No one knew if he had earned his name through his pugilistic exploits or by being the most demanding editor on the Guardian's staff, but everyone knew he did not suffer fools lightly.

"I know. Personally, I would have used 'convoy' or maybe 'armada' for emphasis.' Do you think it might be a code word?" Not for the first time, Declan wondered if Punch might be a watcher.

Punch shrugged. "Flags?"

"Didn't say. Must be British though."

Another shrug. "And nothing about a destination?"

"Nope. Too big for Gibraltar and apparently not turning to the northeast. Malta's certainly a possibility. I hear the situation is pretty bad there. Nothing to eat. But it sounds like a bloody lot of ships for tuck. Didn't go all that well before, did it? I'm betting it's supplies for Monty, maybe some reinforcements, too. Finish off Rommel."

Punch finally looked up at Declan. "Why don't you find out? I'd hate to get caught again with my Irish breeks down around my ankles like some poor bloke I know who doesn't seem to have much respect for proper British decorum. Here's *another* (Punch emphasized the word) chance to redeem yourself. Go over to *Cap Bon*, see what you can see."

Cap Bon was the thumb-like peninsula that formed the eastern side of the Bay of Tunis. Declan liked it over there; very peaceful. He had gone spear fishing there last summer. Got a tuna and an octopus. The headland jutted out into the Mediterranean ; it was only about 300 miles across to Sicily. If the ships—the flotilla—were indeed heading for Malta or into the eastern Med, he might be able to see something.

Declan stared at Punch and Punch stared back. Declan had played this game before and knew he would lose. So did Punch. Declan turned and headed back down to the street. Another tactical retreat. It was getting to be a bad habit.

Back outside, Declan briefly considered swimming upstream to see if his friend was still asleep at his flat, snoring—faintly or otherwise—but thought better of it; she had plenty of other "friends" to visit. He opted instead for a table at a nearby café which served generous cups of *café au lait* and delicious almond croissants. He needed time to think.

Declan did not want to get caught in another (his own emphasis this time) war zone. The first time was in Madrid in 1938, on his first assignment covering the Spanish Civil War for the Guardian. He hated the loneliness of fear, the taste it left in his mouth. The second time he was in a war zone, he was assigned to cover the Italian invasion of Egypt and Libya in 1940. At first, it was hard to take the Italians seriously but he learned quickly that death is death; it doesn't discriminate on the basis of uniform. At a small engagement near Neuzet Ghirba, it became readily apparent, at least to Declan, that the battle for North Africa would be fought by men in tanks, and tanks were nothing more than lumbering steel death traps. The first time he saw the burned-out shell of a tank and the charred bodies inside, his stomach turned over. The other journalists with him understood and gave him room to vomit, then a canteen of water to rinse his mouth.

By now, he knew what to look for, the signs of war. The first was denial, soon followed by grim resignation. Terror came in the third wave, beating against all sanity, eroding everything in its way. For some reason, Declan figured he was somewhere between stage one and stage two this morning; he would do anything to avoid being caught up in stage three another (no emphasis necessary, none whatsoever) time.

But he liked Cap Bon. He'd drive over tomorrow, maybe even take his 'friend' with him.

CHAPTER THREE

Ali

4 *November, 1942; Tunis Medina.* Unlike many of his friends at the University of Tunis, Ali Abbas was not *Tunisois*, someone from one of the city's wealthy and well-connected families. His family was from Kairouan, two hundred kilometers south of the capital and the fourth holiest city of the Muslim world after Mecca, Medina, and Jerusalem. Also, unlike many of his fellow students, Ali preferred to speak Arabic rather than French. He knew too many Tunisians who thought themselves more French than the French and who preferred to speak impeccable French with a Parisian accent rather than lower themselves to speak Arabic. French implied status; Arabic was for the lower classes or the uneducated.

There was one other distinction between Ali and his schoolmates. Whenever they had a free moment, most of them would head off to a favorite café to drink coffee or smoke a cigarette. Ali preferred the tranquility of a small neighborhood mosque adjacent to campus. He was observant, even devout. He said his prayers five times a day, eschewed alcohol, gave what he could to the poor, and had just finished his Ramadan fast. Some day, *Inshallah*—God willing—he would make the Hajj, his pilgrimage to Mecca.

In the cool quiet of the mosque, Ali was always content to sit on the floor leaning against the wall, a string of glass prayer beads running silently through his fingers, reading a school book or sometimes the Holy Quran. He found peace within its pages. He was a tolerant believer—he knew several Christians, even a few Jews; after all, they, too, were monotheistic, they shared a common Patriarch, Sidi Ibrahim, and called themselves People of the Book. But Islam was Ali's guide, his pathway through the complexities of life and as the word itself meant, he submitted willingly to it.

If there were a political edge to Ali's belief, it was only that someday Tunisia would be free of French rule. Ever since France made Tunisia a Protectorate in 1881, there had been a slow but steady erosion of Tunisian identity and culture. Something essential, even precious, in the country's soul was slipping away. Now even little children were reading textbooks about their country's history that began with the words "Our Gallic ancestors..." Islam was another part of that disappearing legacy, but Ali believed it would survive; it was too deeply etched into the hearts and minds of most Tunisians. But Islam could never be the instrument of political change. It was inherently too peaceful, too humane, to incite revolution. Allah and his beloved prophet Mohammed—Peace be upon Him!—never intended Islam to be the sword of God.

The neighborhood mosque where Ali idled in his free time was known as *Sidi BouBakr*. It was hardly an ornate place, not much more than a large unfurnished room with whitewashed walls, its quadrants lit by four bare bulbs suspended from the ceiling, bathing everything within in a harsh white light. A ceiling fan rotated slowly overhead even on this cool November day. The floor was covered with a patchwork of worn and mismatched carpets, many nearly threadbare from years of use under the knees and foreheads of worshipers. A few framed pieces of calligraphy, verses from the Quran, hung haphazardly on the walls, along with one faded photograph of the Kaaba, the large, cube-shaped building in the center of the courtyard of the Grand Mosque in Mecca, the *bayt Allah*—the house of God—the holiest of holies. The eastern wall of the mosque—the one that determined the *qiblah,* the direction of prayer—was identified by a large framed copy of the *Shahada*, the creed that lay at the beating heart of Islam. It declared the oneness of God and the acceptance of Mohammed as His prophet: "There is no God but God and Mohammed is his Prophet." That statement alone was sufficient to make anyone who said it, and truly believed it, a Muslim.

Ali had closed his eyes for a moment and when he opened them, he found himself looking up into the face of the old man who often led the *Fard,* one of the five daily prayer services held in the mosque. He was not a cleric—Sunni Islam had no formal priesthood—merely a first among equals. Ali struggled to recall the old man's name; couldn't.

"Forgive me, *ya Sheikh*. I must have been dreaming."

"We are all just dreamers in this world, my son. The real world is the Paradise to come."

"*Inshallah.*"

"Indeed. God is great. I see you here often but always alone. Tell me who you are."

"I'm from Kairouan; I'm a student at the university. Then, to fill a silence, "My family name is Abbas. I am Ali, *ibn* Kareem."

The old man placed his right hand over his heart. "*N'charfu.* I am honored."

"*W'obeek,* The honor is mine."

"What do you read at the university?"

Ali shrugged. "I am studying to be an engineer, but all knowledge is good knowledge, *al'hamdullah.*" Thanks be to God.

The old man—his name came to Ali; he was called Sheik Hassine—sat down next to Ali. "Recite for me, ya wildi, my son."

"*Enna sura, ya sheik*?" Which chapter? There were 114 *suras* in the Holy Quran, each one the precise words of God as revealed to His holy prophet Mohammed, peace be upon Him. Each *sura* contained verses of varying length. Ali knew many by heart; someday he would know them all.

"You choose. They are all the holy word of God."

Ali began to recite *Al-Ma'un,* The Small Kindness. It was not a long *sura*—only 7 verses—but it revealed the meaning of true worship through devotion and service to others. Sheikh Hassine listened intently, eyes closed, his head nodding with the rhythm of the holy language.

Dust motes twirled and danced, suspended in a shaft of pale sunlight from one of the windows set high in the wall above Ali's head. Later, he would recall that brief recitation and that single moment of sublime peace, the one shattered forever when the door from the street banged open and a man Ali had never seen before staggered into the room. He was pale and sweating; a sickly, sweet smell followed him seconds later. His wild eyes searched the room for another exit; seeing none, he stumbled over to the wall opposite Ali and slid to a sitting position. A bright red smear smear marked his slow descent. For a brief moment, he sat there stunned, his eyes locked on Ali, before slowly toppling over onto his side, his life draining away in a ruby-hued pool of blood that seeped into one of the old carpets, staining it forever.

CHAPTER FOUR

La Marsa

4 *November, 1942*. La Marsa was a quiet little seaside village at the end of the standard gauge light rail line that connected Tunis with its port at La Goulette. Beyond the port, a string of small villages dotted the Bay of Tunis a string of pearl beaches gracing the Mediterranean coast. Before arriving at La Marsa, the tram ran past the ruins of ancient Carthage. Long ago, the site had been part of a vast empire, an ancient Phoenician settlement that had risen to rule the Western Mediterranean for more than six hundred years before it was destroyed by Rome in the Second Century, BC. The victorious Roman army sowed salt into the soil surrounding Carthage so it would never dare to threaten the power of Rome again.

More recently, La Marsa had become the summer capital of pre-colonial Tunisia, but now it was the favored location for the villas of the French and the Tunisian elite who administered the Protectorate. It had seaside charm but very little soul. One never heard Arabic spoken in the restaurants or cafés of La Marsa; the village liked to think of itself as Paris-by-the-sea.

Had it been a few degrees warmer perhaps, Leila BenZayed and Paul Fabron might have been sitting outside drinking their *café au laits* in the thin afternoon sun. But a chill wind curled around the beachfront café, and they were more comfortable sitting indoors where they could look out onto the empty wide beach across the little street that qualified as La Marsa's version of an Esplanade.

Naturally, they spoke French. Leila's Tunisian father only spoke French at home and her French mother had never spoken a word of Arabic. Paul's parents were *pieds noirs,* French citizens who had been born in North Africa, Algeria to be exact, but for the past thirty years, they had lived in La Marsa where it was, according to Madame Fabron, *beaucoup plus tranquille.*

Monsieur Fabron, Paul's father, was a vintner; he owned an estate of more than a hundred hectares in the hills just beyond the nearby village of Tebourda. Tunisians, and the Phoenicians and Carthaginians before them, had been making excellent wine for more than two thousand years and despite the arrival of Tunisia's Muslim conquerors in the Seventh Century, wine-making was still a thriving business along the northern coast where the soil and climate were almost identical to the famous wine-producing regions of southern France. Even the French White Fathers, Catholic priests, had gotten into the act; their unlabeled green bottles of white *vin de messe* were highly appreciated on both sides of the Mediterranean Sea.

Except for Leila and Paul, the café was empty; in fact, the whole beachfront street was eerily quiet. There were rumors everywhere: the German army was nearing the border with Libya, apparently heading for Tunis. They were being chased by British forces bent on keeping the Germans on the run. It only remained to be seen where the battle—or battles—would be fought. The war that had seemed so faraway in Europe was now honing in on gentle Tunisia.

Paul took another lump of sugar from his coat pocket and stirred it into his coffee. Leila watched him and wondered again why they were even friends, if that is what they were. He had no interesting ideas, couldn't even make conversation, really. Someday he would take over the family business, but beyond that, he had no aspirations, no passions. He was racist, too. Once he told her about a sign he had seen in a café window in Paris: "*Interdit aux chiens et Arabs.*" No dogs or Arabs allowed. He had laughed about it. She had reminded him that she was half Tunisian; he replied that it was the other half he adored. It shamed her now to think that she had allowed the remark to pass unchallenged.

"What do you think is going to happen?" she asked him.

Paul responded with the classic Gallic shrug. "Nothing. Nothing ever happens here. But if it did, it would be by the Germans. Rommel is too good a warrior, too smart. The British will lose; you'll see."

Leila knew this was not Paul's idea; he was just repeating what he heard at home. His parents were supporters of the Vichy government that was collaborating with the Nazis who had occupied Paris and the north of France since 1940. The most recent rumor was that the Germans had decided to extend their occupation of northern France into the southern half of the country as well. Leila suspected it was because they wanted to protect the Mediterranean coastline in case Rommel was not as invincible as Paul seemed to think. Apparently, the war planners in Berlin didn't share Paul's *insouciance*.

"Look," Paul continued. "The Americans are losing the war in the Pacific. They can't even defeat the Japanese! They have not fought one battle—not one!—against the Germans and they wouldn't dare. My father says that little raid on Dieppe last summer proved they could not fight. They were crushed. *Ils sont cons*." They're idiots.

"You're certain of that?" It was more a taunt than a question. Paul looked at Leila the way his father sometimes looked at his mother, but he said nothing.

CHAPTER FIVE

Gibraltar

5 November. The weather in England was foul even by English standards: heavy rain, gusting winds, thick, heavy clouds. Ike needed to move his headquarters closer to the landing zones; Gibraltar was the obvious choice for a forward command post. Paul Tibbets, the pilot of one of the six Flying Fortress that would carry Ike and his staff to Gibraltar, was nervous about the flying conditions, but Ike had to get to the Rock. Just after 8 o'clock in the morning, Ike gave the order to take off.

It was only three days before the Allied assault troops were to storm the beaches of Northwest Africa. The move to relocate the Supreme Commander's headquarters had to be done in strictest secrecy. If a high profile American general were suddenly to leave London and set up headquarters in Gibraltar, the Germans would know some major operation was about to happen. Torch would be comprised.

Allied intelligence devised a plan. It tipped off two journalists by hinting that Ike would be returning to Washington "for consultation." The journalists did their part by reporting that Ike was on his way to see President Roosevelt. There was no mention of an imminent operation.

To avoid detection and stay below the weather, the six Flying Fortresses never flew more than a few hundred feet above the ocean. Rain, fog, and zero visibility made for a long and difficult flight; any sudden downdraft would spell disaster. After nearly eight airborne hours, Tibbets finally spotted the unmistakable silhouette of Gibraltar's Rock and had to gain altitude in order to land his heavy aircraft on one of its short runways. At 4:22 in the afternoon, under grey skies spitting intermittent rain, he touched down. Ike was safe.

A coded message went out to Chequers and the White House notifying Churchill and Roosevelt that Ike was safely in command at Gibraltar. You could practically hear their sighs of relief. The Allies badly needed a victory and both leaders knew Ike was the key.

7 November. A little more than two weeks before, on October 22, two huge convoys had sailed out of His Majesty's Naval Base at Faslane on the Gare Loch and down the Clyde before turning south toward the Pillars of Hercules, gateway to the Mediterranean. Consisting of more than 500 troop carriers and supply vessels, the convoy was in reality bound for two beachhead targets in Algeria. A day later, another powerful convoy of more than 300 ships left Hampton Roads, Virginia bound for Morocco. Operation Torch was underway.

Now, in his tiny new office deep within the Rock of Gibraltar, Eisenhower was still consumed with doubt about what the Vichy French forces would do once the Allies landed. Would they side with the British and American forces or at least be neutral observers? Or worse, would they defend the beaches, making an already difficult operation all the more bloody?

Ike knew there was one man who could potentially bring the Vichy French over to the Allied cause. Henri Giraud, sixty-three years old, was a four-star French general. Giraud was a respected military leader who was not associated with either Marshall Pétain, head of the Vichy government, or General Charles DeGaul, commander of the Free French resistance. If he gave his "blessing" to Operation Torch, Ike felt sure the French would stand down.

On the evening of Ike's arrival on Gibraltar, a British submarine was surfacing off the southern coast of France. Its mission was to collect General Giraud and bring him to Gibraltar to meet Ike. To ensure Giraud's cooperation, the British sub, the *Seraph,* flew an American flag. Once on board, Giraud, settled in for the return voyage to Gibraltar. It was D-Day -2.

A little after noon, less than ten hours before the the first wave of the assault was to begin, General Giraud was shown into Ike's offices deep within the Rock.. He was wearing rumpled civilian clothes and had not shaved for two days. Nevertheless, to Ike, he was a life-saver; the Frenchman could make all the difference in how his countrymen would or would not fight.

The meeting between the two generals did not go well. Giraud spoke English but insisted on using a French interpreter. Ike outlined the plans for Torch, adding that Hitler's intention was to seize North Africa and incorporate it into the Reich. Ike wanted to beat him to the punch. Giraud would be essential in convincing the Vichy forces not to oppose the Allied landings.

Giraud listened intently but remained silent. When he finally spoke, he was indignant as only a French aristocrat can be. He did not think much of the American plan; why North Africa? To Giraud, it seemed much more important for the Allies to invade southern France in order to keep Hitler from occupying more of his native soil. Moreover, he did not like the idea of an Allied command for an operation in French territory that did not include him as Supreme Commander. Finally, he thundered about the timing of this meeting. How dare Eisenhower "inform" him only a few hours before the operation was to begin. He should have been consulted months ago! *"Non! Je serais un spectateur!"* No! I will be a mere spectator!

General Giraud was escorted out of Ike's office. A few minutes later, a coded message written in French was sent to General Mast in Casablanca. Signed "Giraud," it indicated that the general would be working closely with the Allies and would arrive in Casablanca or Algiers a few days after the invasion. Aides transmitting the message noticed something strange: the handwriting on the original copy of the message looked very much like Ike's.

But in Ike's Gibraltar command center, the question of how the Vichy French would react to an Allied invasion of North Africa remained dangerously unresolved. It would be another long night for the general and his staff—a very long, cold night.

CHAPTER SIX

Cap Bon

8 November. Declan rose early. He made coffee and tried to rouse Valerie, his *"petite amie"* from a few nights before. She was still half asleep when he practically threw her into the car.

Declan owned a battered Fiat 500 Topolino that had been to hell and back twice and would probably go again if he asked it to. With any luck, today it would get him out to the tip of *Cap Bon* where he hoped to catch a glimpse of a large British convoy heading east. Score some points with Punch.

The road out of the city ran through the village of Ben Arous and along the southern curve of the Bay of Tunis before turning to the northeast and up the length of the peninsula. It was Sunday and there was almost no traffic on the road, not even bicycles or the ubiquitous donkey carts loaded with vegetable for market. Valerie dozed, her head against the window; Declan wondered if it had been a mistake to include her on this outing. She complicated everything. On the other hand, he knew a little beach that was out of the wind and very private.

It would take them more than two hours to reach the little town of El Haouaria near the northern tip of the peninsula. The headland of Ras ed-Dar was another half hour beyond that at the end of a dirt track. Declan had packed a lunch—a baguette, cheese, olives, a tin of sardines— and two bottles of wine. If he didn't see any ships in the channel, at least he could make love to Valerie before driving back to Tunis.

Cap Bon had its own history of warfare and conquest. Near the end of the Fifth Century, a Roman fleet of more than a thousand ships and fifty thousand men commanded by Basiliscus was on its way to attack the Vandals who had established an African kingdom on the site of ancient Carthage. The Roman fleet foundered off *Cap Bon* and was thrown into disarray by a fireship attack that sunk, burned, or captured nearly half the Roman armada and killed more than ten thousand soldiers. It was said to have been the largest amphibious operation in antiquity. Basiliscus fled in disgrace to Constantinople and hid in the church of Hagia Sophia to escape the emperor's wrath. He was eventually pardoned, but spent the last years of his life exiled in Thrace.

Without access to the resources of the former provinces of North Africa, once the breadbasket of Rome, the Western Empire was doomed. Within ten years, Rome had fallen; the Western Empire was no more.

But today, *Cap Bon* was bathed in bright sunlight, seemingly oblivious to anything remotely resembling war. It was hard for Declan to imagine a German army in full retreat only a few hundred miles away. He looked over at Valerie and put his hand on her knee. She smiled coyly and moved it higher up her thigh under her skirt. He obliged and was pleasantly surprised to find she wasn't wearing panties. Maybe things wouldn't be so complicated after all. He extracted his hand to downshift around a sharp turn in the road.

"I need to pee. Is there somewhere we can get a coffee?"

"It's not much farther to Haouaria. We'll stop there. I need to refill the tank anyway."

In the village, there was a small café next to the one-pump petrol station. While Declan went to find someone to crank the fuel pump, Valerie went over to the café. Inside, there were several men gathered around a transistor radio. It crackled with static, but Valerie heard an announcement in French instead of the usual blaring Tunisian music. She listened unnoticed by the men in the café, then went to find Declan who was finally filling the Topolino's tank.

"Something happened. There's been an invasion in Algeria."

"What?"

"An invasion. The radio says the Americans have landed on beaches in Algeria and in Morocco, too."

"What are you talking about?"

Valerie shrugged. "That's what I just heard on the radio." She pointed across the dusty street to the café. Declan handed her the fuel pump and said, "Make sure it's full." He went over to the café.

He came back a few minutes later. "Get in the car. We have to get back to Tunis. Get in!"

"But I still need to pee."

"Hold it."

Punch would be going out of his mind looking for Declan. Or worse.

CHAPTER SEVEN

Torch

8 November. Almost no moon. Overhead in the pre-dawn darkness, Allied bombers out of Gibraltar and Malta were crossing the Moroccan and Algerian coastlines respectively. They opened their bay doors, but instead of bombs, they dropped thousands of leaflets written in French signed by General Dwight D. Eisenhower. The leaflets informed the residents of towns along the coast that American troops would be landing soon, that they came in friendship as liberators, and that they might require assistance.

The American and British troops came ashore at daybreak; the men had been at sea, crammed into troopships, for almost three weeks. The Western Task Force—Patton's brigades arriving directly from Virginia—had somehow managed to avoid detection by German U-boats as it crossed the Atlantic. However, upon arrival off Morocco, it encountered bad weather, high surf, hopelessly snarled communications, and unexpectedly stiff Vichy resistance. Nevertheless, after a siege lasting two long days, Patton's men captured Casablanca as well as a nearby French naval base along with many ships anchored there.

The Center Task Force, the one aiming at Oran, lost a few ships that were damaged in shallow water, but managed to drive off a passing Vichy convoy. Oran itself surrendered after bombardment by British battleships. Oran's deep-water port, essential to any future Allied operations in North Africa, was captured before it could be sabotaged but not before a French battery above the harbor blew apart two Allied cutters, killing nearly everyone on board.

In the East, the Allies came ashore on three beaches near the city of Algiers with surprisingly light opposition thanks to assistance from a cell of Jewish Free French resistance fighters who staged a coup against the Vichy forces defending the city. Within a day, that Task Force was heading east toward Tunis.

Except for the losses sustained in Oran's harbor, Allied casualties were remarkably light for a combat operation of Torch's magnitude. More than 107,000 soldiers had come ashore, yet American and British losses amounted to just over 1,000 men with another 750 wounded. Almost 1,400 Vichy French soldiers had been killed and another 2,000 wounded. Fifteen Allied ships were lost; twenty-four enemy vessels including eight German submarines and two Italian submarines were either sunk or put out of commission.

At a remote airfield in Cornwall on the southwest coast of England, 559 American paratroopers were preparing for battle. They, too, did not know what to expect from Vichy French forces protecting the two airfields—La Sénia and Tafraoui—that were their targets in Algeria. They would ride 39 lumbering C-47 Dakotas into battle; the only question was would they be welcomed as liberators or would they have to fight hostile forces bent on defending the airfields. Two battle plans existed—one called War, the other called Peace; with minutes to go, it was still not clear which battle plan would be in effect.

On the evening of November 7, the order was given to load the 39 C-47s and take off into the unknown. Airborne assault had never been used in combat by the Allies before; now, they were literally and figuratively in the dark. The future of American airborne combat units hung in the balance.

The Dakotas lumbered to an altitude of 10,000 feet for the flight south. Almost immediately, the men, already uncomfortable in their heavy battle gear, began to freeze. Blankets were passed around. It would be ten long, bumpy hours until they jumped into battle over Morocco and Algeria. Midway to the targets, pilots received a message stating that Marshall Pétain, leader of all Vichy French forces had ordered his officers in North Africa to "resist any invading forces with every means at your disposal." Plan War would be the order of the day. A British battleship radioed "Play Ball"—the code for Plan War—over and over to the formation in the air, but the message was never received; the ship was using the wrong radio frequency. The men in the planes were flying into battle blind.

The mission encountered other problems. Bad weather and cross winds over Spain, along with the extreme range of the mission, resulted in the formation becoming separated and navigating independently toward their targets. One pilot became so disoriented he landed in Gibraltar. Thirty other planes were forced to land, fuel tanks empty, in the *Sebhkat d'Oran*, a dry salt lake forty miles northwest of the targets. Three more planes veered completely off course, landing in neutral Spanish Morocco; as a result, 67 men were interned there for three months. Only five planes made it to the targeted airfields at La Sénia and Tafraoui, but the airports had already been captured by ground troops. The usefulness of airborne assault troops on battlefield effectiveness still had much to prove.

Despite the difficulties encountered by the airborne assault force, the success of the amphibious landings were enough to convince the commanders of the Vichy French forces they should cooperate with the Allies, not fight them. Eisenhower could finally breath a weary sigh of relief. Now he could concentrate on fighting the Germans. Hitler obliged him. With the fall and defection of the Vichy French, the Führer, furious over the lack of any effective resistance by Vichy forces, ordered the occupation of most of southern France along with all French territory in North Africa; he immediately sent fresh troops to Tunis to guard the city and secure its port in order to protect Rommel's retreat.

It was just under 500 miles from Algiers to Tunis. The accelerated buildup of Axis forces in Tunisia meant time was of the essence. The British Eighth Army under the command of Lieutenant General Bernard Montgomery had chased Rommel more than halfway across Libya, but had stopped its advance near Tripoli in order to await reinforcements and supplies and to repair the port. Rommel and his depleted *Afrika Korps,* outnumbered and low on fuel and supplies, would have no choice but to retreat into Tunisia and work their way northward toward Tunis. The Allied forces of Operation Torch were heading there, too, from the west. Inevitably, the two forces would collide somewhere in Tunisia.

Within a week, advance elements of Operation Torch assault troops had come within 50 miles of Tunis. In a series of low hills near Djeida, they met their first fierce resistance from a newly arrived German brigade and were driven back. A jeep with American markings took a direct hit from a shell fired from a German tank. It was later determined that the occupants of the Jeep were, in fact, British soldiers.

CHAPTER EIGHT

Djeida

18 November; Northern Tunisia. Rumors had been swirling throughout Tunis for at least a week, but there was precious little hard news and very few facts. Most people understood that there had been an Allied invasion in neighboring Algeria and apparently in Morocco, too, but beyond that, nothing was certain. Where were the Allied invaders? Were the French resisting them or had they joined them? What about the Germans: where were their troops and what would they do?

There were unconfirmed reports of two armored brigades that had clashed recently near Mateur, not even a hundred kilometers west of Tunis. A few days ago, a lorry driver who was delivering fresh fish from the docks at Tebarka near the Algerian border had arrived at Tunis' port of La Goulette at dawn and went for coffee. At the café, he bumped into his cousin who happened to be the *chaouche*—the custodian—of the building that housed the Guardian's office. He told his cousin that somewhere near the town of Mateur, he had passed the smoking shell of a small vehicle and what appeared to be two dead bodies near a dirt road coming from the direction of *Djebel Abiod*. The *chaouche* mentioned this to Punch when the bureau chief arrived at the office a half-hour later. Punch sent Declan out to investigate.

The road running west out of Tunis was not a good one under the best conditions and recent heavy rains had made it worse. It looked to Declan like that there were deep ruts in the road, the kind caused by heavy armor. If that were true, an Axis brigade coming from near Tunis must have slipped out of the city during the night to confront the Allied forces who were moving in from Algeria. Operation Torch, the press wire had called the Allied landings at Oran and Algiers, had apparently been very successful. The Allies had gambled, betting that Vichy French forces would either join their side or at least stand down and allow the Allies to invade. It looked like they had won the bet, but now the Allies would have to take on Rommel's seasoned *Afrika Korps*. For the moment, the Desert Fox had escaped Montgomery's Eighth Army after seesaw battles in the Libyan desert that had finally ended with the fall of Tobruk a few days ago. Now Montgomery had set his sights on Benghazi; Tripoli would surely be next. Once Tripoli fell, it would be two Allied armies converging on Tunisia from opposite directions with Rommel caught somewhere in the middle. Declan wondered if the ruts gouged into the Mateur road suggested that the first wave of that storm had already arrived on shore.

Declan had been around war long enough to appreciate its objectives. Ultimate victory was one thing but that was too big an objective to contemplate in a day-to-day ground campaign. No; what Rommel wanted was a secure supply line for the material he desperately needed too hold out in Tunisia, a North African terminus for a resupply route running from Germany and occupied Europe, through Italy, then ferried across the Mediterranean by boat. Once Tripoli fell, there would be only two deep water ports on the North African littoral: Tunis and, not far to the northwest, Bizerte. Without control of these two ports, Rommel could not hope to keep his troops armed and fed. Without vital supplies, North Africa would eventually fall to the Allies which would clear the way for an invasion of Italy and the eventual retaking of Europe. Then one could think about 'ultimate victory.' Declan knew enough about Rommel to know he would fight more like a trapped rat than a desert fox to keep all that from happening.

Tunis and Bizerte were essential to Rommel's defense of the Axis southern flank. Both were close enough to Sicily to allow Axis supply ships to cross the sea at night, out of sight and range of RAF pilots who would be flying out of Malta or liberated airfields in Algeria and Libya. If Rommel could control Tunis and Bizerte, he could hold out in the *Maghreb,* maybe not forever, but long enough to convince the Allies that North Africa was not worth its bloody human cost.

Near the village of Fontana, the road forked and Declan took the branch road north. In the distance, he could make out several *dawwar*, small nomadic encampments, dotting the barren brown landscape. Good for sheep, he thought, but not much else, certainly not tank warfare. There was almost no cover or high ground, just flat, open space. No commander in his right mind would ever choose to fight a battle on these plains.

But off to the north, Declan could see an ascending series of hills, enough elevation for gun emplacements, with passes between them that could concentrate enemy targets in a devastating field of fire. Plus, control of that terrain would protect the flank of any force that held Bizerte or Tunis or preferably both, a textbook objective surely not lost on well-trained and battle-hardened *Wehrmach*t officers.

The ruts in the road had taken their toll; Declan's back ached and he needed to stretch his legs. He pulled over and turned off the Fiat's engine. As the engine cooled, the stillness of the place engulfed him like the grave; how could war possibly be near? Except for the deteriorated condition of the road and those distant strategic hills, he saw nothing that could independently verify what the *chaouche*'s cousin said he had seen earlier that morning—no scorched vehicles, no dead bodies, nothing that bespoke the cruelty of war. He lit a cigarette and leaned back against the car, closing his eyes to face the the thin afternoon sun. He would push on in a few minutes. If he continued north on this road, he could skirt *Gareat el Ichke*l, a large lake just west of Bizerte, then take the bridge across the narrow isthmus near the port before returning to Tunis by nightfall.

When Declan opened his eyes—had he dozed off?—a dog was barking at him. An old man, probably a shepherd from one of the *dawwar,* was nearby. His burnoose was worn and ragged; bare feet in dusty leather sandals despite the cold air. On his head, he wore a red *chechia*, the distinctive brushed-wool fez worn by all working Tunisians. "*Atini swega,*" he said.

Declan reached in his pocket and produced a pack of cigarettes. He lit two and offered one to the old man. They smoked in silence for a few minutes.

"Shu*ft askari*?" Have you seen soldiers? It wasn't perfect Arabic but Declan hoped it would do.

The old man expelled air through pursed lips and raised his eye eyebrows. Affirmative.

"*Ween? Qa'desh?*" Where? How many?

The man waved his hand in the general direction of the hills to the north. "*Yesser.*" Many; too many to count.

"*Enna askari? Alemani? Inglisi? Americani, mumpkin?*" Which soldiers? German? English? American, maybe?

A cluck of the tongue, a quick shale of the head. "*Rubi yaref.*" Only God knows.

It was almost midnight by the time Declan got back to his flat in the *medina*. He was exhausted and went straight to bed, thankful Valerie wasn't there. He slept soundly until nearly ten the next morning, then went to the office. Punch had been waiting for him for an hour.

Declan knew enough not to interrupt Punch when he got up on his Hyde Corner soapbox. "Bloody Yanks! Just like the last war. Last ones to join the party and then they want to take over everything. Think they know it all! Haven't even been in this war a year now and they actually wanted to sail across the channel and fight Jerry in France two months ago. Bloody suicide! Prime and Brooke told them to sod off so now this Eisenhower chap is running the show. Who the hell is he anyway, and why is he in charge? Why not one of us or at least a bloody Frog officer. Hope old Uncle Joe is happy now!"

Declan started to say something but Punch was on a runaway train. "Stalin, man! Told Prime he needed a second front to keep Jerry occupied in somebody else's garden. No second front, no more Russia. Hitler moves everything to the western front, invades England, war over. Bloody hell!"

Declan tried again. "The Americans…"

Punch cut him off. "Sod the Americans! They're up to their arses with the Nips in the Pacific. They don't have enough men or anything else to fight one war let alone two! They're pulling eighteen year-old boys off the farms, training them with bloody broomsticks! Jerry will make his Christmas pie with that sorry lot. Bloody hell!"

"Well, I'm telling you they're here now. I saw a Willys Jeep all blown to bits. Only thing in one piece was the bonnet with a big, white star."

"No bodies?"

Declan shook his head. "I didn't feel like sticking around. But I did find this." He held up a mangled, blood-stained combat boot, handed it to Punch.

Punch examined it, for some reason sniffed it. "Strange. You sure it was an American vehicle?"

"Big white star on the bonnet."

"This didn't belong to a Yank. One of our boys. Standard issue."

Punch chewed his lip. Muttered "Bloody hell" again. The conversation—such as it was—was over, except it wasn't. Another thought had grabbed hold of Punch. "And another thing: you'd think that if the Yanks were so bloody smart, they would realize that the lights from their coastal cities make their ships perfect targets for Admiral Dönitz and his bloody U-boats. They sank four ships yesterday, five the day before! Bloody hell; at that rate, the Yanks will have to walk across the bloody ocean if they want to fight!"

Now the conversation was over.

CHAPTER NINE

Bourguiba

Ali had not returned to the little Sidi BouBakr mosque since the day he watched a man die there. There were multiple theories about what had transpired that day but the one that made the most sense to Ali was that the man—whoever he was—had been shot by French police after he had been stopped at a checkpoint and the *flics* had discovered a cache of rifles in the boot of his car. A nationalist, probably, one more martyr to the cause of Tunisian independence. Now, only a week later, the walls of the little mosque had been scrubbed of his blood and the carpet on which he died had been exchanged for another prayer rug, just as threadbare, but unstained.

Independence was hardly a new notion in Tunisia. In the aftermath of the Great War, two great European powers, the Austro-Hungarian and Ottoman Empires, had dissolved while two other nations, Britain and France, still stubbornly clung to their far-flung empires. But even they were shrinking. Egypt had become independent in 1922, and in India, an odd little brown lawyer named Mohandas Gandhi who wore nothing but a loincloth and a homespun shawl was leading an anti-colonialist movement that threatened to remove the jewel from the British imperial crown. And who knew what would eventually happen in the Middle East and particularly in the British mandate of Palestine where diaspora Jews were clamoring for a "homeland." That movement was called Zionism and the homeland they craved would be called Israel.

Those ripples were beginning to form a greater wave. In the French protectorates of Morocco and Tunisia, nationalists, modeled on the Young Turks movement of the 1920s, were advocating for political reform. Algeria was different: it was not a French colony, but rather a *départment de la France*, an integral part of the territory of the French homeland. That distinction would make the struggle for Algerian self-determination much more difficult and bloody, but no less vital than the ones in Morocco and Tunisia.

The Tunisian independence movement was being led by a loose amalgamation of organizations composed of everything from farmers to workers' guilds to intellectuals who had been educated at the elite Sadiki College in Tunis. Many of these men, along with a few women, had also earned higher degrees at the Sorbonne or other universities in France. One of the most influential activists was a young lawyer named Habib Bourguiba.

The name 'Bourguiba' meant 'prisoner' in Albanian, one of the many languages once spoken in the now-defunct Ottoman Empire. The Bourguiba family had emigrated to North Africa from Istanbul in the 18th Century, settling first in Libya before eventually making their way to the small coastal town of Monastir in Tunisia. Educated at the exclusive Lycée Carnot and then Sadiki College in Tunis, the best schools the Protectorate had to offer, young Habib had gone off to Paris to earn a law degree from the Sorbonne. After he returned to Tunis in 1927, Bourguiba gradually became convinced that Tunisia should become a nation of opportunity that more resembled France—liberal, modern, and secular—rather than an Islamic colonial backwater. Over the next decade, he modified his views and advocated for a separate Tunisian identity and complete emancipation from France. Then, in 1938, following a violent nationalist demonstration in Bizerte, Bourguiba was arrested and sent to prison for conspiracy against the public order and incitement of civil war. *Le Jeurist*, an Arabic language newspaper published in Tunis, quoted him saying, "Let us be what we are before becoming what we will be."

As World War II raged in Europe and was spilling over into North Africa, Bourguiba was, as his name warranted, a prisoner in a French jail in Marseilles. During that time, he wrote a letter to a friend in Tunis that defined his position on two important matters: the end of the war and the beginning of Tunisian independence: "Germany cannot win this war.

Between the Russian colossi and the Anglo-Saxons who control the seas and whose industrial possibilities are endless, Germany will be crushed in the jaws of an irresistible vise. The order is given, to you and to all the activists, to make contact with the Gaulist French to combine our clandestine actions. Our support must be unconditional. It is a matter of life and death for Tunisia,"

Ali had seen Habib Bourguiba only once before he had been imprisoned. At the time, he thought to himself, "This is Bourguiba?" The man was laughably short, but as Ali listened to him speak, Bourguiba's striking personality, dazzling intellect, and undeniable passion for independence made him seem like a giant. By the end of that day, Ali was a disciple, albeit a silent one.

Now, alone in the quiet of the mosque, Ali's mind returned over and over again to the same question: "What is my responsibility in all this? What is Allah's will?" With the threat of war so imminent, perhaps independence would have to wait. On the other hand, maybe this was precisely the moment to challenge a colonial government riddled with uncertainty about its own future. What would the Vichy French army stationed in Tunisia do—fight on the side of the advancing Allied forces or side with the German army who would fight to the death to defend the Axis' southern flank? Moreover, whichever decision the French made, how would it ultimately affect the fight to secure Bourguiba's—and now Ali's, too—cherished dream of independence for Tunisia?

But war complicates everything; Ali understood this. Now that the war had come to Tunisia, the calculus was different. As much as he wanted to be independent of France, he was certain he wanted no part of Fascist Italy or Nazi Germany. They were inhuman, Godless ideologies; at least France had its *mission civilisatrice,* its civilizing mission. Assimilation could be resisted, even overcome; annihilation was an entirely different beast.

The *mas'baha*—Ali's prayer beads—slipped endlessly through his fingers. There were ninety-nine beads strung together in groups of thirty-three, each one representing one of Allah's ninety-nine names. His hundredth name would be revealed on the Day of Judgement. Ali recited the names silently: *Ar Rahmann* (Most Merciful), *Ar Raheem*

(The Bestower of Mercy), *Al Malik* (The King), *Al Quddus* (The Most Holy)... At the sixty-first name, *Al Mumeet* (The Destroyer), he paused, then continued on to the end: the ninety-ninth name—*As Saboor* (The Patient).

Perhaps independence would have to wait, at least until something else was destroyed.

CHAPTER TEN

Consequences

In war, there are two kinds of consequences: intended and unintended. The Allied invasion of North Africa had created both kinds. As Ike had hoped, the forces of Vichy France in North Africa had eventually sided with the Allies—or at least did little to oppose them. Not unexpectedly, that made Hitler furious. He fumed that he had abided by the terms of the armistice that Germany and France signed in June of 1940 that created a neutral zone in southern France, but now he would teach the feckless French a lesson. He would occupy all of southern France, and in particular, he would seize the port at Toulon, Vichy France's sole naval base on the Mediterranean. The French thwarted that aim by scuttling their fleet, leaving Hitler with nothing but seventy sunken ships and a few small, virtually worthless vessels. The Führer's Operation Lila was deemed a total failure.

That made Hitler even more furious. Beginning on November 9, the day after the Allied landings in Algeria and Morocco, the Nazis began the build up of their forces in Tunisia. The buildup was essentially unopposed: local French forces, commanded by General Georges Barré, were poorly equipped and unable to mount any kind of effective resistance. As a result, Barré withdrew his forces to a defensive position in the hills sixty kilometers west of Tunis and ordered his men to shoot anyone who attempted to pass. On November 19, the commander of a brigade of newly-arrived German forces, Walter Nehring, approached the French lines at a bridge near Medjez-el-Beb and demanded passage. When Barré refused, the Germans attacked the French units. They were driven back, but Barré sustained heavy casualties and was forced to retreat.

By then, advance elements of the Allied forces that had come ashore in Operation Torch had crossed the Tunisian-Algerian border and were headed eastward into Tunisia. In the vacuum created by Barré's retreat, units of the Allied First Army encountered a German force outside Djeida and were driven back. First blood had been spilled.

Now it was a waiting game. In the east, Montgomery's Eighth Army had captured Tobruk and Benghazi in Libya; Tripoli would surely be next. Rommel and his *Afrika Korps* were on the run, heading for Tunisia. The inevitable was about to happen.

Complexity breeds consequences—both intended and unintended—and war is one of the most complex systems known to mankind. As a result, all these actions were consequences of Operation Torch. On the other hand, the unintended consequences of war tend to be somewhat less precise and much more personal. They have to be reckoned in the lives and deaths of the people affected by events that lay far outside the pale of their existence, the thousands of men and women in uniform as well as the millions of civilians caught in the grip of war.

Ike knew all too well that war is the story of unfolding mis-calculations and confusion. Nothing ever really goes according to plan. Still, in his office buried deep within Gibraltar's rock, Ike fretted. He and his staff had spent the last six months planning Operation Torch down to the last detail, but there were unknowns on top of unknowns and thousands of lives at stake. In the days immediately following the landings in Morocco and Algeria, information was scarce. More than one hundred thousand men had come ashore and survived, but that was only the beginning of the North African campaign. Now the long, hard slough would begin.

Reports trickled in slowly, particularly from the Western Task Force under General Patton, which should have landed in Morocco. In between dispatches, Ike wrote notes to himself in his diary. Torch was the largest amphibious operation ever undertaken by the American military. It was also the first; there were important lessons to be learned. Ike knew there might well come a day when another amphibious assault would be required—an even greater and bloodier operation probably somewhere on the west coast of France.

Faraway in London, Winston Churchill went on the BBC to report on the success of Operation Torch. In his inimitable cadence, he told his audience, "Now, this is not the end. It is not even the beginning of the end. But it is, perhaps, the end of the beginning." Ike heard the broadcast in his cubby of an office deep within Gibraltar's massive rock and muttered to himself, "Oh, Winston. Another one of your mood swings?"

CHAPTER ELEVEN

Bismuth

25 November, 1942; Tunis. Every city has at least one person like Bismuth BenDaoud, someone who always kept his lines of communication open and who knew everything and everybody. Someone who was always willing to talk to a journalist and who usually told the truth, more or less. The art for any journalist who wanted to talk to Bismuth lay in knowing what was more and what was less.

Bismuth was a Tunisian Jew, part of a community that numbered more than 100,000 souls and was nearly two thousand years old. Jews had been in Tunisia since the Phoenician era and certainly predated the diaspora of the Jewish people that followed the destruction of the temple and the sack of Jerusalem by the Romans in 76 AD. By the time of the Muslim conquest of North Africa in the Seventh Century, Tunisian Jews spoke their own dialect of Arabic; a synagogue—*El Ghriba*—on Djerba, a small island off the southern coast of Tunisia that was reputed to have once been the mythical island of the lotus eaters described by Homer in *The Odyssey,* was one of the oldest places of worship in the world.

Whatever the truth of the origins of Tunisia's Jewish community, Bismuth felt himself the blessed beneficiary of a rich legacy that allowed him to take occasional liberties with facts. That never bothered Declan who considered Bismuth an amusing, if not always reliable source, someone always ready to provide him with useful information or a good contact or a quote from an anonymous source.

This morning, Declan found Bismuth in his usual habitat, a crowded café near *Bab Souika,* the old gate that marked the northern boundary of the medina. Bismuth saw him coming through the crowd and motioned him with one hand to an empty chair. With the other hand, he signaled a waiter to bring two more cups of coffee.

Before Declan could say anything, Bismuth put a finger to his lips and motioned Declan to lean in. He spoke in a whisper. "It is not a good time, *mon ami*."

Declan sipped his coffee and waited. Bismuth looked around and leaned closer. "The Nazis have arrested Moises Burgel." Declan nodded; he had heard that the President of the Jewish community had been arrested, along with several other prominent Jewish leaders. The Vichy French had been relatively lax in their handling of Tunisia's Jews, willing to find ways to delay or avoid mass deportations to concentration camps in Europe. Tunisian Jews who had been caught in Europe when war broke out had not been so lucky. But now that there was an actual uniformed Nazi presence in the country, the laxity of the Vichy regime could well change. Tunisian Jews were schooled in the art of going to ground when necessary and Declan sensed Bismuth was headed in that direction. Declan would have to strike fast, but first, sympathy.

"*Je suis désolé, mon ami* " I'm sorry, my friend.

"*Merci. Ça ne fait rien.*" Thanks, It can't be helped. "Anyway, I am much too old to enjoy forced labor. How can I help you now?"

"What have you heard about troop movements? When is it likely to happen?" Declan felt he didn't need to elaborate on what 'it' meant.

Bismuth laid a finger on Declan's hand. "*Bientôt. Peut-être aujourd'hui ou demain.*" Soon. Possibly today or tomorrow.

"*Et ou ça*" Where?

"*Pas loin d'ici.*" Not far from here. He nodded west. "*Fait gaffe, mon vieux.*" Be careful. Bismuth rose to go, but Declan placed a hand on his arm.

"*Toi aussi, eh?*" You, too.

***

Punch was in one of his usual less-than-jolly moods. "And what the fuck is that supposed to mean? 'Not far from here.' Nothing is fucking far from here!" He took a breath. "I can look out my bloody window and see it's no bloody far from here." Declan knew that when Punch fell into using his Scottish diction, you were in for it. "Is tha' worth a wee coffee for ya, lad?"

"He paid for the coffee. Now he's going to have to lay low for a wee while." Declan knew he was poking the bear, but Punch seemed to have run out of steam, at least for the moment.

"Aye. I would na' want to be wearin his brogues just now. Jerry's in a foul mood and a wee roundup might be just the thing." The accent began to fade a tad; Punch was coming back down the mountain. "I'd just like to know where it will happen before it happens. Better than bloody steppin' in it."

"I agree. Bismuth thinks to the west, but not far away." Declan wondered if that would set off Punch again, but the Chief just nodded.

"Would make sense. The Yanks are coming from that direction and Jerry doesn't want them getting too close to Tunis. Or Bizerte, for that matter. He's got to stop them somewhere around Béja."

"Béja? Too late for that. The wire says the First Army's already east of that. I think Tebourda, or maybe even Djedeida."

Punch looked at a map he had pinned to the wall. "Djedeida's not more than fifteen kilometers from here."

"Actually, twelve."

"Here we go, laddie. Better pucker up." It sounded to Declan like Punch's accent was working its way back up one of the Munros, Scotland's tallest mountains.

CHAPTER TWELVE

Fabron

27 November; Djedeida. Monsieur Alain Fabron was pruning his vines when the first shell landed a few hundred meters away. The explosion was deafening and the concussion knocked him to the ground, stunned. Clods of dirt were still raining down by the time he was able to stand.

The past few days had been, to say the least, trying for M. Fabron and many of the French community who had been satisfied to ride out the war under the benign wing of the Vichy government in Tunisia. In fact, he was not displeased with the Nazi occupation of his adopted homeland; say what you would, but the Nazis were efficient and entirely predictable. As long as one's papers were in order, one could do business with them—quite good business, for that matter.

But now the Vichy French were losing ground on two fronts: their German overlords didn't trust them and the Free French under their exiled leader Charles de Gaulle now saw an opportunity to assert their own dominance over France's waning colonial empire. Fabron did not admire de Gaulle. He was arrogant and, in Fabron's estimation, far too militant. He certainly did nothing to further the business interests of successful French enterprises who deserved to be left alone if they were to remain profitable. Fabron had spent considerable time and resources courting friends in the offices of Vichy bureaucrats. All wasted now.

But there were more pressing concerns on his mind now, like the ringing in his ears and the taste of cordite in his lungs. Another shell whistled by overhead. *Merde! Ils sont tous fous, ces connards!* Shit! These assholes are all crazy.

Fabron ran for his truck, signaling to a few workers who were huddled together between the rows of vines to join him, but before he could get there, he saw a dull green wave of tanks heading directly toward the southeast corner in his vineyard. His instinct was to wave them away but it was too late for that. They were already at the margin of his property and moving fast. A third of his vines would be gone in minutes.

More explosions, closer now. The smoke from jagged craters in the ground stung Fabron's eyes. He couldn't see but he knew the terrain well enough. He threw the truck into gear and took off, heading away as fast as he could from the chaos of the battle.

The concept of war was not unfamiliar to Fabron. As a boy, he had watched the terrible Great War unfold from the safety and comfort of his family's estate in Algeria. He understood war: might made right; survival of the fittest, an honest assessment, a mathematical calculation: these things all made sense. But the reality of war was something altogether different. It was a fog bank; it had taste, sound, smell. It produced something detached from reason, then replaced that with panic and fear. There simply was no accounting for war, no bottom line, because the costs were incalculable and the gains ambiguous. A few minutes ago, he had a vineyard, a thriving business, something tangible to leave to Paul. Now, he had a smashed estate and his pants smelled faintly of urine. He had lost nearly everything, his life included, but he was not to blame. It wasn't his fault. He was innocent, but nevertheless a victim. Through no fault of his own, had been caught in a trap of someone else's design, someone far away from here. He might escape the trap today but he might die tomorrow. *Ce n'est pas logique.* It didn't make sense.

By the time Monsieur Fabron returned to La Marsa late in the afternoon, he had regained a measure of composure. He had also changed his pants. He told his wife and Paul about the battle, not the truth of it, just its falsehood. The Germany army had met an advancing Allied force and had pushed it back fifteen or twenty kilometers to a defensive position behind their estate near Tebourda. If that was going to be the calculus of this campaign, then the Allies and their new Vichy friends would not be in Tunisia for very long. Thank God! Maybe he would be able to replant in the spring and still have a small production from his old vines in the fall. 1943 might not be a great year for Chateau Fabron, but it would be better than nothing.

Paul listened closely to his father' account of the skirmish—it didn't even sound to Paul like a real battle—with growing irritation. His anger wasn't directed at the participants or even at the loss of forty or fifty hectares of his family's old vines. Paul was primarily angry at the Vichy government who had capitulated to the Allies without putting up much of a fight. Spineless old men! No wonder Hitler was even now moving his armies into southern France as well as ferrying them across the Mediterranean and pouring them into Tunisia. The Führer was a warrior whose time had come; Pétain and his lot of aging egotist generals and admirals were relics of the past. Let the Allies waste time pulling on their brittle puppet strings; Hitler was better off without them.

An idea began to grow in Paul's mind. Perhaps he could be of help to the Nazis. As a *pied noir*, he wouldn't be tainted by the desertion of the Vichy; perhaps, if he played his cards right, he could secure a favorable position in the post-war administration of what would likely become the North African jewel in the Third Reich's new colonial crown. That thought mollified Paul somewhat; maybe those tired old men of the *ancien regime* up in Vichy had done him a favor after all.

CHAPTER THIRTEEN

Leila

Leila put down her fountain pen and stared out the rain-spattered window. Beyond the wall of her family's villa, she could just make out the beach, wide at low tide and edged by a thin line of surf under a leaden sky. Not surprisingly, the beach was empty, a perfect metaphor for the windswept loneliness she felt. It did not look like a war zone, although it was—or soon would be.

Everyone could feel the storm that was coming; in fact, it was already here. German troops and supplies were continuing to land at the port of Tunis as well as at the nearby El Aouina airfield. The *Wehrmacht* was doing everything it could do to build a formidable force to protect Rommel's retreat from Libya and to push back against the Allies advancing from the west. Thus as ever: gentle Tunisia, caught in the middle of a deadly struggle between powers far greater than its own.

There was an old saying in the Maghreb: Moroccans are lions, Algerians are men, Tunisians are women. Leila understood that all-too-well. Tunisia's gentle geography had molded its culture and character, making it a small country wedged between giant neighbors. It had learned to survive by being pliant, accommodating, receptive—just like a woman, Leila thought. Sometimes it felt to her that Tunisia was more of a dreamscape than a country, too peaceful and ephemeral to survive something as inherently destructive as war. An image sharpened in her mind: an old man sitting quietly in the sun, a sprig of jasmin tucked behind his ear, its sweet scent carrying him off on a gentle breeze.

Leila refocused on her reflection in the window pane. How dispirited she looked! It was not easy, under the best of circumstances, to be a woman in a man's world, even a gentle one like Tunisia. But these were hardly the best of times. Now that war had come, she felt more trapped by her gender than ever. Leila's French mother was of no help; she hardly ever left the house. Her Tunisian father still went to work at the Ministry of Education, but now he was home by late afternoon; the presence of so many armed Axis troops on the streets of Tunis made evening café life uncomfortable, if not impossible.

Dismal day or not, Leila had to get out of the house. Her *safsari* was on the chair right where she left it last week. She wrapped the white sheet around her body and pulled it up over her head, leaving only a portion of her face exposed. She didn't like the garment and what it represented, but outside the house, she had to admit it provided her with a measure of ghostly anonymity, almost rendering her invisible to the stares of men.

When she left the house, Leila didn't have a specific destination in mind, but as soon as the raw November wind hit her, she knew where she wanted to go. It was only mid-morning, still plenty of time to go to the *hammam*. Maybe steam, a hot bath, and a good, hard scrub would help lift her mood. Leila's mother would disapprove; she thought the place was filthy, but to Leila, it was an enticing treat, one of the few public pleasures left to women.

Almost every neighborhood, town, and village had at least one hammam, as much a place to gather and gossip as a place to bathe. The morning hours were reserved for women; afternoons and evenings belonged to men. Leila disrobed in the cool anteroom and wrapped herself in a large cotton towel before making her way through a series of dim chambers, each one warmer and steamier than the one before. In the innermost room, she slipped into a waist-deep pool of steaming, hot water. She sighed as the water worked its way into her tense muscles, relaxing them, draining away the tension hiding there. She closed her eyes and let her mind wander, half-listening to the chatter and laughter of the other women in the bath, while her other half relished the solitude of the steamy, dim chamber.

After about twenty minutes, Leila felt light-headed from the heat so she rose from the pool, squeezing and twisting the water from her hair. She retreated into one of the slightly cooler rooms and summoned one of the attendants waiting there. She lay face down on a raised marble slab and closed her eyes. The attendant began to work her strong hands and fingers into Leila's shoulders, pressing her forearms into Leila's lower back. Her calloused hands stroked and flowed across Leila's body in an intimate dance, occasionally slapping her muscles and scraping away old, dead skin with a pumice stone. The massage was both painful and exhilarating; Leila tried hard not to flinch, concentrating on the pleasurable sensations, but there were moments when the attendant was stretching and prodding her in ways that made her want to scream.

Leila's skin glowed; she tingled all over. Back in the cool anteroom, she lay down on a thin mattress while another attendant fetched her a glass of mint tea and a slice of orange. She must have fallen asleep for a moment; she suddenly started and to her delight, felt refreshed—no: more than refreshed; reborn. She rose and dressed quickly; it was almost noon and the hammam would soon close for two hours for cleaning before the men arrived. She gave the attendants a few coins and thanked them profusely. "*Baraka'allufikum, ya ochti!*" God's blessings on you, my sisters.

The euphoria of the *hammam* did not last long. On her way back home, Leila was rudely halted by a German sergeant who was waving along a detachment of troops—six tanks and several halftracks—that were taking up positions along one of the narrow streets facing the beach. The soldier regarded Leila cooly but she pulled her *safsari across* her face so only her eyes showed and continued on her way. She heard him say something to her but she just kept walking. "*Haloof*," she whispered to herself. Pig. She was glad the German soldier didn't speak Arabic.

CHAPTER FOURTEEN

Eid-el-Adha

9 *December, 1942; Tunis.* It had been raining for nearly a week. In the west, almost all the roads from the Algerian border had become quagmires, bringing the Allied advance on Tunis almost to a standstill. German reinforcement divisions continued to arrive in Tunis, taking up defensive positions around the city and the two important northern ports: La Goulette and Bizerte. In the south, Rommel was still in retreat; soon Tripoli would fall to the British Eighth Army and Rommel's *Afrika Korps* would be forced back across the Libyan border into Tunisia.

Despite the impending bloody confrontation, most Tunisians went about their lives in a strange twilight. Food was becoming scarce; so was fuel. Travel between cities was difficult, but not impossible. Ali, on holiday from university, had pushed and shoved his way onto a bus heading south to Kairouan to visit his family. He would have to stand in the packed aisle for more than three hours, but he didn't mind. Tomorrow would be the first day of E*id-el-Adha*, the Feast of the Sacrifice, one of the most important holidays in the year for Believers.

The relationship between *Allah* and his servants was simple yet demanding: man must submit to the will of God. In the time long before *Allah* had chosen to reveal Himself to the seal of the Prophets— Muhammed, peace be upon him!—He had sought to test the faith of His beloved servant Ibrahim by commanding the old man sacrifice his first-born son, Ishmael. It was the cruelest of tests, but as Ibrahim was preparing to slit his son's throat in obedience, *Allah* stayed his trembling hand and allowed him to sacrifice a ram instead.

That story of the first patriarch was almost as old as time itself, but, to Ali, it was still immediate and relevant. It demonstrated the two essential elements of the relationship between Allah and His servants: divine mercy and man's unquestioning obedience—his submission—to God's will. The three-day holiday was festive, but its joy was tempered by the discipline that lay behind it; it was not always easy for man to submit to the will of *Allah*.

As the crowded bus slowly made its way south toward Kairouan through hills covered with rows of ancient gnarled olive trees, Ali had time to think about the events of the last month. He had watched a man die. This war, once so distant, had now come home and Ali had no doubt it would leave an awful scar across much of his lovely, peaceful country. There was also the dream of independence: how would this war affect the inevitable tide that was flowing across all the colonial territories of the European powers? The world was changing, Ali was sure of that, but he was not yet able to discern the shape and substance of the world yet to come.

Home at last, Ali put aside all these imponderables and gave himself over to the excitement and joy of the holiday and to his family. He was the oldest of five children; his father was a mathematics teacher at the local lycée—a good position but *Baba* was hardly a wealthy man. Their modest home was not far from the *Sidi Uqba* mosque, a monument dating back to the ninth century and one of the most renowned places of worship in the Muslim world. It was said that the columns inside the main prayer hall had been taken from the ruins of Carthage, and that at one time it was forbidden even to count them upon pain of blinding.

But as glorious and famous as *Sidi Uqba* was, Ali preferred the quiet intimacy of *Sidi Sahab,* an ornate *zaouia*, or mausoleum, better known as the Mosque of the Barber. A small dim interior chamber contained the sepulcher of the saintly *Abu Zama' al-Balaui,* a venerated companion of the Prophet Muhammed, Peace be upon him, who, according to local legend, had cut and saved three hairs from the Prophet's beard. It was there, at *Sidi Sahab*, that Ali, along with his father and two eldest brothers, all dressed in their finest clothes, went just after sunrise the next morning to recite in congregation with many others the ritual prayers and to listen to the *khutba*, the sermon, that marked the formal beginning of the Eid-al-Adha.

Returning home after the service, Ali was delighted to see a fat shorn sheep tethered in the street just outside the door that opened onto to the small courtyard of his family's home. The sheep had been daubed with red dye, designating it as the *Qurban*, the ritual sacrificial animal whose meat would provide the feast. A friend of Ali's father who for years had been performing the sacrifice for many in the neighborhood stood waiting. As the family gathered to watch, the animal's carotid artery, jugular vein, and windpipe were severed with a single stroke, the blood quickly draining to the east in the direction of Mecca. Ali's mother and eldest sister ululated in celebration.

While the sacrifice was performed to commemorate Allah's mercy to Ibrahim, the meat from it would provide for more prosaic needs. It would be butchered and divided into three equal portions: a third for the family, a third for relatives and friends, and a third for anyone who could not afford to purchase an animal for sacrifice. Thus it was both a family feast and a celebration of the *Umma*, the greater Muslim community, three days of feasting during which no one, not even the poorest of the poor, would go to sleep hungry.

Late in the evening on the third and final day of the Eid holiday, the evening before he would return to his studies in Tunis, Ali sat with his father in the *majlis*, the traditional living room in Ali's home. There were woven carpets and hand-knotted kilims on the floor, pillows strewn about. Ali's father, Bashir, was a traditional Tunisian, not one who favored more fashionable European furniture. He sat with his son, leaning back against the tiled wall, one knee raised, the other flush against the floor, a glass of tea nearby. Ali sat across from him cross-legged, careful not to display the soles of his feet to his father; to do so would be to disrespect him.

"*B'shwoya, ya wildi,*" Little by little, my son. "It is not all bad. We have better roads, hospitals, electricity, schools now. We live a better life. We are a more modern nation."

"No; we are not a nation, father. A colony. Yes, the French have done much but they have not given us the most precious of gifts. Independence. Freedom."

"And you believe we are ready for that?"

"Yes, *baba*, I do. Every day, we are losing a piece of who we are. We are Arabs, Muslims—part of something much greater, a rich history, a culture. We are not French and never will be." Ali was careful not to raise his voice; he did not want his father to think he was just another idealistic young student caught up in the fervor of the struggle for independence.

For a moment, Bashir was quiet. "And how do you propose to accomplish this?"

"First, we ask. Then, we demand. If we must, we fight."

"*Yezzi!* Enough! There is enough fighting now. Anyway, we have no weapons."

There was silence in the room for a moment and then the *muezzin* in the minaret of a nearby mosque began to intone the *salat al-isha*, the last of the five daily calls to prayer for the faithful. Soon, other *muezzin* all across the city joined in, their voices rising and falling in the darkness: Bashir and Ali—father and son—rose as one, faced eastward in the direction of Mecca, and placing their hands to their ears, began to recite their evening prayer: *"Allahu akbar."* God is great.

CHAPTER FIFTEEN

The Road South

16 December; southern Tunisia. Declan stared at Punch as long as he dared but it didn't seem to have any effect on the chief. He didn't even look up from the stack of papers on his desk. "You'll be back in plenty of time for Christmas Mass at the cathedral, not that you care. Bloody Papist!"

"That's not the point! Herr Hitler isn't likely to take—what did you call it?—an 'inspection' of his southern flank very graciously. There is a full-on war here now, in case you didn't know."

Punch shrugged. "And we're paying you to cover it, not sit around here on your arse waiting for something to happen. Anyway, you'll like it down there. A lot warmer than up here. I'll see you in a week. If there's anything worth a story, send it by wire. I'll punch it up it for you just like I always do." Big fake smile,

Another stare, another waste of time. Declan turned to go.

"And make sure your papers are in order. That's all they bloody care about. And take extra petrol; it's getting scarce. Oh; one more thing: no bloody trollop this time!"

"Sod off." Declan shut the door to the office, almost careful not to slam it. Even that extra bit of drama didn't seem to register with Punch. "And remember not to drink the water down there. You'll get worms!" he yelled through the door.

When Declan left early the next morning, he was still in a foul mood. He had packed a duffle and filled two twenty-liter jerrycans with petrol; he could feel their weight taxing the already tired springs of the little Fiat. No matter: the road was crowded with everything from donkey carts to troop lorries; it was going to be a long, slow crawl down to the desert.

Once out of the city, he was on the same road he had taken to Cap Bon, but this time instead of turning north up the peninsula, he continued southeast across its base. At the seaside town of Hammamet, the road tuned south, hugging the Mediterranean coastline. Heavy military traffic and occasional checkpoints made forward progress painfully slow; at least it wasn't raining.

At Enfidaville, Declan stopped at a roadside café to stretch his legs. While he was sipping a coffee, he watched a convoy of heavy lorries roll by, each one filled with troops. At first, Declan didn't think much of it until he realized the trucks weren't German. They were Italian and so were the soldiers riding inside. He had heard that the airlift of Nazis brigades to the El Aiouan airfield had slowed while large troop transports from Sicily were arriving daily at the port of La Goulette. The strategy seemed suddenly obvious to Declan: the *Wehrmacht* forces were being sent west to meet the Allies advancing from Algeria while the Italian troops were being deployed south, presumably to cover Rommel's retreat and to counter Montgomery's Eighth Army, the British hounds that were chasing the Desert Fox.

Declan finished his coffee and hurried around the corner to the PTT, the local post office and public telephone center. He was pleasantly surprised to find the place nearly empty. He went into a phone booth and put in a call to the office in Tunis. Time to make amends. The line buzzed, crackled, went dead for a moment, but then he heard Punch's growl. "Guardian."

"Miss me yet?"

Hardly a pause and Punch said, "Are ye lost already lad?" He didn't sound too angry.

"I don't want to lose the line. I'm in Enfidaville. There is a large convoy heading south. Italians; at least a brigade. Could well be more ahead or behind."

"Messe."

"Say again."

"Giovanni Messe. Italy's best general, if that's not an oxymoron. Won the Battle of Greece with help from the Nazis and for his sins was sent to the Russian front. Heard he was removed a few weeks ago... he complained that his troops weren't properly equipped and outfitted. Undoubtedly right. Must have been reassigned; probably a hell of a lot happier to be here. Won't freeze his balls off."

"What's his rank?"

"He's a Field Marshall, same as Rommel. He knows how to fight in the desert; served in Abyssinia back in the 1930s. If his men are properly equipped, he'll give Monty a time, probably at Mareth."

"Mareth? I thought that was out of commission."

"It was, but I'm guessing it won't be for long. Try and get..." The line went dead. Declan leaned out of the booth and asked the *standardiste* at the switchboard to try again, but the call wouldn't go through. He paid and left.

Back in his car, Declan slowly followed the long convoy south. He had counted thirty-two lorries before calling Punch but there was no way of knowing if more troops were on the way or were already of him. He had only gone a few kilometers when a general staff car, flags flying, sped past him, honking at oncoming traffic and swerving around the lorries in the convoy. Declan smiled; "*Benvenuti in Tunisia, Maresciallo Messe.*"

Declan arrived on the outskirts of Sousse, Tunisia's favorite play-ground on the turquoise Mediterranean, in mid-afternoon. The journey from Tunis, usually a little more than three hours, had taken nearly twice that long. That was the bad news. The worse news was that he had still twice as far to go. He decided tomorrow would be soon enough.

He found a small *fondouk* just inside the old walls of the city. Fortunately, there were no animals stabled downstairs and Declan's room on the upper floor was spare but clean. With luck, he'd get a decent meal and a good night's sleep and be on his way by dawn.

Sousse's roots stretched far back into antiquity. It had been founded by the Phoenicians in the 11th Century BC and eventually became part of the Carthaginian Empire. Julius Caesar once visited Sousse; he stumbled coming ashore but managed to save face by deftly grabbing two handfuls of sand while exclaiming, "Africa, I have you now!"

Now Sousse was a seaside city enclosed by towering stone walls. In the early years of the Protectorate, the French had improved the harbor and many European expatriates had come to prefer the city's seaward orientation, moderate climate, wide beach, and traditional Arab character to Tunis. Declan didn't disagree.

Even with war on its doorstep, Sousse still managed to maintain its relaxed reputation. There were a few Italian soldiers strolling in the winding streets, but they didn't seem all that out of place, the way the strutting Nazis did in Tunis. Declan chose a small restaurant facing the beach and ordered a *brik a l'oeuf*—a thin sheet of folded fried pastry containing spices and an egg yolk—and a beer. He settled in to watch the passing parade: jasmine sellers, young men holding hands, European women out for an evening stroll. He wondered if the convoy he had encountered was still rolling south toward a war that would eventually shatter this peaceful scene.

The following morning, Declan was awakened by the *adhan* of the *salat al-fajr*, the dawn call to prayer, the first prayer of the day. He lay in his bed, listening to God's timeless exhortation to the faithful: "Come to prayer! Come to salvation!" Declan had grown up in a small village not far from Cork where the sound of church bells on a Sunday morning cheered him but did little to remind him of his Christian duty. But here, even in a Muslim country as moderate as Tunisia, the *adhan* punctuated the hours of each passing day, providing an underlying sacred rhythm to the busyness of daily life. Declan had come to appreciate its sound as well as its intent. Few Tunisians rigorously observed the five daily calls to prayer, but perhaps in their collective subconscious, Allah was never very far away.

Downstairs, Declan filled the Fiat's tank from one of the jerrycans in the boot, then walked across the street for a glass of coffee with hot milk and a croissant. Thank God and French bakers for some of life's small pleasures.

At this hour of the day, there were fewer vehicles on the road and Declan made decent time through the Sahel, the verdant landscape that separated Tunisia's Mediterranean coastline from the great Sahara Desert farther south. He had considered taking the coast road through the small seaside towns that dotted the coast, but had opted instead for the more direct route south, through El Jem, then on to Sfax and Gabès. He knew the roads would deteriorate the further south he went but with any luck and enough petrol, he would be in Gabès by nightfall.

A half-hour out of Sousse, near the village of M'Saken, a secondary road that ran west toward Kairouan joined the main highway south. A cloud of dust hung in the air and as Declan approached the intersection, he saw several large trucks lumbering toward him. It was another convoy, but unlike the one he had seen yesterday transporting troops, this one was comprised of heavy construction equipment: bulldozers, earth movers, cranes on flat-bed trucks. There was also a stream of camouflaged canvas-covered lorries riding low on their oversized springs; Declan guessed they were loaded with ammunition or explosives—probably mines. He accelerated through the intersection; the last thing he needed was to get behind that slow-moving train of vehicles. He'd stay well ahead, then do some reconnaissance further down the road. After all, this was the only way south.

After another half-hour of driving, the road curved gently to the left and then ran straight as an arrow toward the horizon. The first and only other time Declan had passed this way, he had been surprised to learn that the highway was literally built on top of an ancient Roman road that led to El Djem. Now, far in the distance, he could barely make out the form—no more than a dot on the barren landscape—of the modern town's Roman legacy: a monumental coliseum, almost as large as the one in Rome. El Djem was originally called Thysdrus, and it had once been a major city in the Roman province of *Africa Proconsularis*. Its amphitheater had been built in the Second Century by the local governor, Gordian, and at one time it could hold 35,000 people who came to watch chariot races or sometimes slaves captured in West Africa who were brought here to be trained in gladiatorial combat, or to face the fierce lions that had inhabited the lush forests of North Africa. Those forests had once covered this landscape and had produced almost all the lumber used to build the barges and triremes of the vaunted Roman fleets, but once they were decimated, the desert had begun its inexorable march northward. Deprived of habitat, the lions of North Africa were long gone, too. Someday, this once fertile land would also be gone, turned to desolate sandy wastes by time and the appetites of men.

Thanks to the dry climate of the Sahel, the coliseum at El Djem was remarkably well-preserved, and on another day, Declan might have paused to wander through its haunted ruins. But not today, not with an enormous convoy pressing him from behind. Better to push on to Sfax, another sixty kilometers to the south. Maybe the convoy would pause to reform and refuel there and he could get a closer look. Declan's stomach growled; maybe he'd get a little tucker, too.

Like almost every other city along the Tunisian coast, Sfax was built atop ancient Roman ruins. At one time, Taparura had been a thriving Roman seaport; a few centuries later, it had served as a base for Barbary pirates. Since the establishment of the French Protectorate in 1881, Sfax had grown to become Tunisia's second largest city and in the last few months, it seemed to have also become the southern headquarters for the Axis command in the country. Field Marshal Messe's staff car was parked conspicuously in front of the *Hôtel de Ville*, the administrative offices of Sfax's French governor. Declan saw two German officers enter the building, but it was the heavily armed Italian soldiers guarding the entrance and patrolling the adjacent plaza that caught his attention. Declan knew the feeling in his stomach all-too-well and it wasn't hunger. He was not going to a war zone; he was already back in one.

Declan toyed with the idea of filing a wire story but decided against it: the copy would surely get censored and anyway, what would it say? That the Italians had invaded Sfax? He decided to wait one more day before sending Punch his copy. He'd been lucky so far. Better to push on to Gabès tonight and hopefully on to Mareth tomorrow. That's where the story was; he felt certain of that much.

It was another 150 kilometers to Gabès and the road was deteriorating fast. Declan hadn't seen any sign the convoy of heavy equipment and reasoned it had stopped at Sfax to await further orders. He was gnawing on an end of the day-old baguette he had brought from Tunis and taking a swing out of a bottle of water when his good luck light flickered once and went out.

A hundred meters ahead, it looked like the road suddenly disappeared. Declan braked hard and as he screeched to a stop, he heard a loud bang and then flap-flap-flap, the unmistakeable sound of a blown tire. He leaned his head on the steering wheel while his heart rate slowed back down to something approaching normal.

When he looked up again, the road had, in fact, disappeared. Declan was staring out over a *wadi*, a dry river bed. During the recent rains, a flash flood must have come roaring down from the mountains far to the west and taken out a section of road almost five hundred meters wide. He could see where the road resumed on the opposite side of the wadi, but getting over there wouldn't be easy. But first things first: change the bloody tire. Fortunately, he had a spare in the boot; it was worn, but it might get him to Gabès—if he could figure out how to get across the *wadi*.

He had the tire off and the car up on the jack when he heard a car approaching fast. He stood to wave a warning about the washed-out road and saw two cars and a motorcycle slowing to a stop fifty meters away. He recognized one of the cars immediately: a black Alfa Romeo Coloniale, with flags on either side of the bonnet.

The soldier on the motorcycle got off and pointed his machine gun at Declan, motioning him to raise his hands. Declan complied in an instant. An officer in the trailing vehicle got out and walked up to Declan, hand extended, palm raised, fingers beckoning. "*Documenti,*" he said, and with just the barest emphasis, "*per favore.*" Declan brought his hands down very slowly and reached inside his car. He kept his papers—his Irish passport and his travel permit—in a leather wallet above the visor; he handed the wallet to the officer who turned and carried it back to the black Alfa, handed it through the window.

Declan could hear a faint clicking as the engine of the motorcycle cooled, but otherwise, everything had gone silent. The sergeant's machine gun was still pointed directly at him. Another minute passed. Then the officer who had taken Declan's papers opened the rear door of the Alfa and General Giovanni Messe stepped out. He said something quietly to the sergeant who lowered his gun before walking over to Declan. "Looks like you have a problem," he said. His English was accented but otherwise good.

"Yes, sir, but I think we both do," gesturing to wadi and stub of road just ahead.

Messe smiled. "That is not a problem. What about your car? Your… *ruota di scorta* is good?" He pointed to the spare tire.

"I hope so. I think so."

Messe looked at Declan's battered car, reached out, and to Declan's surprise, patted it lovingly. "You know, this is just like the first car I ever drove. Topo 500, yes? You have a good taste for *la macin*a, Signor Shaw." He handed Declan back his wallet, turned to the sergeant. "*Aiutalo*." Help him.

Without a word, the sergeant lowered his weapon and unbuttoned his tunic. Five minutes later, the spare was on and the blown tire was stowed in the boot. Declan had not noticed that while he and the sergeant were busy changing the tire, Messe and the other officer had walked down into the *wadi*.

Declan started to thank the general but he waved his hand dismissively. "Nonsense. We are allies, no? You're Irish. According to Mr. deValera, you're a neutral in this war but I don't think you like the British any more than we do. What is it they say here? The enemy of my enemy is my friend? Now; follow me. I will get you to Gabès and get you something better to eat. Then you can tell me why you are here." He held up the half-eaten baguette before tossing it away.

Messe said something to the sergeant on the motorcycle, then got back in his car. The sergeant pushed his bike off the road and down the hillside onto the *wadi* bed. For the first time, Declan noticed that large tire tracks followed a compacted path leading across the dry river bed, fifty meters west of where the road had once crossed it. This was the track the sergeant followed. He went slowly, pushing his motorcycle, stopping every few meters to test the sandy river bed for trapped pockets of underground water that could collapse and break an axel. When he was finally reached the far side, he motioned to the others to follow. They went slowly, the two staff vehicles spaced several meters apart. Declan followed, a wary and distant third.

Back on the rutted main road, the small convoy continued southward toward the oasis at Gabès, Declan struggling to keep pace. At least he would be waved through any checkpoints along the way. And wouldn't Punch be surprised by the company he kept; maybe he would finally sniff out a real story, something almost worthy of editorial delight.

That evening, the soldier and the journalist shared a simple meal, accompanied by a bottle of Italian wine from General Messe's private stock. "You really should visit the place while you're here. There is nothing quite like it. Much more interesting than some worn-down defensive fortifications. More wine?" General Messe reached for the bottle and refilled Declan's half-empty glass. He poured a small splash into his own. "I tell you what: tomorrow, you come with me to inspect the work at Mareth and then we will make a—how do you say?—a *deviazione* to Matmata."

"Detour."

"Yes! Detour. I want you to see this place." Messe sat back and loosened the collar of his tunic another button. "Tell me, Signor Shaw, do you think there will ever be a world without war? Sometimes, I think, war is necessary, but it is never good. We should discover another way of resolving our differences, don't you think? Maybe someday there will be a *deviazione* around war." Messe smiled and took a small sip of wine.

"You sound like a reluctant warrior, sir." Messe looked puzzled. "Reluctant. It means you don't really want to be a warrior."

Messe nodded once and looked out over the oasis that lay below the hotel balcony. Even this far south, it was an unusually soft evening for this time of year. Despite its proximity to the sea, majestic date palms ringed a large cultivated plot of land fed by underground fresh water springs. Olive and fruit trees, vegetables—tomatoes, onions, even watermelon—grew in profusion. "Do you know what makes all this possible, Signor Shaw?" Messe made a sweeping gesture with his hand. He didn't wait for Declan to reply. "Water clocks. Ingenious. A thousand years ago, someone—a farmer—discovered how to distribute the water evenly to all parts of the *oasi* so everything could grow, not just a few things." When Declan didn't respond, Messe continued. "You see, that farmer was not a *riluttante*—reluctant?—man. He did what he had to do in order for everyone to survive. No; not just survive. *Prosperare.* Thrive, I think?"

"Do you truly believe, General, that war can make us thrive?"

Messe laughed. "You tell me, Signor Shaw. You are a writer who understands human nature. I am only a warrior—and, yes, a reluctant one at that. Now, you're tired. You've had a long day. You need to sleep.

Tomorrow, we have much to do, you and I." Messe pushed back from the table. He stood, made a small salute. *"Buena notte."*

"Buena notte, Maresciallo."

Back in his room, Declan scribbled in his notebook. Punch hated soft stories—Declan could already hear him yell "That's not bloody news!"—but the conversation with Messe had added another dimension to Declan's perception of war, of this war in particular. There were so many actors in the play: Free French, Vichy French, German, Italian, British, American, combatants and civilians, not to mention the setting of the play itself: Tunisia. Declan pictured the oasis: the trickle of moving water, the breeze that rustled the date palms, a small watch fire blinking on the perimeter, the murmur of voices from below. This was a delicate little country that did not deserve to be caught up in the currents that were sweeping across the globe. Tonight alone, there were a million men freezing to death on the Russian front, Jews were being sent to death camps, civilians were caught up in the slaughter: how were humans ever going to survive, let alone *'prosperare'* in a world gone so mad? Maybe Messe was right to be a reluctant warrior.

The next morning after cups of coffee, Declan accompanied General Messe on an inspection of the fortifications at Mareth. Like all Italians, when Messe spoke, his hands were in constant motion. "Ironic, is it not? The French built this defensive line six years ago to keep out the Italian army marching from Libya. But they did not maintain it. Now the Italian army is restoring it to defend against the British who are chasing the Germans." Messe shook his head and laughed. He and Declan were standing on one of the cliffs that towered above Wadi Zigzaou, a dry river bed fifty kilometers south of Gabès. Below, much of he heavy construction equipment Declan had seen on his way south were busy as ants, laying barbed wire, digging trenches, building concrete bunkers and casements, and piling earth into high mounds to create firing blinds and provide cover for tanks and artillery.

"Can you really defend this? The Maginot Line didn't stand up so well against the *Wehrmacht*."

"E vero. But Maginot could be easily flanked. This line—Mareth— is not so vulnerable. It extends for almost thirty miles. The sea is to the east and the Matmata hills and the *Chott el Dejrid* salt flats to the west

are impassable, especially at this time of year. That makes this the only viable way north to Tunis. With enough ammunition and supplies, we can hold out against Montgomery and his Eighth Army for a few months, long enough for Rommel to get to Tunis and rearm his *Panzerarmee*. Once he retreats through here, we'll shut the gate and plant anti-tank and anti-personnel mines from here down to the Libyan border. That will slow the British rats down. We are only buying time; I know that."

"Forgive me, General, but why are you showing me all this. Do you want the British to know you're here?" As soon as he said it, Declan saw Messe's motive. "You want him to know you're here. The only way around you is for him to go south deep into the desert and then far to the west where his supply line gets very thin."

Messe shrugged and smiled. *"Può essere."* Maybe.

Later that afternoon, General Messe and Declan were looking down again, this time into someone's house. They were exploring the Berber village of Matmata, a few miles west of the Mareth Line. The Berbers were the original inhabitants of North Africa who predated the Arab conquest of the Eighth Century. They still spoke their own proud language.

"It's incredible, no?"

Declan gaped at the hole in the ground. "How do you suppose they do it...and why?

Messe shrugged. "It's so simple. They dig a big hole and then make caves in the walls for rooms; they're all connected with passageways. The hole becomes the courtyard. Cool in summer, warm in winter. The only problem is when it rains. Then they have a *piscina*, I suppose. But then it hardly ever rains down here."

"I wonder if they know what is going to happen over there?" Declan pointed in the general direction of the Mareth Line.

Messe was silent for a moment. "Not even you or I know what is going to happen there, *mio amico*."

CHAPTER SIXTEEN

Fox and Rat

In another lifetime, Johannes Erwin Eugen Rommel might have been an accountant or a scholar or even a barber, for that matter. He did not look at all like an almost mythical warrior or, as he was popularly known, like a *wustenfüchs*, a desert fox. He had just turned fifty-two and the war in the Libyan desert was taking its toll. He was balding, gaunt, and in poor health, but he nevertheless still adhered to a rigorous daily personal discipline, rising early and avoiding alcohol. His hobbies included engineering and mechanics. A highly decorated officer in the Great War for his service on the Italian front, he was adored by the men he commanded and respected by his fellow officers. His 1937 book, "Infantry Tactics," was required reading for anyone who hoped to advance up the chain of command in the *Wehrmacht*. Even Hitler acknowledged his military prowess although he didn't fully trust him, believing that Rommel's first loyalty was to the *Wehrmacht*, not to the National Socialist Party or to Hitler himself. The Führer even resented Rommel's popularity as a war hero; perhaps that was the reason Rommel always carried a cyanide capsule on his person. Even his adversaries admired Rommel: he was known for his chivalry and for making what Rommel himself called "war without hate."

When World War II broke out, Rommel was promoted to Major General and assigned to guard Hitler and his field headquarters during the invasion of Poland. He attended the Fürher's daily war briefings and often accompanied him on his frequent visits to the front on his personal train. After Poland fell, Rommel pressed for command of one of the German army's ten panzer divisions on the western front; Hitler obliged him by promoting him over more senior staff officers. The Führer liked Rommel's use of innovative tactics. During the German invasion of France, there were days when Rommel moved his divisions so quickly that the Allies never knew for sure where he was; they called his troops the "ghost divisions." Rommel was flattered and he drilled his men constantly in the tactics of surprise and maneuver, the very ones he would eventually use in the desert campaign.

Rommel had been given command of the *Deutsches Afrika Korps* in February 1941. Although initially subordinate to an inherently cautious Italian commander, Rommel's instincts were to advance aggressively against the British forces defending Egypt and Britain's lifeline to its empire, the Suez Canal. Hitler was delighted, but there were consequences to Rommel's offensive impulses. On one occasion, he failed to notify his supply officers of his decision to press an advantage, and was subsequently warned he would only have enough fuel for four more days because no dumps had been prearranged. Rommel had to order a halt and only a massive overnight resupply effort reduced the delay to a single day.

By April, Rommel was on the doorstep of the port city of Tobruk in eastern Libya, less than 400 miles from Cairo. In order to capture Tobruk and advance into Egypt, Rommel knew he would need supplies and reinforcements. His request to the OKW, the German High Command, was denied because the army needed men and material for Operation Barbarosa, the Axis code name for the invasion of the Soviet Union. This internal conflict would plague Rommel throughout the North African campaign.

Every good general needs a worthy adversary. Rommel's British counterpart was Field Marshall Bernard Law Montgomery, better known as "Monty." Montgomery was four years older than Rommel, but like the German general, he had distinguished himself as a junior officer in the First World War. Although shot through the right lung by a sniper during the First Battle of Ypres, by the time the war ended in 1919, Montgomery had climbed through the ranks to become Chief of Staff of the 47th (2nd London) Division, an infantry division that saw fierce fighting all along the Western Front.

Montgomery was a newcomer to the desert warfare of North Africa. He had only arrived in Libya in August 1942 after General Claude Auchinleck had been relieved of the British Middle East Command and his successor, Lieutenant General William Gott, had been shot down and killed by the *Luftwaffe* on his way to take command of the British Eighth Army. Monty was next in line.

His timing could not have been better. In late October, near a small railway stop close to the Libyan/Egyptian border called El Alamein, Montgomery's Eighth Army slugged it out with Rommel's *Afrika Korps* for nearly three weeks. Superior in numbers and with an intelligence advantage that made it possible for British forces to have advance warning of Axis battle plans as well as to locate and destroy supply depots, Montgomery's Eighth Army finally broke through the Axis lines in early November, turning the tide of war in the desert and forcing Rommel to begin the long retreat east across Libya and eventually into Tunisia.

One of the divisions that helped Montgomery win the Second Battle of El Alamein was the British Mobil 7th Armored Division, better known as the Desert Rats. Monty liked their insignia—a big red rat with a long tail sewn with scarlet thread—and wore it proudly on his sleeve. He liked to joke that now it was the desert rat chasing the desert fox, not the other way around.

CHAPTER SEVENTEEN

Ike and George

24, Dcember; near Tunis. On Christmas Eve, Ike was in an abandoned French farmhouse in Tunisia, drenched, hungry, cold. He was coming down with the flu. But this was his first visit to the front—his first real taste of combat—and he was doing his best to bolster morale. It wasn't easy. The relentless rain had forced the Allied offensive to a halt at a place called Longstop Hill. British and American casualties were heavy, almost as heavy as the rain that was turning everything to thick, viscous mud. Just when it seemed things couldn't get any worse, Ike's aide received a phone call from General Clark in Algiers. "Sorry to interrupt, Sir. General Clark on the line." He passed the field handset to Ike.

Ike listened quietly before handing the handset back to his aide. He was silent for a long while before turning back to face a group of officers assembled for a briefing. One of them thought Ike looked tired, almost defeated. "Change of plans, gentlemen. No Christmas dinner for me with the men at the front. I'll be returning to Algiers ASAP. General Darlan has been assassinated. General Anderson, you will make the appropriate decision about the current situation on Longstop."

Stunned silence in the room. Someone coughed. Everyone present knew that only a few weeks before, Ike had appointed Admiral François Darlan Commander-in-Chief of the Vichy army in North Africa. It was not a popular decision—the American press disdainfully referred to it as "the Darlan Deal"—but Ike had been forced to strike a devil's bargain with the collaborationist Frenchman: Darlan would grant the Allies badly needed access to French military bases in North Africa in exchange for recognition of Vichy sovereignty over the entire region. Ike knew de Gaulle and the Free French wouldn't like that one bit; they wanted the recognition. A few days after Ike refused them, a young Free French resistance fighter named Fernand Bernier de La Chapelle took executive action and shot Darlan four times at point-blank range. Now what?

It was a long, hard drive through pelting rain, sliding along slick roads, back to Algiers but thirty hours later, Ike was back in his quarters in the St. George Hotel overlooking old Algiers. He had soaked in a hot bath and was eating his first hot meal in more than two days. "What do you think I should do, Beetle," he said to his friend General Walter Bedell Smith. They were due to attend Darlan's funeral in an hour.

"I know you don't want to hear this, Sir, but what about Giraud?"

Ike grimaced. He remembered the exchange with Henri Giraud that had taken place in Gibraltar just hours before the Operation Torch landings. Giraud had huffed and puffed before refusing to send a message to French commanders in Algeria and Morocco that would allow the Allied forces to land unopposed. In fact, Ike remembered Giraud's exact words just before he walked out, "I will be a spectator!" Now Ike had to swallow a bitter pill and make Giraud the Commander-in-Chief of all French forces in North Africa. Well, Giraud wouldn't be a spectator anymore.

"What do you think de Gaulle will do?"

"I think he will do what you tell him to do, Sir. My impression is that he doesn't think much of Giraud and that the French resistance will ultimately support him. I tend to agree."

Ike was thoughtful. "Beetle, do you remember what Winston said when we first started talking about invading North Africa?"

"What was that, Sir?"

"He said our first battle was to have no battle with the French. God, was he right! This diplomatic bullshit is harder than fighting the war."

Ike turned to look out the window. He could see the *casbah* and beyond, the glint of the sea. He was exhausted. Kansas seemed a million miles away and Washington wasn't offering much comfort either. Earlier in the day, Ike's boss, General George C. Marshall, had sent him a brutally terse cable: "Delegate all political and diplomatic decisions to your subordinates. Concentrate your full personal efforts on battle for Tunisia."

"Giraud," he said wearily. "Well, make it so. Merry Christmas, Beetle."

"Merry Christmas, Sir."

***

George Smith Patton Jr. graduated from West Point in 1909, six years before Eisenhower. It still rankled him that the younger man was his superior officer. Some of his ancestors had fought for the Confederacy. He got his own first taste of combat in 1916 in the Pancho Villa Expedition in Mexico under General John "Black Jack" Pershing, the first time motor vehicles had been used in combat. During World War I, he led tanks into combat before being wounded just before the war ended. Ike had never even been fired on.

But Patton respected Ike, at least to his face. Ike was patient; he had enviable diplomatic skills;. More importantly, Ike was his superior officer, and a soldier's first duty was to his commanding officer. Patton, for all his faults, was a soldier, through and through so Ike would have to be not only tolerated but also obeyed. Their relationship was professional, and sometimes, when talk turned to subjects like military doctrine or tank warfare, even cordial. But the men were not close personal friends. Two men, two soldiers, cut from wholly different cloth: all his life, Ike remained suspicious of war; Patton loved it above all else.

Since commanding the Western Task Force in Operation Torch, Patton had been billeted in a Moorish palace in Casablanca, much too far from the front lines for his liking. Moreover, he was chafing at the slow development of the Tunisian campaign. He wanted to fight the German army now, before more fresh field battalions were put into action and before Rommel's *Afrika Korps* arrived on the scene. Like Rommel, Patton was an instinctive leader: aggressive and bold. He had no stomach for the politics of the Allied cause, and was particularly frustrated by all the in-fighting among the French. He sent Ike a message: "If they're not with us, then get them the hell out of our way."

Patton was only a little less frustrated with some of his fellow officers. He believed in training and discipline, and any lapse in either made him boil. He didn't mince words with his staff officers. "Don't mollycoddle your men! Make them hard; make them tough. They don't need to like you, but make damn sure they respect you. When they do, they will fight like hell for you." He saved particular disdain for Major General Lloyd Fredendall who had commanded the Central Task Force that came ashore at Oran in Operation Torch and was now in command of II Corps, the largest American fighting force in Tunisia. Another of his cables to Ike was notoriously succinct: "That soft son-of-a-bitch should be relieved immediately!"

But for all his bluff and bluster, Patton was wildly popular with his men; the American press liked him, too. He looked and acted like a movie-star version of himself, and he played his part to the hilt of the M1913 cavalry sword he had invented. He knew how to handle the press corps, always knew where the next camera lens was aimed. Jut-jawed and ruggedly handsome, he liked to chew on a cigar; his uniform was always immaculate, from his lacquered helmet right down to his jodhpurs and polished riding boots. He sported twin pearl-handled revolvers. He believed in leading from the front and didn't care if his fellow officers thought he was a vulgar boor; he only wanted to connect with his men. Every day, he made himself more and more of a folk hero as well as a battle field legend to the men who called him "Bandito" or his personal favorite, "Old Blood and Guts."

Ike had only this to say about General Patton: "I'm glad he's on our side, not theirs."

CHAPTER EIGHTEEN

A Case of Wine

24 December, 1942; Tunis. The weather was relentlessly bad. Both armies were bogged down, stymied, every vehicle axel-deep in thick mud. It was a dreary stalemate that would remain so for several weeks until the weather finally changed. Frustrating as the delay was, it was in all likelihood a blessing for the Allies. They had suffered a string of defeats and needed time to regroup.

Life in and around Tunis was getting difficult. The German army fared well enough, but there was hardly any fuel and food—especially meat—was scarce for civilians. People hunkered down; the cafés were almost all empty, waiters stared out windows at the rain-soaked streets. Tunisians took the rain and the cold in stride; "*Allah enube*," they said to each other. God will provide. The Europeans in the city, normally happily preparing for Christmas, were bored, restless, and out-of-sorts from weeks of rain.

Not Paul Fabron. He had set his sights on General Field Marshall Albert Kesselring, Commander-in-Chief of the *Wehrmacht* South, the highest ranking German officer in the Mediterranean Theater of Operations. To Paul, Kesselring was his *billet d'or*, his golden ticket.

It had already been a long war for General Field Marshal Kesselring whose men affectionately referred to as "Uncle Albert." He was a popular commander, primarily because he regularly made unannounced visits to the front in order to spend time with the men who put their lives on the line every day. Since the war began in 1939, Kesselring had seen action in Poland, the Soviet Union, France, and the Low Countries rising in rank each time. He had commanded the largest *Luftwaffe* air fleet in the Battle of Britain, raining deadly nightly fire on London during the blitz. Since assuming command of the Mediterranean Theater of operations, Kesselring had been consumed with obliterating British airfields on the island of Malta which were hampering efforts to resupply Rommel in Libya. He almost succeeded in bringing the island to its knees after a violent air campaign destroyed thousands of buildings and left the civilian population of the island at near starvation levels. Only conflicting German priorities and British determination to resupply this island thwarted Kesselring's goal. Now his task was to defend the deep water ports at Tunis and Bizerte and— most importantly—to ensure the survival of General Rommel and his retreating *Afrika Korps*.

It was late on Christmas Eve and Kesselring was clearing his desk, getting ready to leave his office. General Walther Nehring, commander of German forces in Tunisia, knocked once on the Field Marshall's door and entered, saluted. Kesselring noted his old comrade still limped, the result of a wound he had sustained in an air raid earlier in the year. "Anything else, Walther? If not, let's go home and celebrate another Christmas."

"There's a young man who would like to see you, Sir, a Monsieur Fabron. It should only take a minute. He has something which might help you celebrate a little better tonight."

"To be honest, I'd rather sleep than celebrate. What does he want?"

"He says he has a Christmas gift for you. From the looks of it, it just might help you sleep better, too."

"A Frenchman bearing gifts on Christmas Eve? You think there are any trustworthy ones left?"

"I think this one is harmless, Sir."

Kesselring sighed. "Show him in. If he's still here after three minutes, then please show him out."

***

Paul took the *tire-bouchon* from his pocket and opened a second bottle. Kesselring had invited Nehring to join them for a glass. "This is really quite good, M. Fabron. *Mes félicitations*!"

Paul gave a slight shrug and a modest smile. "There are still some things we do well, Sir."

"It would seem you are better winemakers than fighters, that's true. *Prost!*"

Paul raised his glass in response. "Actually, Sir, if I may, I am not truly French. My parents were born in Algeria, but my mother's family is Alsatian, from Metz. Her father was German. He was the first in our family to bottle a Riesling. The grapes in this bottle are from cuttings from his vines. I am glad you gentlemen approve." The last part of Paul's little speech wasn't technically true, but it probably didn't matter. Kesselring seemed quite content to take another sip.

"Forgive me, M. Fabron; where did you say your family's vineyard was located?"

"Near Tebrouda, Sir." Paul noticed that Kesselring shot Nehring a quick look. "I'm afraid we lost a portion of our estate last month. I'm sure it couldn't be helped."

"Forgive us, Monsieur. We shall be more careful next time. Walther, remind me to tell General von Arnim to be more careful in the future." Kesselring paused, looked over at Nehring. "Tell me, Herr Fabron: if you needed to replant a portion of your estate, when would you do that?" Paul was pleasantly surprised by the change of title.

"It is too wet now, Sir. Maybe in the spring, perhaps the beginning of March, if the rains stop. May I ask why?"

Kesselring looked again at Nehring who shrugged, nodded slightly. The two spoke rapidly in German. Paul couldn't follow much of the conversation but he did pick out one word: '*Jüden.*' Jews. Kesselring turned back to Paul. "Perhaps we could be of some assistance." Paul waited.

"We have some…volunteers…simple folk who need something to do. A little hard labor is good for the soul, no?"

Paul understood. He had heard the rumors. "Yes. Yes; that would be very helpful and I would be happy to give these people something useful to do."

Kesselring smiled. "You are most kind, Herr Fabron." He raised his empty glass. Paul refilled it.

"Prost!"

Paul refilled his own glass; Nehring's, too. *"Vielen Danke, meine Herren. Und Fröliche Weihnachten! Pros*t!" Thank you, gentlemen. And Merry Christmas! Cheers!

Two high-ranking German "friends" and a work gang to repair and replant the destroyed portion of the vineyard. For free! All for a case of wine!! Maybe he would have another case delivered for the new year. Paul was sure father would approve.

CHAPTER NINETEEN

A Christmas Truce

Christmas Day, 1942; Tunis. Ever since the war began, The Guardian published a front-page story on December 25th called "A Christmas Truce." It recalled the unofficial truce that fell across the Western Front in 1914, one of the few serene moments of the Great War. This year, the fourth since the tradition began in 1939, the honor to write the Christmas article fell to Punch, perhaps because he was there when that first, brief truce was declared. Punch's original copy was a bit too colorful for The Guardian's editorial taste, but overall, he was pleased with what would appear on the front page later that day:

"War is many things, but much of the time, war is waiting. Waiting for tuck, or what our American cousins call chow. Waiting to use the latrine. Waiting for mail call. Waiting to go over the top as we once did, or waiting to clamber down rope ladders to pack like sardines into a landing craft as our boys did just last month. Waiting to hit a Moroccan or an Algerian beach. Waiting for the next bullet or the next shell to kill you, or worse, leave you mangled for life.

War is waiting, but it is many other things, too. It is fear and bravery. It is silence and chaos. It is the utter stillness before battle and the pitiful cries of the wounded when the shooting stops. It is the camaraderie and the killing. It is the reek of blood and cordite and the aroma of hot soup. It is wet socks and toe rot and fungus powder. It is the pit you feel in your stomach on your way to the front and the miracle of life you cherish when it is your turn to move to the rear.

It is the death of the man on your left and the survival of the one on your right. It is everything while you are alive and nothing when you are dead.

The Prime Minister has said that the landings in North Africa are not the end of this war or even the beginning of the end of this war. Maybe, if we are fortunate, they represent the end of the beginning. We have been fighting for more than three years already and we may well be fighting for three more, or thirty more. Who knows? Not this old soldier. But I do know this: we will continue to fight for however long it takes to defeat tyranny; the rule of despots will end someday and the sun will shine again.

War may look like hatred, but it is love, too. It is love of country, love of an ideal, love of our fellow man. And, God willing, when this war is over, it will be love of our enemy, too. For the world that lies beyond this terrible war must be remade in peace, a lasting and just peace this time, not one that punishes the defeated or exalts the victors, but one that incorporates the lessons of the war-torn past into the hope for a war-free future.

This old soldier is in Tunisia today. There are armies gathering here and they will fight soon enough. But at least for today, all is calm, all is bright. Those of us who fought and survived the Great War—the war that was supposed to end all others—salute those of you now fighting this war in Europe, in the Pacific, and here in North Africa. Forgive us: we won our war but then we lost the peace. We failed you lads. We could not keep you from going back to war, but God willing, together, we will soon end this scourge and calmly carry on into a more peaceful tomorrow.

God bless you and may He keep us all safe. Merry Christmas!"

Punch put down the telexed copy of his article and lit another cigarette. "Bit of rubbish," he said to himself.

Declan read Punch's article later that afternoon. He had returned to Tunis two days previously and he had spent those forty-eight hours catching up on sleep. He had a lot to think about as he drove north, this time up through the central valley just to see some different terrain. It was a more mountainous route and that, along with the constant rain, made for slow going. He broke his journey in Kairouan, but the mattress in his room was infested with fleas so he slept restlessly on the floor. He was on his way before dawn the following morning.

Once home, Declan worked up a story about the Italian presence in the south and the restoration of the Mareth Line. He wondered what Punch would think about the access provided to him by Field Marshall Messe and whether Punch would choose to deliver the Italian's message to Montgomery in print. Maybe it would be smarter to get that intelligence to Montgomery in a less public forum.

There was something else on Declan's mind. Before he had turned west to take the road to Gafsa, he had stopped in Sfax to get a closer look at the port's shipping activity. At a small, café, he was surprised to see his friend Bismuth. As soon as he saw Declan, Bismuth got up and walked away, motioning Declan to follow. After several twists and turns, he entered a small shop, and when Declan followed a few moments later, the shopkeeper led him into a back room where Bismuth was waiting.

Bismuth appeared shaken; it was not like him. "I did not expect to see a familiar face here."

"I'm sorry if I startled you. Is everything alright?"

"I hope so. I am leaving Tunisia. It's no longer safe for me here."

"Where will you go?"

"God willing, to Palestine. There is a ship heading there, leaving tonight. I have passage on it."

Declan was well aware that large numbers of European Jews were desperately trying to reach Palestine to avoid being caught in Hitler's 'Final Solution.' He was also well aware of British immigration policies—White Papers they were called—which were trying to appease the Arab residents of the British Mandate in Palestine by strictly limiting Jewish immigration. Many influential people in Britain—Jews and Christians alike—supported unlimited Jewish immigration but there was also a strong contingent in Whitehall who thought it was essential to align Britain's interests with Arab interests to keep vital oil supplies flowing. That dilemma was called 'riding the tiger' and Britain was dangerously close to being eaten by the beast.

"Are you sure you will be allowed to disembark—assuming you make it," Declan asked.

Bismuth gave a shrug. "It's worth a try. Better than remaining here and sent to a slave labor camp. Or being sent off to France. That is a death sentence. From here, at least I have a chance."

"What are you taking with you?"

Bismuth patted his belt. "Everything I need is sewn in right here."

"Is there anything I can do for you?"

"Say kaddish for me. Hopefully, not the version for the dead."

"How will I know if you make it to Palestine?"

"Maybe one day when this war is over, you will come to Palestine to write a story about the birth of a new nation, one called Israel. You'll be walking down a street in Jerusalem or Tel Aviv or Haifa, and there I'll be, drinking a coffee. It will be just like old times. But do me one favor, please."

"Of course. What?"

"Don't tell anyone you saw me. This is an anonymous exit. It's better that way."

Declan understood. *"Bon voyage, mon ami."*

"Shalom, ya habibi." Peace, my sweet. Bismuth gripped Declan's hand, kissed him on both cheeks, and was gone.

***

Sadly, the Christmas truce was nothing more than an editorial in a British newspaper. In the hills to the west of Tunis, Allied and Axis forces continued to clash sporadically as they grimly maneuvered for position. The constant rain and freezing nights made life miserable for infantries, and air cover was either haphazard or non-existent. On the day after Christmas, Allied forces were forced to draw back to a defensive position near the town of Medjez El Bab —only 60 kilometers west of the prize: Tunis. But now the position they occupied was exactly the same one they had occupied at the beginning of the month. They had not gained a meter of ground but in the meantime, they had suffered nearly 21,000 casualties.

At one time, there had been hope that the landings in Morocco and Algeria would enable the Allies to make a fast run to Tunis, effectively trapping Rommel's forces who were retreating through Libya. But a quick infusion of German and Italian forces, plus drenching rain that turned the roads in the western half of the country to impassable muck, had dashed that hope. Now the Allies, just now beginning to learn the hard lessons of warfare, would be forced to fight Rommel's battle-hardened divisions somewhere in Tunisia—sometime in the new year, sometime very soon.

CHAPTER TWENTY

Pancakes and Champagne

31 December, 1942; La Marsa. Leila's mother clung fiercely to her French traditions. On New Year's Eve, she was preparing an intimate supper for some friends to celebrate le Revéillon de Sainte-Sylvestre: pancakes, foie gras, and champagne. The menu was supposed to bring good luck and prosperity to all in attendance and at least for one evening, With such fare, Madame BenZayed figured her family and friends would be able to forget about *"cette guere enmerdante,"* this shitty war, at least for one night.

Leila was half-heartedly helping in the kitchen. She was tired of the constant rain and bored beyond belief; her house felt more like a prison than a home. When she had been a student in Paris, she had been able to lead an exciting, happy life—the theater, night clubs, unchaperoned evenings with handsome men. But back home in Tunisia, she felt like a bird in a *cage à oiseaux*, one of those elaborate Tunisian bird cages, lovely to admire but never free to fly away.

The ingredients for the supper had been surprisingly easy to procure. Flour, butter, and eggs were still available in the market. A local French farmer had supplied—for a price—the engorged liver of one of his male geese; he added some rendered duck fat at no additional cost. The champagne came from the Fabron estate; it wasn't true French champagne, but it would do. Leila knew that Paul had given her mother several bottles of the sparkling wine in implicit exchange for an invitation to the dinner. That was yet another reason she felt trapped.

Normally, a New Year's Eve celebration would start late in the evening and extend well beyond midnight, but with the German curfew in effect, it would have to start and end much earlier. Madame BenZayed hoped the early hour would not dampen spirits too much. As for when it came time for her guests to leave, she had a plan. She had reserved two bottles of champagne for the local gendarme who could be persuaded, she felt sure, to look the other way.

By five o'clock, the guests began to assemble: Monsieur and Madame Fabron; Paul; a young French Tunisian couple who had been friends with Leila at Lycée Carnot. They had asked if they might bring a friend with them, a quiet but pleasant young man whose family lived in Kairouan and who would be alone that evening. Mme. BenZayed had been gracious: *"Plus on est de fous, plus on rit."* The crazier we are, the more we laugh.

The evening launched well. It was immediately apparent to Madame BenZayed that the young man from Kairouan—what was his name? Ali, perhaps?—did not drink champagne, but he was pleasant enough, even if his clothes weren't very fashionable and his French was heavily accented *à la Tunisienne*. But Leila's mother had to admit he was quite handsome and more importantly, Leila seemed to be enjoying his company. She had brightened considerably and when it was just the two of them sitting together at the table, she chatted away in that mix of French and Arabic that young people favored these days. Even M. BenZayed appeared to like the young man. The two men were both fans of *L'Etoile*, one of Tunis' better football clubs, and men never required more of a bond than that.

As the evening went on, It was also apparent to Madame BenZayed that Paul was getting quite loud. He seemed upset about something and quickly downed several glasses of champagne. At one point, he mentioned he had recently made two new acquaintances, both German generals. His father tried to steer the conversation in a different direction but Paul turned to M. BenZayed and asked him if he happened to know either of his new acquaintances, Albert Kesselring or Walther Nehring. Leila thought she saw her father stiffen at the names but he answered mildly enough, *"Je n'ai pas eu le plaisir."* I haven't had the pleasure. Paul responded casually, "I would be happy to introduce you someday" but it sounded condescending and now Leila was sure her father was irritated. She knew he did not like the new German occupation of Tunisia and that he wanted everyone—Germans, Italians, British, Americans, and even the French—to just go away. The young man from Kairouan, Ali—that was indeed his name—listened impassively. If he was at all political, he gave nothing away.

By the end of supper, Paul was quite drunk. His parents did not seem the least bit embarrassed, and when it came time to say goodnight, they were lavish with their *remerciments;* it had been a most delightful evening, a very happy way to end a somewhat sad year. Leila's friends from school stayed a few minutes longer, but the curfew made them uneasy and they thought it wiser to make their way home sooner rather than later. They would celebrate midnight at home. Ali was going to spend the night there, then take the tram back to the city tomorrow. As he was saying goodbye, Madame BenZayed noticed that Leila leaned close and whispered something in his ear. Ali simply smiled and said, *"Bon soir. mademoiselle."*

Madame BenZayed was tired so she said goodnight to her husband and daughter and went upstairs. Leila asked her father if he would like her to make him a glass of mint tea, but he preferred a small whisky and his pipe. While Leila's tea steeped, the two sat together contentedly, talking about nothing and everything.

"That young Fabron is an ass. It will not go well for him. I hope you're not associating with him."

"Mathafesh, Baba." Don't worry, father. The more I see him, the more I don't like him. He is not the least bit *interestant*. What did you think of the young man from Kairouan, Ali?"

"I like anyone who is an *'Etoilist.'*"

"Vraiment? C'est tout?" Really. Is that all?

"No, that's not all. He's respectful and perhaps very clever. I have the impression that he cares deeply about his country. He strikes me as a Destourian. Maybe even one of Bourguiba's disciples—a Neo-Destourian."

"Is that a bad thing, Baba?"

Leila's father shrugged. "No; but he should be careful. No one knows how this will end. The Germans? They will lose the war someday;

93

they will be gone. But the French? They will want to stay as long as they can. It may not go well for the nationalists; someday perhaps, but not right away."

"What about you, Baba. What do you want?"

"I want to sit here and talk with my beautiful daughter, sip this Scotch, smoke my pipe and then go to bed. That's good enough for me."

"*Enna zayda, Baba.*" Me, too.

"By the way, your mother told me you whispered something to that boy. What did you say to him?"

"I told him my father liked him."

CHAPTER TWENTY ONE

Hogmanay

1 January, 1943; Tunis. In his dream, Declan was with his father, fishing for salmon on the Shannon. It was a Sunday afternoon and the clouds were flying—"quite the dynamic sky," the gillie said. Then for some reason, the fish started banging on the door; the noise woke Declan and the dream quickly fades. Now the banging was only getting louder.

Bleary-eyed, Declan got out of bed and went to the window, poked his head out to look down at the street. His first thought was he was still dreaming dream; it was a bright morning and the street was unusually quiet. Then Punch looked up at him and said, "Get down here and open the door, ya wee wanker. I've brought you yer breakfast." Declan blinked. So it wasn't a dream, but maybe he was having a nightmare. Punch held up a package, kicked the door this time.

Declan padded down the stairs and unbolted the door. Punch stuck his boot across the threshold. "There! You're first-footed! " Declan just stood there, utterly lost. "It's Hogmanay! Give us a wee dram, ya Irish bastard!"

"What time is it?"

"It's nearly eight. I would have been here hours ago but Jerry wouldn't have been too pleased." Punch looked past him, up the stairs. "Is she here?"

"Who?"

"You know very well who."

Declan was beginning to wake up. "Your sister?" Bad idea. Punch stuck a stubby finger on Declan's nose. "Watch yourself, laddie.

95

We wouldn't want to start the year off on a bad foot, now would we? Come on; I'm hungry. Put on the hob and leave the rest to me."

The world was starting to come into focus. New Year's Day. Hogmanay. Very important holiday in Scotland. But how in God's green earth did Punch know where he lived? Declan couldn't remember ever telling him, and he was sure Punch had never set foot, first or otherwise, in his flat before. Ever the man of mystery.

It was chilly in the flat. Declan threw on a jumper and lit the kerosene heater. He filled a pan with water from the cold tap—the only one there was—and turned on one of the two small burners on the bottle-gas hot plate and set the water to boil. He reached for the tea tin—Twining's "Irish Breakfast;" Punch stared at it. "That the only one you have? Good cuppa for the ladies in the afternoon. Make it extra strong."

Punch had found the frying pan. "Plates? We'll need forks, too, or do you papists eat with your hands?"

"What's in the package?" Whatever it was, it was wrapped in old, oily newspaper.

"The butcher didna have any haggis so this will have to do." Punch peeled back the newsprint, revealing four small kippers, salted, gutted, and split from tail to head along the dorsal ridge. Something else, too: a string of bloody *merguez* sausages made from ground lamb, very spicy. Punch looked very pleased with himself. He reached into his overcoat pocket and produced four brown eggs. "*Hara athum*. Right out of the hen's bum. Never understood why the wogs sell eggs in fours; must be a Mohammedan thing. You do have bread for toast? Maybe even a little butter. I expect marmalade would be too much to hope for."

Declan looked at him and reached into the bread box on the counter. Out came half a loaf of brown bread, a small butter dish. "No marmalade, but will this do?" He held up a jar of marmite, a pungent, black paste made from yeast extract with some vitamins and minerals thrown in for good measure. "Invented by a German; only good thing they ever made. Well, that and beer, too."

Punch's eyes were wide with amazement. "Bless me, St. Andrew. There's hope for the Irish yet! Hurry up the tea! Put another spoonful of leaves in the pot and let it steep. Oh…and what about my whisky and none of yer God-awful poteen, either. Fetch, boy! The new year is hurrying by!" Declan rummaged in a drawer, produced a bottle of Jameson's, almost full. Punch looked at the label. "Poor Micks. You're such a sorry lot. Can't even spell. Oh well, can't be helped. Better than nothing. Slainte!"

Cigarettes after breakfast, plates in the sink, bottle almost empty. To Declan's surprise, Punch seemed almost reflective. "Always this quiet in your neighborhood?"

Declan laughed. "Never. French holiday and on a Friday to boot. Perfect storm. No buying and selling today. Everybody's in the mosque."

Punch shook his head, stared into his glass. "Nineteen-forty-bloody-three. We've been at it more than three years now. Yanks just a little more than a year in. Still in their nappies, but got their noses bloodied, they did. They'll learn."

"What happens next?"

"Libya's almost over. Fiver says Tripoli falls in the next two weeks. Then old Mr. Fox will be on his way here, looking for the exit. We'll have to keep our heads down then. Heard anything more from your Italian chum?"

"Didn't send a Christmas card. Can't imagine why."

"No, imagine he didn't. Too busy getting Mareth ready for Monty." Punch divided what was left in the bottle between the two empty glasses. "We need to know."

"Know what?"

"Their plan. Will the Desert Fox go straight up and out or will he stay and pick a fight? Knowing Rommel—and I'm not saying I do, but if I did—I'm betting on the latter. Things aren't looking so good on the Eastern Front these days. Wire report this morning has the Red Army surrounding the Germans at Stalingrad; more than 300,000 Germans already dead or wounded. God knows how many Russians have died— they say at least a million—but that doesn't matter to Stalin; the more dead, the fewer mouths to feed. But Hitler can't afford to lose on the Eastern Front and in North Africa, too. Bad for morale."

"A million dead? You can't be serious."

"Och, man. Listen to this: a friend of mine, a stringer based in Moscow—saw him in London last summer—told me a story. Uncle Joe is meeting with some party bigwigs around a table and he has to take a shit. So he gets up, goes over to a corner of the room, drops his pants, squats, and does it right there on the floor. Nobody says a word, not a peep. Don't know if it's a true story or not, but that's not the point. The point is nobody dares say anything to Joseph Stalin. It's his country. His army, too. Maybe someday, his world."

"A million dead! Jesus, Mary, and Joseph."

"Son, by the time this is all over, a million won't begin to matter. We're headed for oblivion. There isn't just one war going on out there; there are three."

Declan waited. Punch raised a finger. "One: we're fighting the Nazis, but that war will be over in a year or two. That's our war and we'll win it. Two: the war for independence our little Arab friends are fighting here and in Algeria and Morocco, too; that one will take longer because the French are just like us; they'll cling to their empire until their fingers bleed. Violent decolonization…North Africa, West Africa, Indo-China…" His voice trailed away.

"So what's the third war?"

"Son, that's the worst one of all. It's like one of those sandstorms that come up out of the desert—what's it called?—a *sirocco*; you can close all the shutters and the doors you want, but the sand will still get into the house. It gets in your hair, your ears, your nose, in between your teeth and up your arse." Declan was listening carefully; political speeches were not Punch's usual fare. "It's the war just beginning here in Africa, in Asia, in Latin America; a battle for the hearts and minds of all these worthy little yellow, brown, and black people; a war of ideas… of ideologies. East versus West. That war will last for a hundred years." Punch swallowed the last of his whisky, clinked Declan's glass. "And on that cheerful note, wanker, I'll be on my way. *Auld Lang Syne* and all that."

At the door, Punch turned to Declan. "Which side will you be on, Comrade Shaw? We will all have to pick one. Right, then. Cheers! See you tomorrow, bright and early."

The flat was suddenly quiet. Declan stared out the window, watched Punch make his way down the narrow street, turn a corner. Then he took out his notebook and wrote for almost an hour before reading what he had written, tearing out the pages and ripping them into little pieces.

He was attempting to make some sense of the slaughter on the Eastern Front, to distill some small measure of reason and truth from all that terrible madness. But the tiny pieces of paper in the wastebasket told the story: no words could truly describe the frozen horror unfolding just outside the gates of Stalingrad. And what if Punch was right, that this current war was just the beginning of an even more deadly confrontation to come? Everyone said that the last war was the war to end all others, but maybe this one was the beginning of the end for all of us.

CHAPTER TWENTY TWO

Secret Steps

1 January, 1943; Tunis. After he left Declan's flat, Punch walked down through the quiet streets of the Medina. All the shops were shuttered; his footsteps echoed through the empty, winding alleys. Twice, he turned around because he thought someone was following him, but both times, he found the street was deserted. When he passed through the Sea Gate and into the more modern French section of the city, he felt as though the broad avenues and regular plat revealed too many of the secrets that had been hidden in the shadows of the twisting, narrow streets of the old Arab Medina. Given what he was about to do, it was not a pleasant feeling.

Punch knew the Guardian's offices would be deserted. He unlocked the outer door and once inside, relocked and bolted it. He did the same to his cluttered, small office. He sat quietly for almost half an hour, partly to make sure he would not be disturbed and partly to compose a message in his mind. Once that was clear, he unlocked a cabinet in his office and extracted from it a small telegraph key and a book. The book was "Rebecca," the popular 1938 novel by Daphne du Maurier. The book had just been made into a Hollywood film directed by Alfred Hitchcock, his first American production; it starred Laurence Olivier and Joan Fontaine.

For the next half hour, Punch used the book to encode a message that would be decoded by cypher experts in the Kremlin in Moscow. It contained information about the size and movements of Allied troops in Tunisia, as well as Punch's assessment of Italian and German forces.

He added some of the details Declan had observed during his visit to the Mareth Line with General Messe, as well as what he could surmise about the timing of Rommel's retreat, the state of his army, and his intentions once in Tunisia. The last part was intentionally vague because no one yet knew what Rommel intended to do.

When Punch had gone off to fight in the Great War, he didn't give a tinker's damn about politics. The Russian Revolution was not his problem. But as his personal war progressed, he began first to question, then resent, orders given by men far from the front that resulted in the wholesale slaughter of his friends in the trenches, men who did the actual fighting and the actual dying. The system of old alliances that brought about the war in the first place, along with the British social order that desperately sought to maintain itself in the blood of the common soldiers, seemed to Punch grossly out of place in the Twentieth Century. It was time for things to change.

When the war was finally over and the boys came home, maimed, sick at heart, and robbed of their youth, Punch, like so many others, felt abandoned, tossed on the rag pile of the past and forgotten. With help from his father, he managed to get work on the docks at Tayside in Dundee. It was there, working alongside men like himself, that Punch got a taste of the hopelessness and disappointment of the dock workers who put in long hours without much hope of ever breaking away from a life of hard labor and subsistence wages. In searching for something better, Punch began to read about the Russian Revolution—Trotsky, Lenin, John Reed's masterpiece "Ten Days That Shook the World."

Punch never fully embraced Communism, but he became a sympathetic fellow traveler. Given his family's strong faith in the Church of Scotland, he kept his leftist leanings to himself. He began to write for the local newspaper and when the Spanish Civil War broke out in 1936, he saw the brass ring and grabbed it. He convinced his editor to let him cover the war and some of his first dispatches caught the eye of one of the Guardian's Senior Editors who offered Punch a byline. Punch jumped ship and for the next three years, he filed stories about class struggle, religious warfare, revolution and counter-revolution. He was careful not to overtly side with the Republicans, but he made friends with many British and American members of the International and Abraham Lincoln Brigades. One of those close friends was Jock Cunningham, a Glaswegian, who rose to the rank of Lieutenant Colonel and who played a key role in the Battle of Jarama, one of the principal actions of the war where he caught the attention of a young American war correspondent named Ernest Hemingway. Things began to get a little heady for Punch.

If Punch was lukewarm in his sympathies before heading off to Spain, he was a much more committed believer upon his return to Britain in 1939. He never pretended Communism was a perfect ideology, but he did see it as a valid alternative to the forces that brought the world to the brink of catastrophe in 1914 and seemed bent on doing it all over again in 1939. When Hitler invaded Poland, Punch was assigned to Tunisia to head the Guardian's small North African bureau. Now, three years later, thanks to Operation Torch, he was in the thick of it.

By this time, Punch believed he had a role to play on both sides of the political fence. He told the truth in his articles, never sugarcoating it for a British audience who desperately wanted to read some good news. And he made contact with handlers in Moscow who were delighted to have reliable eyes and ears inside Vichy France colonial territory, and who could observe at close hand events sweeping across North Africa. When Stalin was pushing Churchill to open a second front to relieve pressure on the beleaguered Russia army, Punch's Kremlin stock rose quickly. Rommel's retreat pushed his stock higher, and the Allied landings in Algeria and Morocco made him Moscow's man on the ground.

Punch kept this all very private. The world was complicated enough as it was and Punch was careful to keep his political worlds compartmentalized. When he wrote or edited articles for the Guardian readership, he was careful not to list too heavily to port. When he passed along information to his Soviet handlers, he did not feel he compromised the work or trust of his reporters; he just felt he widened their sphere of influence. And if, in the process of dealing with both sides of the ideological coin, he helped to defeat Fascism, well then, so much the better. The world had enough "isms" as it was.

Punch put away his telegraph key and his code book, locked the cabinet and then the office, and headed home. The rain had started again, a drizzle at first, then a steady downpour. By the time he reached his flat in an apartment building near *Cité Jardins*, he was soaked to the skin.

He peeled off his wet clothes, toweled his hair and put on a thick, tartan bathrobe. He poured himself a wee dram to take away the cold and picked up the book he had just purchased the day before: *Anna Karenina* by Leo Tolstoy. "Happy families are all alike; every unhappy family is unhappy in its own way."

There were only two windows in Punch's flat; both were grimy and streaked with rain. The light outside was already getting winter thin. He settled into his worn leather chair, pulled a an old afghan over his legs, took another sip of whisky, and dove in.

CHAPTER TWENTY THREE

Five Generals and a Soldier

New Year's Day, 1943. Back at his headquarters in Algiers, Ike spent the morning trying to fix a broken supply chain and looking at weather forecasts. There wasn't much he could do about the weather, but he was damn sure he would get the supply SNAFU straightened out. Before he left the front lines back on Christmas Eve, he had listened to one of his tank commanders tell him about the shells that were being fired from the American Honey tanks during the battle for Longstop Hill. At first, the colonel could't figure out why his ordinance could barely dent, let alone penetrate, the hulls of the new German Panzer MK IVs, the Tigers, that were pounding his men so murderously. It was only after he was forced to withdraw that the group commander realized his tanks had been firing practice rounds used for training; all the live explosive shells were lost somewhere along the supply chain that stretched back more than five hundred miles to the port of Algiers.

Ike fumed but at least he wasn't dickering with French politics. He had taken his orders from General Marshall to heart; all the political bullshit (as Ike called it) was now someone else's problem. He was determined to concentrate on winning the coming battle for Tunisia; its outcome could make or break him. At least he had his trusted assistant, "Civilian First Class" Kay Summersby, his red-headed Irish personal secretary, and his dog Telek, to keep him company.

***

More than a thousand kilometers to the west of Ike's headquarters, General George Patton paced like a caged lion in his seconded palace in Casablanca, looking at the same damn weather forecasts. He was going stir crazy. Second Corps was literally stuck in the red Tunisian mud, and its commanding officer and Patton's personal nemesis, General Lloyd Frendendall, wasn't doing a damn thing about it. Patton had read Frendendall's Christmas message to the troops who had fought so bravely in such miserable conditions on Longstop Hill; he found it depressing and defeatist. "Who would want to fight for that miserable son-of-a-bitch?" he fumed to his valet one morning. Every other day, he sent a cable to Ike promising to "get us moving again, with or without Lloyd, preferably the latter!"

Without anything better to do, Patton spent hours each day writing in his diary. He particularly liked to contemplate his past lives: as a soldier in Alexander the Great's army; fighting Parthians for Rome; a Viking bound for Valhalla; an English knight at Agincourt; a Highlander fighting for the House of Stuart; a pirate raider; a decorated officer in Napoleon's army. An American general bound to defeat the Nazi horde was only the next logical lifetime.

***

Field Marshall Erwin Rommel, the vaunted Desert Fox, lay in the back of a truck, despondent and sick. He had been in the desert for more than two years; his face was covered in sores and he was ill with another bout of dysentery. At one time, he had been feted as Germany's greatest general, but ever since his defeat at El Alamein, he had been on the run, literally and figuratively.

The previous month, he had flown to Berlin to meet with Hitler and the Führer's second-in-command, Hermann Goering. The Führer had berated him: "But you were superior in every way; you had more material, more tanks, better artillery and air superiority," he had screamed at Rommel.

"But we ran out of fuel, Mien Führer," Rommel responded.

"You had enough fuel to retreat," Goering taunted.

"We ran out of ammunition, Air Marshall."

"And yet you left thousands of shells at Tobruk and Benghazi!"

Hitler was now in a rage. "Your men had rifles, didn't they? Didn't they? They just threw them away! A soldier without a weapon deserves to die!"

That was one straw too many for Rommel. He told Hitler and Goering that it was a miracle that his army had been able to mount a fighting retreat almost two thousand kilometers long; that unless his men were withdrawn to Italy immediately, while there was still time, they would all be destroyed and so would Germany if the Allies were able to capture Tunisia and then land in Italy.

Hitler exploded. "Not another word from your mouth, Field Marshall!" he screamed, red with rage. "Your men will fight with their bare hands if they have to! You will defend North Africa like the Russians defended Stalingrad! You will destroy Eisenhower's army before they have a chance to invade Italy! If you die, so be it. At least you will die with honor! THIS IS AN ORDER!" and he left the room, slamming the door behind him.

Now Rommel was back in Libya and on the brink of defeat. Victory in North Africa was a dream and Rommel knew it.

***

Despite the rain that was falling on Libya, too, General Bernard Law Montgomery smelled blood. His Eighth Army had captured the city of Sirte on Christmas Day and now it was poised to take Tripoli, the last German stronghold in Libya. Mile by mile, he was forcing his opponent to retreat into Tunisia where he would be caught and crushed in the vise-like grip of two Allied armies. The end was in sight.

Following his hard-fought victory over Rommel at the Second Battle of El Alamein, Monty had been advanced to the List of Knight Commanders of the Order of the Bath, Britain's highest military order. As Rommel's star was falling, Monty's had risen to dazzling heights. There was no doubt in his mind that Rommel was beaten; Monty had more men, more vehicles, more supplies, and more fuel. It was only a matter of time before he would accept Rommel's surrender.

***

General Giovanni Messi, Commander of the Italo-German First Army, had completed the restoration of the Mareth Line and was waiting, as patiently as possible, to play his part in the battle for North Africa. He knew Rommel was in desperate straits and that his own job was to buy the time that would enable his German ally and friend to resupply and rest his men or to escape intact to Italy. Messe knew his friend well enough to know that Rommel's first thought would be for the well-being of his men, now numbering less than 5,000. He also knew that the politicians in Berlin and Rome would expect Rommel's exhausted and poorly supplied army to fight and die in Tunisia, bare-handed if necessary.

The natural defensive line at Mareth stretched almost thirty miles, from Tunisia's Mediterranean coast to a line of high ridges inland. Broken terrain and dry salt flats, impassable in rainy winter months, made flanking maneuvers difficult, if not impossible. The line would be defended by 73,500 men, 455 pieces of artillery, 480 anti-tank guns, and about 200 tanks. Messe knew he would be outnumbered in every aspect but he hoped the difficult terrain and the superior German Tiger tanks would be able to sufficiently delay Montgomery's advance, allowing Rommel to escape and Messe's forces to make an orderly withdrawal.

While Messe awaited the inevitable, he used his time wisely by making trips to Gabès and Sfax to shore up defensive positions around those two cities and their ports, and to consult with advance divisions from Rommel's army. Despite Hitler's irritation with Rommel, more supplies were beginning to arrive in Tunisian ports. The problem was that in delivering these supplies to Rommel who was still several hundred miles away, truck convoys used almost ninety percent of his fuel resupply, hardly an answer to Rommel's prayers.

***

No doubt the generals—German, British, Italian, and American—had real problems, but Private First Class Dennis Plaza, a member of the First Infantry Division (United States), the 'Big Red One,' had more immediate concerns. The first of these was staying alive; the second was not freezing to death; and the third finding something to eat. None of these were easily solved.

Plaza came from Worcester, Massachusetts. His Puerto Rican father had abandoned the family when Dennis was four; he had been raised by his Greek mother and grandmother. He had been a high school football star with hopes of a scholarship to Holy Cross, but that dream died on the day he received his induction notice. He had been sent for training to Fort Riley, Kansas in April 1942. Now, eight months later, he sat shivering in a slit trench near Medjez-el-Bab, cold, hungry, and with a bad case of the shits. And yet he was one of the lucky ones: there were 700 men in his unit that landed at Oran in Operation Torch; now there were less than 300.

Ever since the American withdrawal from Longstop Hill to this defensive position a week ago, things along the line had been relatively quiet. There were still a few mortar rounds and occasional sniper fire, but if Plaza kept his head close to the mud, he'd survive another day—that is if he didn't freeze or starve first. What kept him alive and relatively sane were the nightly visits from skinny, ragged Arab kids who brought eggs and even an occasional scrawny chicken to exchange for bits of chocolate or chewing gum or cigarettes. Plaza was even teaching one kid to speak English; already the boy could say "get-the-hell-out-of-here-you-god-damn-son-of-a-bitch," all in one breath. He laughed when he said it; Plaza did, too.

Dangerous and difficult as life was at the front, Plaza didn't mind. He had two sisters at home, but no brothers. Now, wherever he looked, he had as many brothers as he wanted, each one wearing the same shoulder insignia: a big red "1." If he was really lucky, Plaza would have some of these brothers for the rest of his life…however long that was.

CHAPTER TWENTY FOUR

Oud

Even in war, where there is so much destruction and death, life goes on. For most Tunisians, the war on their home soil was an inconvenient distraction; it wasn't deadly. For a few, the war provided opportunity— for advancement, for money, for temporary comfort, even for a way out of a miserable existence. That little Arab boy bartering eggs for chocolate with PFC Plaza near Medjez? A half hour later, he was telling a German artillery officer exactly how many men he had seen on the ridge and where they were dug in. To him, the war was a simple trade : information was just as good as an egg: it was always worth a bit of chocolate or maybe even a cigarette, even if it came with a box to the ears or a kick in the rear.

But for a few others, the war was perhaps a way out of the colonial conundrum. For more than sixty years, France had been Tunisia's "Protector." With its "civilizing mission," France had brought a measure of progress and prosperity to Tunisia. There were schools, doctors and hospitals, more roads and bridges, public transportation, a higher standard of living—for some, anyway. But there was a hidden cost to all this 'progress,' if that's what it was. Count it in the cultural malaise of the elite who were caught between two very different worlds or in the lives of the poor who were falling farther and farther behind. Either way, Tunisia's colonization was as dehumanizing as war; it just wasn't quite as bloody.

Ali now found himself drawn more and more to those who saw a glimmer of hope on the horizon, a place for a new and unique Tunisia in the post-war future. France had undoubtedly been weakened by their defeat at the hand of the Nazis, and maybe when this was all over, the nascent independence movement would be able to finally fulfill its promise. In the meantime, Ali had decided he would do anything he could to foster his Tunisian identity by embracing his religion, his language, and his culture.

And so here he was, standing outside the *Théâtre Municipale* on the Avenue Jules-Ferry, the main thoroughfare of colonial Tunis. The irony of the situation was not lost on Ali: Jules Ferry was a French statesman who was a devout proponent of colonialism and its ecclesiastical cousin, laicism; perhaps that was why the Cathedral of St. Vincent de Paul was directly across the street. No matter tonight. Ali was going to the *malouf* concert.

Malouf—the word meant 'customary' or 'familiar' in Arabic—had its roots in the melodies of the Andalusian region of southern Spain, the center of the Moorish occupation of the Iberian Peninsula. Since it came to prominence in the Fifteenth Century, *malouf* had been influenced by other musical styles most notably by Turkish music during the Ottoman era. There were offshoots of *malouf* in Libya, Algeria, and Morocco, but in Tunisia, where *malouf* had risen to become an artistic emblem of national identity, its unique rhythms were driven by the *'ûd tûnsī*, the Tunisian oud, a fretless lute-like instrument derived from the Persian barbat, that had been in use in North Africa for more than a thousand years. To the attuned ear, the oud was more than a musical instrument; it was its own perfect art form.

Outside the theater, the concert-goers were enjoying a brief but welcome respite from the rain. Normally, the concert would have been held in the evening, but due to the German-imposed curfew, it was scheduled to begin at 4 o'clock. Ali noted that unlike most events at the theater which catered to French and European tastes, this audience would be almost entirely Tunisian. He was especially pleased to see a few men in traditional dress wearing winter-grey *jebbas*, long embroidered linen tunics worn over a vest and baggy trousers called *sarouel*. Because of the cold, wet weather, a few of the men also had a *burnoose*, a long cloak made of brushed wool, draped over their shoulders, or a *kachabiya*, similar in style but with brown and white stripes. Many of the older men in the crowd wore a *chechia*, the uniquely Tunisian brimless cap made of red felt. One or two even had a coiled sprig of jasmin peeking out from behind their ears, the scent heady and sweet.

As Ali was surveying the crowd, he was surprised to see Kamel BenZayed. His back was turned to Ali, talking to a small group of friends that included a few women, all dressed in fashionable European-style gowns. Ali wanted to go over and greet Si Kamel, but he felt a bit intimidated in his plain student attire; also, he wasn't sure someone as distinguished and important as Si Kamel would remember who he was. He started to go into the theater, but just as he did, he felt a hand on his arm; he turned and found himself face-to-face with Leila.

She took his breath away. Ali was even more stunned when she gave him a light kiss on both cheeks; fleeting as it was, he reddened; he had never felt a woman's lips before.

"*Aslema*, ya Ali. *Keefek?* " Hello, Ali. How have you been?

"*La bes, al'hamduallah. Wenti?*" Fine, thanks be to God. And you?

"*La bes, barak'allahowufeek.*" Fine, the blessings of God on you. "Come say hello to Baba; he will be glad to see you."

Ali felt he had fallen into a dream, but he allowed himself to be led over to Leila's father. To his astonishment, Si Kamel seemed genuinely happy to see him again. He, too, kissed Ali on both cheeks, an unusually familiar gesture while they exchanged endless traditional greetings in Arabic. Leila watched, smiling. "*Ajbetic malouf?*" Si Kamel finally asked. So you like *malouf*?

Ali blushed slightly, looked down. "I do. In fact, my cousin plays in the orchestra; he gave me a ticket."

"Really? What does he play?"

"He is a violinist, but he also plays the *oud*. He is teaching me to play—or trying to."

"*Allah einik!*" May God bless your eyes!

"It's not my eyes, Sidi, that need blessing. It's my ears and fingers and they need every blessing God can give."

"I would love to hear you play someday," Leila said.

"*N'challah.*" God willing.

It was time to go in. Ali began to excuse himself, but Leila turned to her father. "Mother's ticket; do you still have it?"

Si Kamel nodded; she looked inquiringly at her father. He nodded again.

Leila turned to Ali. "*Ochod ba'thayna*," Sit with us. "*Menfathlik.*" If it pleases you.

Ali was speechless. The ticket in his hand was a student ticket that only gave him a place to stand at the back of the hall.

Si Kamel broke the silence. "*Haya, wildi. Nimshu*!" Come on, son. Let's go. He took Ali by the hand and led him into the hall.

Malouf is not for the faint of heart. It is played by a small orchestra consisting of violins, flutes, drums, and zithers, with occasional solos played on the *oud*. Its rhythms are based on the *qasidah*, a form of classical Arab poetry that contains a highly structured *nuba*, a two-part suite organized around quarter tones which can easily last for an hour or more. A portion of the *malouf* is sung by musicians in the orchestra who are backed by the heavily syncopated beat of *qanun*, drums. The effect is a mesmerizing repetition of instrumental and vocal music that can transport the attuned listener to an almost rapturous trance-like state. To the uninitiated, it can sound like the musical equivalent of havoc.

But on this particular night, Ali was only listening to the music with his ears. All his other senses were privately focused on Leila who was sitting next to her father, just two seats away. Never had he been so close to *al-jeina*, to paradise.

CHAPTER TWENTY FIVE

Rivals

24 January, 1943. In the earliest days of 1943, the war was not going well for Hitler. Sirte in Libya had recently fallen to the British Eighth Army and Tripoli would certainly be next. That meant Rommel would be pushed back into Tunisia where Allied forces were not-so-patiently waiting for him. But the scale of that retreat was nothing compared with the Battle for Stalingrad in southern Russia where the *Wehrmacht* was about to encounter a humiliating defeat on a scale almost defying human reckoning. The horrific battle had been raging for five months and with more than 2 million soldiers and civilians already dead, Stalingrad was about to become the longest and bloodiest battle in the history of warfare. Moreover, the losses sustained by the German army meant that vital forces had to be drawn from the Western Front to replace those lost in the east; Hitler's *Zweifrontenkreig*, his two-front war, was truly a double edged sword, mighty yet vulnerable. The debacle at Stalingrad also meant that North Africa was almost a sideshow to what was unfolding in Russia. But by no means could it be ignored. If the Allies were victorious in Tunisia, then an invasion of Italy would surely follow. Rommel would have to stand and fight. And win.

And then there was the battle within the battle. For almost two years, Rommel had been in total command of all German forces in North Africa, but now, his health failing and on the run, he was being pushed aside by General Hans-Jürgen von Arnim, a Silesian Prussian with a distinguished military pedigree dating back generations. Rommel detested him; for von Arnim, the feeling was mutual. Rommel thought von Arnim was a priggish aristocrat; von Arnim found Rommel to be a loud, offensive boor who liked to blow his own horn.

General Albert Kesserling knew the two men were more than bitter rivals; they were bitter enemies. One's star was rising, the other's was waning. As long as the infighting continued, the chances for success in North Africa diminished day-by-day.

One important element worked favorably for the German armies: the inexperience and ineptitude of the Americans. Yes; they had pulled off a major amphibious landing, and yes, they had secured help from the French forces stationed in North Africa, but they had yet to face a seasoned German army in a major battle. The skirmishes in the north had resulted in what amounted to a costly stalemate, but that was mere foreplay. Once the rain finally stopped and the armies could begin to maneuver again, the real test would come soon enough.

Kesselring had a plan. His intelligence officers told him that American morale was good but the men not only lacked experience, they were also badly led. Moreover, they loved to chatter away on their radios which made it easy to follow their progress and know their intentions. Their artillery and tanks liked to stay far back of the front lines and more than once, there had been disastrous friendly-fire accidents. Captured British and French soldiers went so far as to refer to their American allies as "our Italians," a not-so-backhand reference to the poor reputation of Italian soldiery. Rommel knew about this all too well; he had been in command of some Italian troops in the desert and found them wanting.

Kesselring's plan was beautifully simple: strike the Americans hard and fast. General von Arnim would sweep in from the north while Rommel attacked from the south through Gafsa. The two would join forces at a dot on the map: the Kasserine Pass. Once through the pass, the German forces would turn north and head toward Bône on the Algerian coast, effectively cutting off the Allied First Army. That would not only force the Americans and their French friends to withdraw but it would also give the Führer his badly needed victory.

There were a few logistical problems—von Arnim and Rommel both worried about having enough fuel for such a large-scale operation— but the reward would be well worth the risk. It might not be measured in territory gained, but it could certainly be measured in the damage inflicted on enemy troops. And it would enable the orderly withdrawal of German forces to the Italian peninsula to protect Germany's southern flank. Rommel had another, more personal, reason to favor Kesselring's plan. After months of fighting a defensive retreat, he instinctively wanted one more chance to take the offense, to attack his enemy. A great victory would save his tarnished reputation, and just might win back the Führer's favor.

War, in addition to its primary military mission, always has an attendant political personality. In early January, plans were underway for a secret conference to plot the future course of the war. Code named SYMBOL, the Casablanca Conference assembled the heads of government of the United States and the United Kingdom—President Franklin D. Roosevelt and Prime Minister Winston Churchill—along with the commanders of the Free French Forces, Generals Henri Giraud and Charles de Gaulle. Premier Josef Stalin of the Soviet Union was understandably otherwise engaged.

The conference was held on the grounds of the Anfa Hotel in Casablanca. Roosevelt took the lead with Churchill as his self-described "ardent lieutenant." The two Frenchmen who, like Generals Rommel and von Arnim were bitter rivals, were not party to any military planning, but offered pledges of "mutual support" to the Allied cause.

The Conference agenda addressed issues of tactical procedures, resource allocation, and a catchall category called "diplomatic issues." Over ten days, the Allied leaders, with input from their respective military and political staffs, hammered out the terms of a declaration of principals that would become known as the Casablanca Doctrine. The central theme of the Doctrine was contained in a phrase President Roosevelt borrowed from Civil War hero and former President, General Ulysses S. Grant: "unconditional surrender." Its meaning was absolutely clear: the Allies were unified in their commitment to fight the current war to its bitter end—the unconditional surrender of the Axis powers: Germany, Italy, and Japan.

Although "Unconditional Surrender" was the headline, other topics were discussed, topics like the eventual invasion of Europe, the leadership of Free French Forces, the postwar independence for the three French colonies in North Africa, and even limiting Jewish immigration into North Africa once the war was over. This last issue was a delicate one, designed to allay concerns that if immigration to newly independent countries were left unchecked, Jews would hold a disproportionate number of professional positions—doctors, bankers, lawyers—in relation to their size in the overall populations in Morocco, Algeria, and Tunisia. This may not have been a comfortable position for Roosevelt, but he felt it was a practical response to the rise of the kind of virulent anti-Semitism seen in Germany.

Just before the conference adjourned, Roosevelt sought out de Gaulle and Giraud. He could feel the palpable tension between the two men who were in joint command of the Free French forces, but in his inimitable style, he cajoled them into posing for a photograph shaking hands. They agreed but the handshake was so short and quick that it had to be restaged for the benefit of the photographers present. Afterward, Roosevelt confided it felt like "a shotgun wedding."

Meanwhile in Tunisia, the rain continued to fall. Plans were one thing; activating them was another. That would come soon enough.

CHAPTER TWENTY SIX

Shakespeare in Africa

4 February, 1943. Even before he opened his eyes, Declan knew something was different. It took him a moment to determine what was so strange: it was eerily quiet. Specifically, rain wasn't pounding on the roof of the flat, splashing across the window, running in rivulets down the street. To make matters even stranger, the sun was out—thin, but nevertheless shining. The street below was returning to life.

Unaccustomed to the sunny silence, Declan turned on the wireless BBC broadcast. Tripoli, the last surviving capital of Mussolini's "Roman Empire," had fallen a little more than a week before and on the morning of January 23, the pipes and drums of the First Gordon Highlanders and the Second Seaforth Regiment had marched into an abandoned city. Declan remembered Punch's New Year's Day wager: "A fiver says Tripoli falls in two weeks." Well, it had taken exactly twenty-three days, but never mind; Declan knew he would never have seen that five pound note.

Now, Churchill had flown to Tripoli to welcome Montgomery's victorious Eighth Army. Declan stopped to listen to the Prime Minister's unmistakeable growl and flowery prose. He ended with typical Churchillian flourish:

"The days of your victories are by no means at an end, and with forces which march from different quarters, we may hope to achieve the final destruction or expulsion from the shores of Africa of every armed German or Italian. You must have felt relief when, after those many a hundred miles of desert, you came once more into a green land with

trees and grass and I do not think you will lose that advantage. As you go forward on further missions that will fall to your lot, you will fight in countries which will present undoubtedly serious tactical difficulties, but which none the less will not have the grim character of desert war which you have known how to endure and how to overcome.

Let me then assure you, soldiers and airmen, that your fellow-countrymen regard your joint work with admiration and gratitude, and that after the war, when a man is asked what he did, it will be quite sufficient for him to say, 'I marched and fought with the Desert Army.' And when history is written and all the facts are known, your feats will gleam and glow and will be a source of song and story long after we who are gathered here have passed away."

Over the airways, there was a moment of silence, then Declan could hear thunderous cheering from the assembled troops. He imagined the Prime Minister, a cigar clenched between his teeth, waving his bowler in the air, saluting the newest British heroes. "A bit Shakespearean," he mumbled to himself, "but feckin' good."

At the Guardian office, Punch has listened to the PM, too. He professed to be an admirer, albeit a slightly reluctant one, but it was hard for a man, even a working man from Dundee, to quibble with Churchill's rhetorical skills. Much of leadership these days lay in the public's perception of a man's way with words, and it was hard to deny that Churchill was the right man for this critical moment in British history. Punch knew his time would come, but he kept that to himself.

When Declan walked in fifteen minutes later, Punch was standing by the window, head bent over the latest news story that had come in over the wire. He barely looked up. "Nice of you to drop by."

"Sorry. I stopped to purchase some of that new sunscreen."

Now Punch looked up and gave Declan one of his 'don't-be-smart-with me' gazes. He let the remark hang in the air just long enough to make Declan uncomfortable. Punch was a master at this game.

"Intermission's over if this keeps up. We'll be getting back to war soon if we aren't careful. Speaking of which…" Punch let another thought hang in the air. Declan fidgeted. "Speaking of which, my sources tell me the game's afoot with von Arnim and Rommel. Apparently they met with Kesselring in Sfax…"

"I heard."

Punch looked at Declan. "And said nothing?"

"Not much to say, really. Other than they had a meeting. Lots to discuss, I imagine. What have you heard?"

Declan knew Punch liked to keep his sources to himself but ever since their little New Year's Day party, he sensed Punch might be softening a little. He was wrong.

"Only that Rommel and his *Afrika Korps* crossed into Tunisia this morning. By tomorrow, he should be sharing a bowl of spaghetti with your friend General Messe." When Declan didn't rise to the bait, Punch took a more serious tone. "Not sure I would want to be one of Monty's engineers or sappers over the next few weeks. That will be a bloody business." Mine detectors had just become available, but because they used sensors to detect variations in the earth's magnetic field caused by a mine's metal, they weren't very reliable. Most sappers still relied on their bayonets to probe for mines, a slow, tricky—and highly risky—method of clearing a field.

"There will be barbed wire, too. Miles of it. We're back to the First War."

"Except this time, we'll blow a hole in the wire with a Bangalore torpedo, not make a human stile with a body or two."

"Not sure I'd want to be the one screwing sections of pipe together with a mess of explosives in my hand with shells and bullets flying over my head. Bloody hell."

Punch nodded, chewed his lip. "Messe will hold up the Eighth as long as he can. Meanwhile, what will Rommel and von Arnim get up to? That is the question."

"More Shakespeare. 'To be or not to be.' You and the PM. Remember a man is judged by the company he keeps. Who said that?"

Punch shrugged. "Hardly Shakespeare, is it now?"

CHAPTER TWENTY SEVEN

Epictetus

Albert Kesserling loved to smile, even when he was delivering bad news. A smile usually softened the blow a little, and this blow would need a lot of softening.

Paul looked stunned. The color drained from his face as he sat staring at the German general. "What exactly do you mean 'expropriate'?"

"It is only a temporary measure, Herr Fabron. We will return everything to you intact, better than before. You will be safer in La Marsa anyway."

"But I thought we were working together, that we were…friends."

"And we are! We are! That's why I provided you with all that nice, free labor. I'm only sorry it was too wet to get much work done. All will be well again, I promise you!"

Paul didn't know what to say. He sat in front of Kesserling's desk, dumb as a fish. Kesserling waited patiently; he knew the expropriation of the Fabron estate—only a temporary expropriation—would upset Paul and his family, but that was not his problem. They had assumed too much and anyway, Kesselring fully intended to pay for all of the wine he consumed…in Reichsmarks. The house and the land was another matter. War was difficult on everyone.

"Are you familiar with the writing of Epictetus, Herr Fabron?"

Paul blinked. "I'm sorry. What? Who?"

Kesselring's smile broadened. "Epictetus. A Greek philosopher. A stoic."

"A Stoic?" Now Paul looked both hurt and confused. What did a Greek Stoic have to do with having his family's estate expropriated by the Nazis?

"Yes! He began life as a slave, then lived in Rome until he was banished. His *weltanshauung*—such a good German word, is it not?—was most enlightened."

"*Weltan* what?"

Now Kesserling actually laughed. "His *concepion du monde* as you would say; his view of the world."

Paul was struggling to recover his portion of the conversation, if that's what this was. "And what exactly was this Greek's *concepion du monde, mon General*?" Paul's use of French was a deliberate strike, but it seemed to fall on deaf ears. In fact, Kesselring actually seemed to brighten.

"That philosophy is not simply a theoretical discipline; it is a way of life! That external events are beyond our control and therefore we should accept calmly and dispassionately whatever happens. In other words, while we cannot control everything in our lives, we can only control our reactions to events. Do you see the connection, *Monsieur Fabron*?" Now it was Kesselring who turned the linguistic table back on Paul.

Kesselring continued. "I have studied Epictetus because I believe he has much to teach a soldier. Do you know what he said?"

Paul waited.

"He said—he actually said!—that we should not be troubled by any loss, that nothing really belongs to any of us anyway so nothing can ever be truly taken away. Only our opinion of events matters! Only our reaction to external events is real. Everything else..." Kesselring widened his hands, made them flutter bird-like, "is illusion. Let me put it his way, my young friend. There are some things in life you cannot control, can never control, but you can control how you respond, how you react. Dignity lies in how one responds." Kesselring's smile faded away. "Do you understand, Monsieur? You will get back what you think is yours when I deem it appropriate. Until such time, *mon ami*, I suggest you choose to respond wisely." Now the smile returned. "A la Epictetus! *Bon journée, Monsieur*." Dismissed.

Paul had dreaded telling his father about Kesselring's expropriation of the family estate, and with good reason. Monsieur Fabron had never been very supportive of Paul's attempts to curry favor with the Germans—he didn't trust them anymore than he trusted the Arabs who worked in his vineyard. And as for the Jews who had showed up one morning to "work," they were worse than useless. Not one knew the first thing about viticulture; they were all lawyers or bankers. even a doctor or two. He had wasted an entire two days trying to teach them the most basic tasks, to no avail. He had sent them away to God knows where, and, to be honest, he didn't care.

Now he stared out the dirty window of the family's villa in La Marsa. It was his wife, Paul's mother, who asked the first obvious question. "Did he say what he intended to do with the property?"

"He wants to use it as field headquarters for some of his general staff. Barbed wire everywhere, guards. Land mines. Land mines! I had the impression that something is about to happen. Something big." Paul sat glumly staring off into the distance, shoulders slumped, his affect flat as a *crêpe*.

Her next obvious question: "When?"

Paul shrugged. "For all I know, it's already done. When was the last time you were there, father?"

"A week ago. No; four days ago. Everything seemed fine. It had even stopped raining. Not that it makes any difference now…" His voice trailed away. At least the anger seemed gone. He looked back to Paul. "You said 'something big.' What did you mean?"

"I'm not sure. People were running in and out of his office. I'd never seen activity like that before. It was something…" he searched for a word, "electric. But nobody actually said anything, at least while I was there, but you could just tell…"

Another question from Madame Fabron, not so obvious this time. "Will they compensate us? Will we get anything?"

"He said he will pay us for any wine from the cellar that gets drunk. In Reichsmarks, whatever good that will do us." Paul looked up at his father. "I'm sorry, father. I was only trying to help."

Madame Fabron looked at her husband, wrung her hands. "We'll be ruined. This war, it's like a nightmare and I can't wake up. What are we going to do?"

Her husband laid a hand on her shoulder. It wasn't like him to be gentle but this time, he was. "Something good may yet come of all this." He looked away. "The Levant. Maybe South America; Argentina…" His voice trailed away. He turned to look at Paul. "Help? You thought you were helping? Really? I thought you were trying to drum up business with the Nazis." The gentleness was now gone. "The next time you feel like trying to help, go see someone who has a reason to offer us help. Kesserling…the Nazis…they don't give a damn. They don't want to help people like us. They want one thing, one thing only."

Paul looked at him, the question obvious.

"To defeat their enemies, boy! To win the war." He turned back to the window and to the sea beyond.

Paul was looking at something else: a faded photograph on the opposite wall taken years ago that showed him with his mother and father on the veranda of the Tebourda estate, "Chateau Fabron." Everyone was smiling, everyone looked happy. Even his Tunisian nanny in the background—he suddenly remembered her name, Khadija—looked like they hadn't a care in the world. Now, he struggled to make sense of his conversation with General Kesselring—one-sided as it was—about some ancient Greek philosopher—Paul couldn't remember his name—who believed that all external events were beyond one's control and it was only one's reactions to them that mattered. He had two reactions to the events of today—fear and anger—and sometimes, it seemed to Paul, it was impossible to distinguish between the two.

CHAPTER TWENTY EIGHT

The Fourth Star

10 February; Algiers. The word spread quickly but quietly. One by one, the staff gathered in the outer office. They shook hands or squeezed a friend's shoulder. They were happy for him. He deserved it.

Lieutenant-Commander Harry Butcher had been the first to hear the news. He had received a call from a friend, Captain Barney Fawkes on the submarine mother ship 'Maidstone' that was at anchor in the harbor below Ike's headquarters in the St. George Hotel in Algiers. Fawkes had just heard a report over the BBC that General Eisenhower had just been promoted to a four-star general; he was calling to congratulate the Supreme Commander. Then Beetle Smith came in grinning, followed closely by Ike's personal staff: Mickey, his body servant, Hoaney, Williams, and Foster, his house boys. "Civilian First Class" Kay Summersby was last to arrive; she had a bottle of champagne. "Does he know yet?" she asked.

No one knew. Ike hadn't said anything to anybody. Beetle Smith said, "Let's all go in. You tell him, Butch."

Butch knocked and they heard Ike's raspy voice. "Come." They all entered, Butch first, then the others, Kay last, with the bottle of champagne behind her back.

Ike looked up from a stack of papers on his desk. "What's all this?"

Butch snapped to attention, saluted, then stuck out his hand. "Congratulations, General, Sir!"

"For what?"

They all looked at each other. "Well you're now a real general, sir; the real four-star kind!"

"What are talking about Butch?"

"You got your fourth star. It's on the news!"

Ike put down the papers in his hands, leaned back in his chair. "I'll be damned. Nobody told me! You sure about this? You better not be joking; I'll break all of you—even you, Summersby!" Ike glowered at Kay, but then he was grinning, laughing.

"It's true, sir and we're here to celebrate." Kay held out the champagne.

Just then, the telephone on Ike's desk rang. It was the message center. A telegram had just arrived. The signaler read it to Ike: "Congratulations on your fourth star! Love, Mamie."

Ike put down the receiver. "Well, if Mamie knows, I guess that makes if official. I'll be damned," he said again.

The cork flew out of the bottle with a loud Pop! Mickey had glasses for everybody. Kay poured.

Glasses filled, Butch raised his and said, "To General Eisenhower: four hips and a hooray!" The party got started.

After that first bottle of champagne and then a second that just somehow appeared out of thin air, they all trooped over to Ike's villa for more drinks. Foster built a fire in the fireplace and someone put a record on the phonograph. There were endless toasts; for a moment, the war was over and won and life was good again.

Ike was in heaven and all his friends were there with him. All his life, he had been working toward this moment, from one fort to the next, always pushing paper, taking orders, far away from home and family. A soldier's lonely life. It had taken a world war to change all that, and now he, a boy from the plains of Kansas, had reached the pinnacle of his profession. Four stars. Washington, Grant, Sherman, Pershing, Marshall, MacArthur; a few others, but not many.

Butch put another record on the phonograph, "One Dozen Roses," It was Ike's favorite song. He loved to sing but he had a soldier's voice; tonight it didn't seem to matter. When the song was over, Ike told Butch to play it again and this time, he joined in on the chorus. Only Mickey caught him looking at Kay Summersby as he sang *"Gimme one dozen roses, put my heart in beside them, and send them to the girl I love."*

Later that night, the party over and everyone finally gone to bed, Ike sat on a bench in the privacy of his little garden, wrapped in his great coat. The tip of his cigar glowed red in the darkness. He heard the door to his villa open and close and when he looked up, Kay was standing there wearing his old woolen bathrobe, the same one that had been issued to him at West Point more than thirty years ago. She shivered. He patted the bench and she sat down next to him. He put his arm around her, pulled her close.

"I'm so happy for you, darling." She kissed his cheek, snuggled closer.

Ike was silent for a moment, took another pull on his cigar. "You know, Kay, in another lifetime, you and I…"

Kay put her finger on his lips. She turned to him, put her face close to his. "Ssh," she whispered. "This. This is our lifetime." When she kissed him this time, it wasn't on the cheek.

"I'm cold," she said. "Let's go back in."

CHAPTER TWENTY NINE

Lions, Men, Women

January,1943; central Tunisia. In Arabic, the word *k'sar* means 'fortress.' By using the dual form of the Arabic language, two fortresses become *k'sreen* and referred to the local ruins of two fortresses, old Roman outposts that once guarded against Berber marauders coming up out of the desert. The forts had long since crumbled to dust, but shepherd boys roaming over the land still found an occasional artifact or coin. When the French finally decided to make a map of the region in the late 19th Century, they used its original Arabic name, only now, they spelled it 'Kasserine.'

Kasserine was the center of an overlooked corner of the country, maybe even a forgotten one. The region was not nearly as lovely as the Mediterranean coast; not as fertile as the Sahel, the thin agricultural band that lay between the coast and the mountains to the west and the desert to the south; not remotely as enchanting as the vast Sahara that covered most of the south. The mountainous regions in the western third of Tunisia got very little official or, for that matter, unofficial attention. There were some sheep herded by nomads and a few apricot trees that struggled for purchase in the thin, rocky soil. It was a thirsty, poor place. But in war, topography is paramount, and suddenly, military eyes were on the mountains, specifically on the passes between them.

There is a saying in the Maghreb that Moroccans are lions, Algerians are men, and Tunisians are women. Gentle, pliant, receptive Tunisia, once again caught in an oncoming human storm, about to be gutted by two great armies—two warring empires—more blood and salt sown into its already depleted soil. For military purposes, tacticians on both sides knew that old saying might as well be a description of the chain of mountains—the High Atlas—that run from Morocco on the west, through the center of Algeria, into Tunisia on the east. As they move east, the mountains seem to dissipate and soften, so by the time the range reaches Tunisia, it is composed more of high hills than steep mountains. Still, for armies, they are important obstacles either to overcome, circumvent, or defend.

The village of Kasserine was barely a dot on one of the newer French maps. There was a dusty central square, a few shops—more stalls, really—a café where men came to play cards and drink tea, and a tiny mosque. The population of the village was less than 500 souls, but that number swelled on Tuesdays, *souk* day, when local shepherds brought their flocks to market or nomadic traders set out their meager wares in the village square. Only one main road ran through the village on its north-south axis; another single track road intersected that road a few miles away to the south. It led off into the mountains toward the Algerian border, less than a hundred kilometers away.

A single geological feature loomed over the entire lonely, arid landscape: *Jebel Chaambi*. It was the last gasp of the Atlas Range and, at just over 5,000 feet, the highest mountain in Tunisia. Its gently sloping limestone slopes were covered by thick pine forests, and other than a few hidden caves and shallow gorges, the rocky path up to the summit wouldn't have posed any significant challenge to a casual hiker let alone a serious alpinist. But to the military planners on opposing sides of the war, it was key high ground. For the Americans, the narrow pass just to the north of *Chaambi* would have to be defended by Lieutenant-General Lloyd Fredendall's Second Corps. For Rommel's *Afrika Korps* and von Arnim's Fifth Panzer Army, it would be the sharp end of the stick.

CHAPTER THIRTY

Prelude to a Battle

12 February. Gone were the days when Ike could just take a drive, Kay at the wheel of his sedan, while he read dispatches, smoked a cigar, relaxed. Now he had to travel in a convoy, armed personnel fore and aft, an emergency spare vehicle trailing, an aide in the back seat passing papers back and forth. The new reality for a four-star general on his way to visit the front.

It was a long and bone-rattling drive: at least twenty-six hours from Ike's headquarters at the St. George Hotel in Algiers to Lieutenant-General's Lloyd Fredendall's new command post in central Tunisia. Along the way, the general's convoy had to contend with British and American truckers who were careening along the "Red Ball Express," the long-haul supply chain that connected the front lines in Tunisia with the Allied-controlled ports in Oran and Algiers, both over five-hundred miles away. The truckers didn't pay much attention to the four-star flags flying from Ike's car, but they sure-as-hell paid attention to the pretty redhead driving it. At first, Ike didn't like all the wolf whistles and catcalls, but as the hours passed, it became something of a joke between chauffeur and passenger.

Fredendall's headquarters were dug deep into a box canyon located more than eighty miles behind his front line that occupied a position near a small village called Sidi Bou Zid. Ike didn't like that one bit. Nor did he like the fact that although British intelligence was repeatedly hearing radio traffic that hinted at an imminent attack from the north,

Fredendall had not bothered to order his men to dig defensive lines or to mine the area north of his position. He seemed to think it more likely that an attack would come from the south through Gafsa, but his intelligence officers felt that was more likely a diversionary tactic, not the main event. The whole situation made Ike uneasy.

Leaving Kay behind in a VIP tent to get some sleep, Ike set out with a driver to inspect the front. He wasn't any more satisfied there. Second Corps was spread out all over the place, exposed and woefully unprepared for any attack from either the north or the south. It seemed to Ike that despite all the warnings from increased radio traffic and some intermittent sniper fire, a dangerous lack of concern lay like a thick fog all along the Allied lines. Returning to Fredendall's command post at three o'clock in the morning of St. Valentine's Day, he bluntly said as much to the Lieutenant-General before heading off to the VIP tent to get some badly needed sleep of his own.

While Ike was fitfully dozing in his sleeping bag, Field Marshall Hans-Jurgen von Arnim gave the order to launch Operation *Frülingswind,* Spring Wind, by ordering four battle groups forward to positions just to the north and east of the village of Sidi Bou Zid and the nearby Faïd Pass. Intelligence had informed him that the Allied troops in the area were under joint British and American command and that they were dispersed in small pockets that would make mutual support difficult, if not downright impossible. Moreover, many of these units were composed of largely untested American combat troops, and who knew how they would react to their first real engagement?

Von Arnim's knew he held another high card in his hand. The American's tanks—Shermans and Honeys—were no match for his Tigers. The Americans would be disastrously out-gunned. Von Arnim smelled blood.

Less than fifty miles to the south, Field Marshall Erwin Rommel, the Desert Fox, was peering through his field glasses at the Gafsa oasis. He was exhausted from his ordeal in the desert, sick with jaundice and dysentery. He longed to go back to Swabia: eat spaetzle, drink cold beer, smell a pine forest again, that is if he could ever get the sand out of his nostrils. But before he could that, before he returned home, he wanted one more chance for glory, one more opportunity to reclaim the hero's mantle. He knew he had fallen from the Führer's favor and he did not like the feeling one bit.

He had expected to find American troops in the oasis, but to his surprise—and his disappointment—the place looked serene and empty. It was nearly dusk and all he could discern were small watchfires from some of the Arabs who lived in the oasis or tended small plots there. Even more to his surprise as he adjusted the focus, they seemed to be celebrating something.

"What are they doing?" he asked his aide.

"Eating. It seems they've been looting, Herr Field Marshall."

"Looting? Looting what?"

"American supplies. Rations, Herr Field Marshall. Look over there." He pointed to a different spot in the oasis. "Abandoned *Ami* vehicles. I think they've withdrawn. They're gone."

"Think it's a trick?"

"No, Herr Field Marshall. I think they're gone. They didn't want to fight you."

"Gone? Gone where?"

"Withdrawn to the north, Herr Field Marshall. To the mountain pass near a place called Kasserine, I think."

Rommel continued to study the scene through his field glasses. Except for the farmers, the oasis certainly looked deserted. It was not what he had expected to see: a few ragged Arabs celebrating their good fortune instead of battle-dressed American soldiers dug into defensive positions, ready to fight. After the long months of a fighting retreat against a formidable British army, Rommel had hoped to finally engage American units. Not just engage; to attack! From what Kesselring and von Arnim had told him, the *Amis* were poorly led and untested. He much preferred those odds.

CHAPTER THIRTY ONE

Head Down, Eyes Open

13 February. Much to Declan's astonishment, the conversation had been unusually soft and civil. Almost democratic. Punch had even ended his pitch with, "I'll understand if ya dinna want to go." Declan was so taken aback that he almost didn't believe the words he heard coming out of his own mouth:

"Of course I'll go. 'War correspondent' has such a sexy ring to it. But tell me again: how am I getting to the Americans? I don't think the Nazis will just open the gate for me."

"There are still a few trucks running the coast road for food and supplies. I have a friend. He'll get you to Tabarka and from there, someone else will drive you over the hump to Sbeitla. Might take a few hours, but you shouldn't have any problems."

"Sbeitla?"

Punch nodded. "You'll meet up with the Yanks there. Probably some other correspondents, too. Just take care of yourself, boy" he said, almost gently. "I doubt you'll find a way to wire copy from down there so think in terms of a feature story, a long one that could run over a few days after you get back. Details, scene, quotes. Color. Not just facts on this one. Show your readers; don't just tell them. This will be different."

"What do you know that I don't?"

Punch shrugged. "Just an old soldier's hunch. There's too much going on now, too many moving pieces. Keep your head down and your eyes open. To the extent you can, tell both sides of the story. I'll back you up. You'll have plenty to see. Remember: this is likely the first action against a real army for the Yanks. The Vichy French—that was just foreplay. This time it counts."

"What about Monty? Where's he?"

"Bit of a sideshow, I'd say. He'll be the next wave, probably at Mareth but not for a week or two. Your friend General Messe is waiting for him there. But right now, the main attraction is in the mountains. A place called Kasserine." Punch looked at his watch. "You'd better get your kit and go. You'll get battle dress there." He extended his hand. "Good luck, lad. See you in a few days."

Declan felt that familiar knot in his stomach. "Aye-aye, captain."

"And remember: head down, eyes open. *Rubi mak.*"

Declan frowned. "What does that mean?"

"*Rubi mak.* It's wog; means 'God be with you'."

Now Declan was really worried. He had never heard Punch refer to anything remotely divine.

"*Anglais? American?*" the lorry driver asked Declan. The cab of the truck smelled of cigarettes and fish.

"*Irlandais.*" Apparently, that was good enough. The driver ground the lorry into gear and off they went. He didn't say another word until they were just outside Tabarka, three hours later. Only once had they seen any Germans; a small convoy moving back toward Tunis. The driver had waved at the trucks as they passed, but kept going. Now, a small grey Peugeot truck was waiting by the side of the road. The driver slowed and stopped, motioned for Declan to get out. "*Yimshi il Sbeitla. Ma'aslema.*" He's going to Sbeitla. Goodbye. The lorry drove off.

The road over the mountains was nearly empty, but the twists and turns made for slow going. By the time the truck reached Sbeitla, it was late in the afternoon and Declan was stiff and sore. The sun was just starting to set behind the mountains, now only a few miles off to the west. It was cold and the temperature was dropping fast. The Peugeot turned down an unmarked road and pulled to a stop in front of a checkpoint manned by a group of soldiers, American flags on their flack jackets. The driver—he hadn't said a word to Declan all afternoon—handed over a letter; the sergeant scanned it and came over to Declan's side of the truck. "Identification, please." Declan handed over his passport and his Guardian credentials.

"Thank you, Mr. Shaw. Welcome to our little slice of heaven." He pointed to a tent marked *Press.* "The other correspondents are already here. Lieutenant Conley will get you squared away." He saluted and turned away.

Lieutenant Conley tuned out to be an enthusiastic young information officer who didn't look like he was old enough to shave. He showed Declan where to stow his gear, then introduced him to three other correspondents, all from American newspapers.

"Welcome to Sbeitla, gentlemen. This is Mr. Declan Shaw from The Guardian. It's getting late, but I'm hopeful that tomorrow you'll be able to meet General Fredendall and maybe have a chance to inspect the Roman ruins of Sufetula, just over there. Very impressive." He pointed vaguely to the south. "As you may know, in addition to the well preserved forum and the many interesting temples surrounding it, Sufetula is also remarkable as the site of a great battle which initiated the Muslim conquest of North Africa in 647."

"*Plus ça change,*" Declan muttered to himself.

"I'm sorry, Mr. Shaw?"

"My apologies, Lieutenant. '*Plus ça change, plus c'est la même chose.*' It's French: the more things change, the more they stay the same."

Conley gave no indication he understood; the remark just didn't seem to matter. He glanced at the others in the group before looking straight at Declan. "Looks like it will be a cold night. I'm afraid we only have some C-rations for you. Better than nothing! Would you gentlemen like some hot coffee? Perhaps you'd prefer tea, Mr. Shaw."

Declan gave a polite nod. It had been a long day and what he really wanted was something a lot stronger, but tea would have to do.

Later that night, Declan, still fully clothed except for his boots and wearing a woolen cap, lay on a cot in the thin sleeping bag provided by his hosts. All the other correspondents in the tent were, by the sound of their snores, sleeping soundly. Declan envied them.

Around 4:30 in the morning, Declan heard what he first thought was thunder, but he knew it was too cold to be thunder. It didn't take him long to realize that it wasn't thunder he heard; it was the sound of artillery. German artillery from the sound of it, coming from the direction of Sidi Bou Zid.

In the dark, he fumbled for his notebook and a pencil, turned on his flashlight and began to write:

February 14, (St. Valentine's Day!), 0500 hours: *We are encamped near Sbeitla, a small town in the remote, mountainous region of central Tunisia. A few minutes ago, I was roused from semi-sleep (God it's cold here!) by the rumbling thunder of artillery, the opening salvo of the next tragic opera in this war? Earlier in the evening, we were briefed by a freshly creased and clean-shaven American Lieutenant who told us that German troops were moving into position to attack the village of Sidi Bou Zid, about twenty-five miles to our east. The American Second Corps has come here to defend Sbeitla and, more importantly, to control the road running south and west toward the Kasserine Pass. That pass is of strategic importance to both the Allied and Axis armies because it guards the way northwest into Algeria. Were it to fall into Axis hands, the Allied forces now in northern Tunisia would be exposed and cut off from reinforcements and resupply. That would be nothing short of a disaster, making the recent Allied landings in Morocco and Algeria— Operation Torch—for naught. The Allied attempt to open a second front in this war would likely fail.*

Declan paused. It was still pitch black outside the tent but there were more and more bright stabs of light from the American guns now returning fire. Something else, too. A fierce wind was rattling the canvas walls of the tent. There would be no sleep for Declan this night.

***

From Declan Shaw's journal, entry dated *14 February, 1700 hours: There was no clarity with the thin morning light, only chaos and confusion. To make matters worse, it was almost impossible to see anything. A sandstorm, thick as a swarm of locust, has enveloped us here in Sbeitla, making observation difficult and communication almost impossible.*

From what I can glean from random conversations with army personnel and after an aborted visit to observe the military action near the village of Sidi Bou Zid, it appears that German forces (tank and infantry) under General Hans-Jürgen von Arnim have routed the Americans and that our position here in Sbeitla is now tenuous. We have been told to prepare for withdrawal at any moment.

Unable to confirm any details yet, but according to unofficial reports, American forces have suffered grievous losses, both men and material. Two infantry battalions and portions of an armored division have been isolated and still surrounded; many officers and men have been captured and local Arabs have been observed looting the dead. One tank commander told me that his gasoline-powered Sherman tank had been hit by a shell and immediately burst into flames. He called his tank a "Ronson" after the windproof cigarette lighter carried by almost every American soldier.

The 10th and 21st Panzer Divisions under the command of Field Marshall Erwin Rommel—the 'Desert Fox'—was reported to have been involved in today's fighting.

General Eisenhower, Supreme Allied Commander for North Arica, recently inspected American positions in the area. I'm told he was less than pleased. Command positions too far to the rear, lack of coordination between British and American units, faulty communications. He is now en route back to his headquarters in Algiers and may not yet be aware of what is happening here. I'm not sure anyone really knows what's going on.

From Declan Shaw's journal, entry dated *15 February, 2230 hours: Overnight, the decision was made to counterattack German positions in and around Sidi Bou Zid. Around noon, Lieutenant-Colonel J.D. Alger led the attack with an armored battalion that included 52 tanks across a wide plain flat as a billiard table toward the German lines. We (4 war correspondents) were driven to observe the counterattack from a hill west of the village.*

The American column had already encountered enemy fighters and Stuka dive bombers. As we watched, Alger's tanks advanced single file across a dry wadi. Halfway across, they encountered enemy air-burst artillery; the rain of shrapnel from the exploding shells caused tank commanders to close their turrets and reduced their speed of attack from 30 mph to less than 5 mph. It also made the tanks blind; now they could only see through a small forward window. We could not help but think of that textbook formation as a line of sitting ducks, blind to anything on their flanks. But this is not textbook warfare, as the Germans know all-too-well. As the Americans proceeded to cross a second wadi, unobserved enemy tanks attacked in force from both the north and south. Shelling was vicious. Of the 52 tanks that set out this morning, I counted 46 wrecked and burning, thick black smoke billowing into the sky, still in single file. The few tanks that were still operational retreated, leaving more than 100 other vehicles and self-propelled guns plus countless dead on the battlefield. The two entire infantry battalions and the remains of the armored division that were surrounded yesterday are now completely cut off from rescue. They will certainly be captured or killed. We observed German tank crews celebrating their victory while local Arabs emptied pockets of cigarettes, candy bars, and other personal items and even stripped clothes off the dead Americans before looting their abandoned vehicles. Boots, cigarette lighters, and jerrycans of gasoline were the most prized booty.

We have been able to confirm that Lt Col Alger was captured and is now a Prisoner of War. We have not been granted access to Generals Ward, Fredendall, or Anderson or any of the other general officers in the chain of command. Everyone seems stunned at the scale of the defeat. Americans aren't used to losing.

From Declan Shaw's journal, entry dated *16 February, 2400 hours. It has been a long and merciless day. At 0500 this morning, approximately 230 men, remnants of the infantry battalion that was surrounded on Djebel Lassouda, came straggling back to friendly lines. They were led by an exhausted Major Robert Moore. After receiving orders to withdraw, Moore had marched his men through the night, often coming with hailing distance of German soldiers who did not realize they were Americans.*

The men surrounded on the other hill, Garet Hadid, were not so lucky. They had been without food or water for two days and were almost out of ammunition. Their commander, Colonel Thomas Drake, did not receive orders to withdraw from his position until yesterday at 2000 hours. According to the few survivors who made it back to American lines after marching more than 20 miles across the desert, Drake and 400 of his men were within a mile or two of American lines when they were surrounded by German tanks and infantry. Drake refused to surrender; put up a three-hour fight. He along with all his men are presumed dead or captured.

Declan put down his pencil. He was cold, hungry, and exhausted from lack of sleep and from what he had witnessed over the last three days. He could smell himself—never a good sign. The battle of Sidi Bou Zid was over; the American position at Sbeitla was no longer tenable. Now he was part of the American retreat to a new defensive positions in the Kasserine Pass.

CHAPTER THIRTY TWO

Panic

"I guess he thinks he's Hannibal."

"Who thinks he's Hannibal?" Declan had just returned to the tent after a hasty visit to the latrine. The other correspondents were stuffing gear into their duffle bags, hurriedly getting ready to leave.

"Fredendall. I just saw a copy of a message he sent to Robinett. "Move the big elephants to Sbeitla," it said. "Move fast and come in shooting." Jesus! Tanks are now 'big elephants'?" It was Will Lang, the Time-Life correspondent, senior journalist in the tent, talking. He usually knew things others didn't. Declan learned long ago that photographers always got the first slice of cake.

"Where's Robinett?" Declan asked. "Why come in shooting now? The battle's over."

"Fredendall needs him to cover our asses but he's thirty miles north at Sbiba. He'll buys us time—that is, if he can get here. Robinett knows what he's doing. He's the one who told Ike that Sbeitla was not defensible and that we should dig in somewhere over in the Western Dorsal, probably right where we're headed. The Kasserine Pass. Must be where the Germans are headed, too. They want to get to our supply depot in Tebessa or head north to the coast to cut us all off. Or both. Rommel is one smart bastard."

Conley stuck his head in the tent. "Let's get going, gentlemen. No bacon and eggs this morning; mess tent closed an hour ago. The general's in a bit of a hurry."

"I bet he is," Lang whispered. "Ike's not going to like this one bit. Old Lloyd might as well keep going all the way to Washington. He's just not fit for command. In my opinion, he's arrogant, jumps to conclusions; a cocky little shit. Even General Anderson thinks he is incompetent and that should tell you something. The problem is Marshall doesn't think so and he's the boss. He once told me he liked Fredendall's swagger, that he could 'see determination' in his face. Ike liked him at first, but after visiting Fredendall's concrete bunker complex 80 miles to the rear, I'm hearing that's changed. Fredendall even ordered a bullet-proof Cadillac like Ike's—not that he would ever need it. Now Ike wants to put Patton in charge of Second Corps. Maybe he will after this set-to is over, but he doesn't want to change horses in midstream. Let's go." He headed outside and threw his kit into the waiting half-track. The motor was running. Declan climbed in beside him.

It was one thing to be a correspondent brought out to see the aftermath of a battle but quite another to be part of an army in full retreat. Declan could almost smell the fear swirling around him; everyone seemed to be looking over a shoulder, expecting to see the entire German army right behind him. Some of the men were actually running, desperately trying to climb aboard anything moving south.

Declan pointed to the camera hanging from Lang's neck. "Good camera?"

"The best. It's a Leica. German. Excellent optics. You should see their field glasses. Far superior to ours." Lang pointed the camera at a GI getting hauled aboard a truck like a beached whale, clicked the shutter. "Doubt that one will make it past the censors."

"Probably not."

"Stinks, doesn't it?"

"What?"

Lang was watching the men, the trucks, the choking clouds of dust. "Panic. Panic stinks. Smells like shit. Literally smells like shit."

***

The village of Kasserine—if the little mosque and the motley collection of stalls and hovels could even be called a village—was less than thirty miles southwest of Sbeita but with all the vehicles and men on the road, it took more than two hours to get there. The ragged convoy didn't bother to even slow down. The entrance to the pass between the mountains was still ten miles away.

It was already cold but as the half-track entered the shadows of the pass and began to climb the first long hill, it got even colder. Declan pulled up the scarf he wore around his neck to cover his face and nose, partly to keep out the dust but mostly for some extra warmth. It didn't help much. "Where do you think we'll stop?" he asked Lang.

"At the northern end of the pass; another ten miles. That's the logical defensive position. This is the only road through and the pass narrows at the northern end. We'll need to hold the high ground on both sides. I don't know if we'll have enough men to do that. There are two other passes through the dorsal—one at Sbiba, one at Bou Chebka—and those will have to be defended, too. We'll be stretched pretty thin. But I think this is highway one. If Rommel gets through here, he can go west right into Tebessa or cut north to the coast. Either way, he's got us by the balls."

Declan stared out at the landscape. It was more lunar than earthly, barren, rocky, frigid. The valley floor was a narrow band, not more than few miles wide. On either side, steep inclines rose to nearly 5,000 feet. There was hardly any cover. At Sidi Bou Zid, the plain was shallower, broader; there were gullies that could hide a dozen tanks, but not here. This would be a brutal frontal assault, an incoming tide rushing up the beach against a sea wall that might or might not hold. So far, the performance of the American army and its suspect leadership did not bode well.

"Been under fire before?" Lang asked.

Declan looked at him, shook his head.

"Then you know how a lot of these men feel." That was the end of the conversation. Declan pulled his neck down into the collar of his flack jacket and pushed his hands deeper into his pockets, a turtle going into its shell. Except he didn't have a shell to protect him.

CHAPTER THIRTY THREE

Orders

Sometimes, it seemed to Field Marshall Erwin Rommel, he was not fighting one war, but two. The Allies were the easier enemy; his own army was a much more complicated opponent. Rommel sensed opportunity in the victory at Sidi Bou Zid, but for reasons he could not begin to comprehend, the Wehrmacht was stalled, its momentum lost. Every neuron in his warrior body told him to press the attack, seize the advantage. Any delay was deadly.

Von Arnim was part of the problem; he wanted to turn north and strike at the British army menacing Tunis. So, surprisingly enough, was Kesserling who was now in Italy conferring with *Il Duce*, that strutting clown. Rommel wanted badly to hit the Americans again and hit them hard. They had been battered at Sidi Bou Zid; now they could be beaten.

In frustration, Rommel sent a message to Kesserling requesting both the 10th and 21st Panzer Divisions be assigned to him immediately. He would use them to spearhead an attack on the major American supply and command center at Tébessa, just inside the Algerian border. If he could capture Tebessa, the American army in North Africa was finished.

Kesserling's reply was encouraging but not definitive. He wanted to confer with Mussolini before giving his final approval to Rommel's plan. More delay. Then, just before midnight on February 18, Rommel received his orders in a cable from Kesserling. He scanned the message, then read it carefully a second time.

"In view of the ascertained inferior combat value of the enemy, a unique opportunity is now offered to force a decisive victory in

Tunisia...all means to exploit former successes...The objective of this operation will be to threaten the rear of the British First Army by means of a broad thrust to the north and, if possible, to isolate it or at least force it to withdraw.

With this view, the following is ordered: F.M. Rommel with all available troops and the 10th and 21st Pz. Dias., will attack over the general line Sbeita-Tebessa, via Le Kef..."

Rommel stopped reading; he was stunned. He had been given command of the two divisions he had requested but instead of attacking the Americans at Tébessa to the west, he was being ordered to go north, take the Tunisian town of Kef, and menace the British rear. It was von Arnim's timid plan, not the decisive stroke—the final blow—he had proposed. The fools! It was a thrust much too close to the front and would surely result in the enemy bringing in strong reserve forces. He would have to fight a tougher, better trained and equipped foe—not the crippled Americans. Madness! When boldness and the cunning of a fox was all that was required, the Comando Supremo in Rome had opted for the battle plan of a mouse!

Just twelve hours after receiving his orders, Rommel stood at the southern entrance to Kasserine Pass. He didn't like what he saw: troops spread out, waiting for someone to tell them what to do. Earlier that morning, his own *Afrika Korps* had sent several small units into the pass to probe American positions, but the reconnaissance was not very useful. The 21st Panzer Division was already heading north toward the Sbiba Pass which was the more direct route north. Von Arnim had ordered the 10th Panzer Division back to Kairouan after their victory at Sidi Bou Zid; they would have to be recalled—another costly delay.

***

"Where exactly is Rommel? What is taking him so fucking long?"

"It looks like he's moving a division toward Sbiba, General. Maybe he's decided to go north through that pass, not use the pass at Kasserine. Not like him, though."

"Damn right, not like him. Not his style. Get me Stark on the phone!"

Colonel Alexander Stark and his First Infantry Division were camped just south of Tébessa, thirty-five miles away over rough terrain. Stark's aid handed him the field telephone. "It's General Fredendall, Colonel."

Stark raised his eyebrows imploringly. Now what? "Yes, sir."

"I want you to go to Kasserine Pass right now. Pull a Stonewall Jackson. Take over there!" Fredendall barked down the line.

"Stonewall Jackson, sir? Now?"

"Tonight, Stark! Get moving. And stop by my CP post on your way!" Fredendall hung up.

***

From Declan Shaw's journal, entry dated *19 February, 1400 hours*: *We wait. Colonel Stark has arrived from Tébessa and established a defensive line about three miles into the northwestern terminus of the pass. Earlier this morning, we received a report from French troops that Germans had been spotted getting out of their trucks and scaling the hills at the southern end of the pass. No actual sightings of these advance forces have been sighted.*

However, it has been confirmed that F.M. Rommel is now at the entrance to the pass. He has apparently decided to make his main assault here as the 34th Infantry Division under General Ryder has made a spirited defense of the Sbiba Pass to our north. At this time, it does not appear that the Bou Chebka Pass (the southernmost route through the Dorsal) will be the focus of any significant Nazi attacks. Allied troops stationed there could be brought here if the American position needs to be reinforced.

Stark seems a capable commander. He has established defensive positions on the two djebels on either side of the road through the pass, and he has mined both the road and hillsides leading to his lines. The problem seems to be that our line is very thin; we do not have much in the way of reserves in case the Germans make a frontal assault which now seems certain.

Last night, German units were able to infiltrate our lines and got between Stark's troops and his CP. They were able to use artillery to cut Stark's lines of communication. He was forced to move his CP back several miles.

And so we wait. Time is on our side to the extent that we can use it to reorganize and dig in that much deeper. Meanwhile it's freezing cold; the wind through the pass makes life on the line miserable. Morale seems to be holding, but between the men who tasted such bitter defeat at Sidi Bou Zid and the newly arrived units that haven't yet seen any combat, who knows what tomorrow will bring?

***

Later that afternoon, while the sun was setting behind the mountains, Declan was in the press tent, trying to get warm. Lang came in and saw him, then went over to his cot and began rooting through his duffle bag. When he found what he was looking for, he stood up and said to Declan, "Let's be civilized!" He was holding a bottle of Cutty Sark. It was half full.

"Jesus, Mary, and Joseph. Where did you get that?"

"Friend of a friend. It's strictly rationed but you look like you might need a nip." He poured a finger into two dirty coffee cups. "Cheers!"

"Slainte!" Declan took a sip, tried to let it slide down his sore throat, one drop at a time.

"Did you hear?"

"What?"

"Stalingrad. The great battle is finally over. German 6th Army has surrendered. Half are dead, the other half taken prisoner. They'll be dead, too, soon enough. Here's to the Russians. Tough bastards!" Lang raised his glass. "You can bet Rommel knows. Now the pressure is really on him. The little fucker with the mustache can't lose two battles in a row."

"What's the body count?"

"Half a million, either dead now or dead next week if they're lucky. I'd hate to be a prisoner there. Don't imagine the accommodations or the food are half as nice as this." He swept his hand around the tent. The wind rattled the canvas walls.

Lang took a sip. "Anyway, Punch should be pleased."

"You know Punch?"

"Do I know Punch? Spent a lot of time in a foxhole with him so, yes, I know old Punch."

"What are you talking about?"

"Spain! Punch and I spent a couple of years together in the Lincoln Brigade. Had more than a little Red in him then; still does from what I hear. But then so do I." Declan was suddenly all ears. "You know, this war—the one we're in today—is just preamble to bigger ones still to come. This war is just about some governments and a few men holding on to power and privilege while making a shitload of money. The next one will be about independence, the end of empires. Think these people—Tunisians—will still want to be mixed up with France when this is all over? No; no way. They're through with Europe's colonial bullshit. Then, when that war's over, there'll be the really big one—a world revolution, a war of ideologies. Hearts and minds, in Africa, Latin American, Asia. Everything will be changing. That's gonna be Punch's war. Maybe mine, maybe yours. If we get through this one, that is."

Declan felt like he had just been tossed overboard in the middle of an angry ocean. Punch. A communist? Three wars? So many dots to connect... suddenly, he needed space.

Lang was looking into his almost-empty glass. "Think they'll attack tomorrow? Rommel, I mean, " Declan asked. Anything to change the subject.

"Count on it, buddy. You meet me here or wherever we are this time tomorrow and we'll have another finger to celebrate. Or two to commiserate. Cheers!" Lang drained his glass and walked out.

CHAPTER THIRTY FOUR

Der Nebelwerfer

The night seemed endless; freezing temperatures, artillery, fighting panic and the urge to flee. Declan's mind was racing back and forth, trying to make sense of everything Lang had told him, about Punch, about the world on the brink. Declan didn't consider himself to be a historian but he knew enough about the aftermath of the Great War and all the changes that followed in its wake. Everything from a virulent epidemic to profound social and political changes on the home front and around the world. He assumed these changes would build a new world order that would last at least for a century or two. But maybe Lang could see over that horizon to some polarized planet where there was no middle ground. You were on one team or the other, East or West. Today's allies would be tomorrow's enemies. Meanwhile, it was too cold to sleep so Declan just stared into the darkness.

At 0730 hours on the morning of February 20, Field Marshall Erwin Rommel stood at the southern terminus to Kasserine Pass, almost too angry to speak. Only half of the 10th Panzer Division had arrived to begin the attack and Rommel surmised that his rival von Arnim had held back the other half for "his own purposes," he shouted. Worse, von Arnim had also held back at least a dozen of the newest 56-ton Tiger tanks, the ones the Allies admitted were unstoppable with anything in their arsenal. And then, just when he thought things couldn't get any worse, Rommel was informed that a motorcycle battalion that he wanted to use in the frontal assault had been kept in reserve. Rommel's head throbbed; delay upon costly delay. He was fast losing patience as well as the advantage of momentum.

By noon, everything was finally in place and Rommel gave the order for an all-out assault up the pass. Within the hour, there was fierce hand-to-hand fighting as little-by-little, the first waves of the German army advanced. Now was the time for Rommel to land a crucial blow.

Most of the American troops in the battle had not yet seen any real combat, but none were prepared for the surprise new German artillery weapon—the *nebelwerfer*. It consisted of six metal tubes, each containing an 80-pound rocket bomb; when the electrical trigger was pressed, all six rockets screamed skyward simultaneously, shrieking, spewing flames before landing on targets as far as 4 miles away. The noise the rockets made was deafening and their effect on green American troops was devastating, especially when rumors broke out that the incoming German shells contained chemical weapons. Some units broke and ran, others were simply overrun by advancing infantry. By the end of the afternoon, the entire length of the Kasserine Pass was in German hands. It was another bitter and bloody defeat for the Americans, this time at the hands of the legendary Desert Fox. He watched expressionlessly as German tanks rolled through the pass and truckload after truckload of American prisoners, bloodied and beaten, headed southeast, back down through the pass, on their way to POW camps in Poland or Germany.

***

From Declan Shaw's journal, entry dated *February 20, 2000 hours*: *The Kasserine Pass is now controlled by the German army. Rommel has his revenge. The only question that remains is now where will he go from here? West (toward Tébessa) or directly north to the coast through Le Kef? The road at the northwestern terminus of the pass has two branches: one runs west toward Tébessa in Algeria, the other turns north and runs through Thala and on to Le Kef. The Allied defense is now a gambler's choice.*

Tonight, it is strangely quiet, almost as if Rommel is gathering his forces, making up his mind about which way to go. Our fresh-shaven Lieutenant Conley (not quite so fresh-shaven these days) hints that the Allies have developed a capability to read coded German messages and that Rommel has been ordered to go north to take Le Kef instead of the big supply depot at Tébessa. We have thrown up a blockade on the northern route, but it will not be able to hold out for long.

The other major rumor making its rounds is that Fredendall's command days are numbered. He is still back at his CP giving orders, but he does not seem to fully comprehend how bad the situation is here. Our forces are scattered and there does not appear to be a comprehensive plan about a counter-attack or a method to stop the German onslaught. No soldier will say it outright, but one feels a growing lack of confidence in Fredendall's leadership. Unlike Rommel, he never appears at the front, prefers to lead from behind. The men sense an unsteady hand on the tiller.

Final note from today: this new German artillery piece—the nebelwerfer—has a bark much worse than its bite. It appears to be highly inaccurate but its God-awful sound makes it a fearful battlefield weapon. The men have already nicknamed it "Moaning Minnie."

Lang came into the tent; Declan put down his pencil. The Cutty Sark appeared. "Looks like it's a two-finger night. Oh; and I brought you this." He handed Declan a thin package. "Arrived with yesterday's mail call."

There was no mail delivery to the medina so Declan used the Guardian office as his postal address. Punch must have forwarded this somehow. There wasn't much: a letter from his mother in Cork and a postcard. The picture was of a seaside café in Haifa; the stamp was from British Palestine. On the reverse, it simply said: 'Arrived. Come have coffee.' It was signed with the initial 'B.'

Lang handed Declan a paper cup. "Cheers!"

For the first time that day, Declan smiled. *"L'Chaim!"*

CHAPTER THIRTY FIVE

Divide and Conquer

The Hatab River rises in the Atlas Mountains in Algeria. In its geological infancy, it cut a wide swath through the mountains, creating a gorge that flowed in an easterly direction down through the Kasserine Pass to the grassy coastal plains below. Now, however, for most of the year, the Hatab was just a dry river bed—a *wadi*—but during the rainy months, there was enough water to form a running shallow channel. Once or twice a season after particularly heavy rains in the mountains, the river actually fills the *wadi*, flowing rapidly before eventually dissipating into the sandy wasteland east of the pass.

The *wadi* is no more than a few hundred yards wide; its banks are steep, rising as much as fifty feet high in some places. It forms a natural barrier but with the rains now slacking, there was still enough water in the channel to make crossing the Hatab a logistical problem—not an insoluble one, but complicated enough to impede communications and coordination between two divisions of the same army or to delay an enemy.

***

From Declan Shaw's journal, entry dated *February 21, 2300 hours*: *Overnight, the decision was made that British forces under the command of Brigadier-General Charles Dunphie would be stationed north of the Hatab River, in effect defending the road to Thala, a small town about halfway to Le Kef. American troops under the command of Brigadier-General Paul Robinett would deploy south of the Hatab to defend against a German push in the direction of Tébessa. Neither command has much firepower; they will have to depend on infantry and limited artillery to preserve the few Allied tanks that are still serviceable.*

Rommel did not make his move until almost noon. He sent part of the 10th Panzer Division north toward Thala while his Afrika Korps moved west toward Tébessa. Lang says it was risky for Rommel to split forces instead of massing them for an assault, but perhaps the Fox thinks that by deploying troops in two different directions, he will cause us to split our forces more than his own.

Reports from the north have been coming in for the past few hours. Dunphie has lost almost all his tanks but has heroically slowed the German advance on Thala, pulling back ridge-by-ridge. At one point, the Germans actually entered the town but have apparently decided to pull back, but not before taking nearly 600 prisoners. There is almost nothing to stop them from moving onto Le Kef in the morning.

Fighting has also been fierce south of the Hatab. German Stuka dive bombers strafed American artillery positions, but anti-aircraft fire appears to be highly effective against them because of their long, straight dives. Given the assaults by German forces, any counterattack by Allied forces seems highly unlikely.

The bottle of Cutty Sark was almost empty. "Don't be so pessimistic, Shaw. There's so much confusion out there right now, no one knows his ass from a foxhole, not even Rommel. Everything is scattered to hell and back and anyone who can figure out how to coordinate all the pieces has a chance to come out on top. We're still in the fight."

Declan shook his head. "I don't know. It all just seems so inevitable."

"Look. They say a sailor can feel the tide turning before it actually does. If Rommel was so sure of his objective, he wouldn't be hesitating like this. Just not like him. Plus he knows we can bring up reserves and he can't. All those soldiers dead or imprisoned in Russia can't fight. He's stuck with what he's got. Every hour we hold the line, more of our men move up. Irwin has come over from Tlemcen; he'll be in Thala tonight—might already be there. He's got more guns and tanks to reinforce the line. Rommel might be thinking twice." Lang tipped the bottle for the last few drops. "I heard something else just now. Guess who's coming to dinner."

Declan waited while Lang held the glass over his mouth, inhaling the vapors.

"Smiling Al has flown in from Italy."

"Kesserling's here?"

Lang nodded. "Met with Rommel this afternoon outside Thala. Seems strange to me. Nothing happened; no attack. Wouldn't you think that if the Boss came to see you, you'd want to put on a show for him? Here's what I think: Rommel's worn down, maybe even worn out—you know he's a hypochondriac—and his men are exhausted. There are no reinforcements, no reserves. It wouldn't surprise me if Rommel wanted to turn around and go back to Mareth for another crack at Monty. This feels more and more like a dead end to him. Plus, it's not his terrain. He's a flatlander, a *w'ild Jenuub*."

Declan gave him a blank look.

"It means 'son of the south.' He hates these fucking mountains. Not good tank terrain. Plus it's too fucking cold up here. The desert's warmer."

You really think he'll withdraw? After all this?"

Lang kicked off his boots, rolled over on his cot, pushed himself deep down into his sleeping bag. "Let's see what tomorrow brings. Feels like a turning tide to me."

Declan laughed. "What's so funny?" Lan asked.

"You just reminded me of something my mum once told me. 'When the tide gets really low, you'll find out who's swimming naked."

"I would have liked your mum." Five minutes later, Lang was snoring.

CHAPTER THIRTY SIX

Changes

It's a common misperception that war smothers everything in its path, that life comes to a screeching halt amid the ebb and flow of battle. But that's not the case; life does go on for soldiers and civilians alike, maybe not as it was, but as it must. As one wag put it, "Morning will come; it has no choice."

Lang was right. Maybe because he was exhausted from his long retreat across the Libyan desert, or maybe because he didn't like the odds in the mountains, Rommel decided to withdraw. The way north through Thala was now blocked and if he turned west toward Tébessa, he risked being cut off from any potential support he might need. It was bitter wisdom, but it made sense to consolidate his forces, go back down through the pass and turn south to join up with General Messe at Mareth, the old French wall built to keep out the Italians but now refurbished to stop Montgomery and the British Eight Army from marching to Tunis.

Lessons had been learned by both sides, bloody ones, costly ones. The Germans learned about American resiliency and about a seemingly endless supply of men and material. The Americans learned about German anti-tank and screening tactics, about the need for close air support, about the dangers of positioning forces too far apart for mutual support, even about things as simple as not creating exposed positions on ridge lines or men digging shallow slit trenches instead of deep foxholes. Those mistakes wouldn't be made again.

The cost of these hard lessons was largely born by a few American commanders. The battles of Sidi Bou Zid and Kasserine Pass had revealed flaws in the Allied command structure that needed to repaired or resolved if victory in North Africa was to be won.

No one knew this better than Ike. Worried about the defeats in the mountains and about reports of friction between Generals Fredendall and Ward, he dispatched Major-General Ernie Harmon to get a first-hand look at the front and assess the situation. Harmon wasn't impressed. On his way to the front, Harmon had passed countless American vehicles heading in the opposite direction; it looked to Harmon like a rout. Fredendall seemed almost relieved when Harmon arrived; it was almost as if he wanted someone else to be put in charge. Even after Rommel's withdrawal, no one seemed to know what to do next. Harmon proposed plans for a counter-attack, but by the time the plan was operational, the German army had made, in Harmon's words, "a clean getaway."

Back at his headquarters in Algiers, Ike asked Harmon, "Well, what did you think of Fredendall?"

"He's no damn good, General. You ought to get rid of him."

"Do you want command of Second Corps?"

Harmon hesitated. He didn't like the idea of giving a negative report on a fellow officer and then taking his job. "No, Sir." When Ike didn't respond right away, Harmon added, "What about Brad? Or George?" 'Brad' was General Omar Bradley, Ike's classmate at West Point, another member of "the class the stars fell on." He was another mid-Westerner, competent, loyal, level-headed. 'George,' of course, was General George Patton who was cooling his heels in Morocco where he was in charge of planning the eventual Allied invasion of Sicily. That operation, of course, rested on the assumption that the Allies would win in Tunisia. Now maybe it was time to overhaul Second Corps. He would bring both Brad and George forward and send Lloyd Fredendall back home. Ike made his decision. He installed General Patton as Commander of Second Corps and named General Bradley as his deputy. He also made it clear that Brad would be his personal representative on Patton's staff, Ike's personal reins, as it were, on the Patton war horse.

Ike was not vindictive by nature. Fredendall had done his best; he was a good peace-time officer, but he was not cut out for the demands of the battlefield. Ike put him in charge of a training army and sent him home with a promotion. He never saw action again.

A few days later, General George S. Patton arrived at Second Corps headquarters at the head of a small armada of Jeeps and half-tracks, flags flying, sirens blaring. Patton stood in the lead vehicle, white helmet polished, his gunslinger's pearl-handled revolvers strapped to his waist. He looked for all the world like a man on a mission...and he was. Things were about to change.

Ike made one other command change. Following up on a decision made by Roosevelt and Churchill at the Casablanca Conference, he named General Sir Harold R.L.G. Alexander the Commander of Army Group 18, a new entity combining the British 1st Army and Montgomery's 8th Army which was now in southern Tunisia preparing to take on the Italo-German defensive line at Mareth. Alexander was an experienced, competent officer. He was one of the last men to leave the beach at Dunkirk in 1940, and he had served with distinction in Burma and Cairo. His new job was to oversee all British operations in Tunisia and to improve relations and promote cooperation between British and American forces. It was high time for that.

CHAPTER THIRTY SEVEN

Entre'acte

Declan peeked at his watch. He had been sitting in front of Punch's desk, watching him read for almost thirty five minutes. Punch's red pencil had been suspiciously quiet. Declan didn't know what to think.

Finally, Punch looked up. "This is good. I'm going to suggest it run on the front page over four or five days. Good job, lad."

Declan waited. There was always more.

"Too bad we don't have any photos to run with it. Should have thought of that."

"Maybe Lang would let you run some of his. I'm sure he got some good…"

Punch's head jerked up. "Lang? You were with Lang?"

Declan nodded. "Really good bloke. I had no idea you and he…"

"What did he say? What did he tell you?"

"Take it easy. Not much. That you and he shared a foxhole in Spain…"

"Did he now? Anything else?"

"Maybe that you had a little Red…"

"Stop. Red? Lang said I was Red? Compared to him, I wasn't even pink."

"Not to worry. Said you were a good mate. Nothing but praise."

Punch unwound a notch or two. "Be careful about Lang. When this is all over, there'll be new lines drawn. Watch what side you're on then. A lot of people in this business don't want a red scare. Bad for readership. Lang. Damn! Where is the bastard?"

"No idea. We parted ways after Thala. He was heading back to Algiers to file, maybe wrangle an interview with Ike. I wanted to get this to you." Declan pointed to the copy in front of Punch. "Talk about snatching defeat from the jaws of victory. Rommel had us beat and he just quit."

Punch shook his head. "Comedy or tragedy; hard to know which. I guess it's intermission. Any interest in going south again? I hear the cast has changed and the third act is about to start. You're on a roll, lad. You might have a career in this business yet."

"I'll let you know. Give me a day or two to sleep on a real bed and get warm again. My cock's still frozen stiff." Declan immediately regretted that remark, but Punch let it pass. Odd.

"Lang," Punch said, more to himself than to Declan. "Said I was the red one?" Gave a snort. "Go home, boy, get some sleep. Mind how you thaw out that wee thing; wouldn't want to snap it off." Declan should have known better; the last word always belonged to Punch.

***

Armies may march on their stomachs, but civilians aren't so lucky. There were now periodic food shortages in Tunis. One day it might be grains or vegetables, the next day, meat. The biggest problem was when there was no bread. On those days, the poor didn't have anything to fill their stomachs.

Tunisians coped, did what they had to. They bartered with soldiers: a handful of dates, some cherries, an apricot or a tangerine for some chocolate. Two eggs for a cigarette or maybe some tea. (Real coffee, flavored with ground cardamom seeds, had long ago become more rare than gold.) Soldiers who had rations to spare or trade were like Pied Pipers; children followed them everywhere, begging for a handout. Pilfering became an acceptable means to an end and if you knew the right people, you could still eat well. The black marketeer was king... for a price.

People ate when and what they could, but often it was only one meal a day and not much of a meal at that. Sometimes, it was only a bowl of *shorba*, a thin spicy soup flavored with a few grimy vegetables or fatty pieces of meat floating in greasy broth. The French *colons* could still get plenty of food or dine in a restaurant, but too many Tunisian families often went to bed hungry. Resentment simmered just below the surface; someday that resentment would rupture like an ugly open wound.

Ali could feel the resentment all around him, the tension of it. It rubbed at him, the way a blister does under the skin before it breaks, raw and angry. The war was keeping the resentment at bay for now, but someday soon, when the war had passed through Tunisia like a swarm of locust, the blister would break open and bleed. It would demand attention. If left untended, it would become infected, poisoning everything in its path, but by then, it would be too late.

Ali thought of Leila constantly. It had been more than a month since he had seen her at the *Malouf* performance and the thought of her, the very scent of her, stayed with him like a dream from which he didn't want to wake. She occupied his being. He studied, he went to the mosque to read or to pray, but she was a flooding tide he could not withstand so he might as well just succumb. He had heard the stories of *jinn*—intelligent spirits just slightly lower than the angels—who could assume human form and possess a man, heart and soul. She had that kind of power over him. She mattered more to him than his family in Kairouan or his studies at the university—almost as much as his cherished dream of independence. He still believed in that and the absolute oneness of God, but Leila was becoming a close third... and that frightened him. It frightened him because in this world, she lay beyond his reach like a mirage in the desert: the closer the traveler came, the more ephemeral the vision, and ultimately, the more bitter the disappointment.

***

Paul was able to scrounge just enough gasoline to fill the tank of the family car. He had not been able to visit his family's estate near Tebourda since the Germans had confiscated the property to use as a field command post. It had served its purpose for the last few weeks, but a few days ago, the Germans had vacated the villa and the surrounding vineyard. They were pulling back, tightening their defensive positions around the crucial deep-water ports at Bizerte and Tunis. If Messe and

Rommel were not able to hold out against Montgomery's Eighth Army at Mareth, and with Alexander and Patton now able to advance from the west, those ports were essential to the survival of the Axis armies in North Africa, as well as the defense of Europe.

Paul was devastated by what he found at the winery. Almost all of the old vines had been uprooted or smashed by heavy vehicles; last year's new plantings had been bulldozed to make room for tents and slit latrine. The house, once a lovely, peaceful place of business and comfortable retreat, was in ruins. Windows were smashed, furniture broken; someone had built a fire in the corner of the family's living room and fed it with wood from the bookcases that had once lined the walls of his father's study. The nearby cellar and the warehouse, once filled with fragrant cork-oak barrels of aging wine and row upon row of bottled vintages, had been sacked. There was broken glass everywhere and the place reeked of spilled or spoiled wine. The vinegary fumes made Paul's eyes water; he pulled his scarf up around his mouth and nose but he gagged anyway.

"Do you think they will ever compensate us?" Paul asked.

Monsieur Fabron stood behind Paul, surveying the scene. He scoffed. "What do you think? Why did you ever think the Germans would give a shit about us?"

For a moment, Paul didn't answer; what could he say? Just a month or two ago, It had seemed like doing business with Kesserling and the Germans was a smart decision that would ensure a prosperous future. Now it looked like it had brought the family ruin.

"Do you think we can rebuild?"

"With what? There's no money to rebuild all this. To replant…it would take at least ten years until we had a harvest."

"So what do we do? How will we live?"

"*Sais pas, mon fils.*" I don't know, son. "*Peut-être ailleurs.*" Maybe somewhere else.

"*Je les detests. Je les destes tous!*" I hate them. I hate them all.

Paul's father nodded but said nothing. After a moment, he put a hand on Pauls shoulder. "*Moi aussi,*" he said. Me, too.

***

These days, Leila Ben Zayed had nothing but time on her hands. She dabbled at Arabic poetry, read French novels, and when the weather was pleasant, took walks along the beach, careful not to enter the areas where the Germans had posted signs decorated with a crude skull and crossbones overlaid with one word: "Achtung!" Its meaning was patently clear.

Over the course of the last few months—the cold winter and the wet spring, Leila's mother had withdrawn into a silent shell. If asked, she would say she missed "the old days," but Layla suspected it was more than that: her family home in France, maybe even more. Her youth. She would turn fifty at the end of the summer but already, she seemed to be wilting, a faded flower. Layla had once heard the women in the *hammem* talking about what they had called "the change of life;" now she understood what they meant. She knew her father felt the change in her mother, too. Where there had once been evident love, now there was simple companionship. She wondered if that would be enough for her one day.

And that thought had brought her to Ali. She wondered what he was doing this afternoon; what book was he reading; what he was having for supper. She had to admit that when she had been going to university in Paris, she had enjoyed flirting with the French boys who found her exotic. But it had always been a game, nothing ever taken remotely seriously. Ali was different. He had ideas. He had goals, He knew where he came from and who he was. Someday, when this war madness was gone and Tunisia was ready, he would become an important part of its new national identity. That thought excited her, excited her mind and her body. She wondered where Ali slept at night; what did he wear?

***

Declan slept for an entire day. Then almost another. He was happy to be home, warm, fed, safe. But when he finally didn't need anymore sleep, he felt something else, too. He was missing something, the adrenaline rush produced by an incoming mortar round, or the camaraderie of men, or the feeling of being part of something extraordinarily bigger than one's self. He didn't miss the war but, he had to admit, he missed the purpose it gave him, purpose in his work and meaning to his life. That was it: even amid all the dying and the pain, the war was giving him a reason to live.

CHAPTER THIRTY EIGHT

Kings and Pawns

By early March, Tunisia resembled a giant chessboard with officers as set pieces and entire armies arrayed as pawns. Montgomery and the British Eight Army had finally crossed into southern Tunisia from Libya and were massing near the town of Medenine to launch an assault on the Mareth Line, the opening salvo of a drive north toward Tunis. Patton, now in command of the American Second Corps, wanted to come storming out of the mountains near the Algerian border and move rapidly due east toward the coast, thereby trapping the Italo-Germany forces commanded by Generals Messe and Rommel between two deadly Allied forces. In the north, General von Arnim was positioning his troops to defend the deep-water ports at Bizerte and Tunis in the face of growing pressure from the British First Army under the command of General Anderson who seemed to have an almost endless supply of fresh reserves.

There was also an unseen hand in the game, one operating in secret thousands of miles from the battlefields of Tunisia. British mathematicians and scientists had been working around the clock at Bletchley Park outside London to break the Enigma Code used by the Axis Powers General Command. That highly secret effort—Code Name 'Ultra' because of its ultra secret nature—had finally succeeded, and it gave the Allies the inestimable ability to read German cipher traffic and to effect operational counter measures that saved countless lives. Now, Ultra would be employed against Axis forces operating in Tunisia.

Field Marshall Rommel was delighted to put the mountains of central Tunisia behind him once and for all. Not because there was an Allied army there who had taken his best punch and withstood the challenge; not because of the relentless rain and cold; not even because, as some surmised, that he was only good at fighting in the desert or because he hated mountains for mountains' sake. That last notion was particularly ludicrous! He was Swabian, for God's sake, and he had grown up riding and hunting in green forests under snow-capped peaks. He wanted to turn south for one reason and one reason only: he wanted one more chance to defeat Montgomery, the man who had hounded him like a bad dream for nearly two years; he wanted that nightmare to end.

***

In pre-colonial times, a traveler coming up out of the great Sahara desert might have arrived at the Tunisian town of Medenine. It had several caravansaries and *ksars*—fortresses—where he would be able to unload and store his trade goods in safety. The town also had a permanent water source where he could rest and refresh his camels. He would likely encounter other traders who had descended from the great cities along the coast bringing wares to trade and looking for new markets in the great African empires that lay far off to the south. Medenine was both a beginning and an end, a door that opened and closed on an almost unimaginably empty expanse, a timeless ocean of shifting sand.

Rommel understood deep in his bones that Montgomery was preparing a frontal assault on the Mareth Line. He also knew that Montgomery was a meticulous planner, and so it was Rommel's intention to disrupt his enemy's battle plan with a spoiling offensive aimed at Montgomery's position near Medenine. He discussed the idea with Giovanni Messe; cables flew back and forth between Rommel, Messe, and *Commando Supremo* in Rome. Montgomery was able to read every one.

On the morning of March 6, fog shrouded the hills above Medenine. Warned of Rommel's intentions by the codebreakers at Bletchley a week before, Montgomery had spent the last three days and nights moving troops forward; on the morning of the anticipated attack, he had 400 tanks, 350 field guns, and almost 500 anti-tanks guns hidden and waiting. He had also increased the number of British aircraft in the area to double the number available to Rommel. At 0536 hours, Montgomery received a cable from Bletchley notifying him that an attack would begin in less than half an hour. At precisely 0600 hours, Rommel launched his attack. Montgomery—who always kept a photograph of Rommel over his desk—turned to an aide: "This is an absolute gift. The man must be mad!"

British artillery were under orders to withhold fire until German tanks and infantry were well within range in order to maximize its effect. That it did, and more. More than thirty thousand shells flew over the battlefield during the course of the day and by dusk, Rommel, in consultation with General Messe at Mareth, made the decision to call off the attack. German casualties outnumbered British casualties more than five-to-one. Moreover, Rommel lost more than 50 tanks; the British lost but two. He could ill afford to lose anymore. What had begun as an offensive sortie meant to harass Montgomery and relieve pressure on Messe's position behind the Mareth Line had turned into a rout.

Three days later, on March 9, Field Marshall Johannes Erwin Eugen Rommel, citing exhaustion and poor health, quietly took off from an airfield near Sfax and flew back to Germany for a "rest cure." The truth, however, was that both Albert Kesserling and the Führer had lost faith in the man. Command of the Axis forces in North Africa was handed over to General Hans-Jürgen von Arnim, Rommel's bitter arch-rival. The Desert Fox would never return to North Africa.

CHAPTER THIRTY NINE

Coordination

War, like nature, abhors a vacuum. The German defeat at Medenine was but a prelude to Montgomery's drive north directly through the Axis defenses behind the Mareth Line. No one understood this better than the Commander of British Army Group 18, General Sir Harold Alexander. He was Ike's second-in-command in North Africa and, as such, it fell to him to oversee all Allied operations in Tunisia.

For Alexander, the first question was what to do with the Americans. Their performance at Kasserine Pass had not exactly inspired great confidence in their commanders, but Ike had taken steps to repair the damage. Alexander knew that Patton was a proven warrior and a charismatic leader, but could be contained? Alexander needed to know if the Americans could still be a battlefield asset, and so he devised a strategy in which he would give Patton and Second Corps a series of limited objectives by which they could prove themselves. Although "limited objectives" was not a concept Patton naturally subscribed to, he understood what Alexander wanted. With Montgomery preparing to push north directly through Mareth, anything the Americans could do to draw attention away from that line would help Monty achieve his objective. As much as Patton didn't like it, supporting action was better than no action at all.

Patton was a thirsty student of military history. He read it, studied it, applied its lessons. He found precedent for his role in the coming battle in, of all places, the American Civil War, specifically at the Second Battle of Bull Run, or as Patton preferred, Second Manassas. There, in the hills and valleys just outside Washington, Stonewall Jackson and only 25,000 men held the attention of the entire Union army, permitting General Robert E. Lee to maneuver his troops into position astride the Union flank and inflict a crushing defeat. That was language Patton understood.

Acting under orders from General Alexander, Patton divided his forces into three operating groups, each with its own limited objective. One group joined with British forces to launch an attack against a German position near Fondouk el Aouareb in the Eastern Dorsal, a thrust that would draw Axis troops away from their heavily fortified position at Mareth. Two other infantry divisions would move south to retake Gafsa and its oasis, which had been abandoned by the Allies prior to the fighting at Kasserine. If Patton were able to control Gafsa and its oasis, he would then be in a position to resupply Montgomery once he had broken through the Mareth Line.

***

"Hello, old sod. Good to see you again. Bit warmer down here, eh?"

Declan was glad to see Lang, too. It hadn't even been three weeks since they had parted company after Kasserine, but three weeks is a long time in war. Now they were back together, assigned to cover the next round of fighting, this time in the desert. There was even an understanding, brokered at higher levels of journalism, that they would work together, sharing copy and photographs. After the fiasco at Kasserine, it seemed everyone was learning how to work a little more cooperatively.

It wasn't just the weather that had changed. Montgomery planned carefully. His army was well supplied and rested; it hadn't seen serious action since Tripoli fell more than a month ago and they were spoiling for a fight. The Germans didn't scare them one bit; the Italians, even less.

"Did you get to interview Ike in Algiers?"

"Yes and no. We talked, but nothing for the record. Let me take a couple of photos. I'll say this, though: he looks a whole lot better. Not so pale; Medenine really put a spring in his step. He seems a lot more confident now. He feels like he's got his A team in place: Alexander, Monty, George, Brad, Pinky Ward. He couldn't wait to see Fredendall get the hell out of here. I got the impression he thinks we'll win Tunisia and move into Europe through Sicily, but he won't say so. You just get a feeling."

"What about Patton? Get anything from him?"

"He's a piece of work. Looks at you like you're something on the bottom of his shoe, then laughs and slaps you on the back. Brad's always nearby, watches him like a hawk. But the men worship his ass. He's whipped Second Corps into shape and he's not done yet. Oh; and guess what he gave me; told me I better make him look good in the magazine." Lang opened his kit to let Declan peek inside. Green bottle, familiar yellow label. "See you at the club at 5 for a high ball. Leave your golf shoes at the door. Your job is to get some ice. Check with Cookie; tell him it's for the general. If he asks which one, just say that's classified." With a wink, Lang was gone.

Later that night, well into their second glasses, Lang and Declan were feeling expansive. The mess sergeant had laughed at Declan, then told him to sod off which was the precise moment Declan realized that Lang had sent him on a fool's errand for ice in the desert. He'd find a way to repay in kind.

"So how is old Punch holding up? Still in search of a better world?"

"He warned me to be careful of you. Told me to watch the company I keep. Thinks that one day the world will line up and choose sides and that I had better be on the proper team."

"He's absolutely right. It's tricky. Freedom is good but too much of it doesn't work. Capitalism is built on the back of the working poor. The trouble is Uncle Joe's alternative, his 'workers paradise,' is inefficient and not much of a paradise, but at least everyone suffers equally. I'd like to think there's a middle ground, but I've yet to see it. Meanwhile, there's this little war…"

Declan reached for the bottle. "May I?"

"One more, then into our sleeping bags. Tomorrow's another day. Where was I?"

"This little war…"

"Right. This is nothing. I know it seems like everything to you right now, but this is nothing. Or maybe the beginning of something... something in Italy, in Europe. Look: the Eastern front has collapsed. Stalin defended the motherland. Think the war's over there? No fucking way. It's just beginning. Remember: this all started when Hitler invaded Poland. That's Stalin's backyard and, trust, me, he wants it back, with interest. Soon as winter's over, Joe will start to roll west. Eventually, we'll invade Europe, maybe through Italy, maybe across the Channel, maybe both. Put Hitler's balls in a nutcracker. Meet in the middle, maybe downtown Berlin, divide the spoils. That's when it'll get interesting."

"What's in it for you?"

"For me? For us? America? Your days are over. Well, not yours; England's. Egypt is gone. India's next. The Middle East? Hardly the stuff of empire, and anyway, England's too tired. Warn out, costs too much, can't afford it." Lang rubbed his fingers together. "Anyway, that will be all about the oil. You'll have to make friends with the Arabs." He laughed. "Probably the Jews, too. Good luck with that!"

"You still haven't answered my question. So America just packs up and goes home?"

Lang swirled the liquid that was left in his glass. "Oh no, son. You're going to want us to stay. Who's going to keep Stalin out of London if not us? The French? England and the rest of Western Europe will have to rebuild, and you will want to hide behind our skirts. We're too big, too strong, too much money. We may not be worldly smart yet, but we will be. When this war's over, the next one will have already begun. That's ours to fight and you'll thank us for it. It's getting late, time for bed, such as that is." He held up the empty bottle. "See? This is what I'm talking about. I'll resupply us in the morning. Too big, too strong, too much money. You need me, poor bastard!"

"You sound a lot more confident than you did a few weeks ago."

"That was then; this is now. Oh; by the way..."

Declan waited.

"Ike did tell me something interesting...off the record, of course."

"What's that?"

"Rommel. Gone. Flew back to Germany a week ago."

"There's been no announcement."

"No, and there won't be. Germany's most popular general, the Desert Fox, the hero of the El-Alamein, defeated? No, there won't be any official announcement. Hitler doesn't need any more bad press on the home front right now."

"How does Ike know?"

Lang shrugged. "Doesn't matter. He just knows."

CHAPTER FORTY

Scopa

"Wake up, Sir! C'mon, get up! It's past 4."

Declan's head hurt and the corporal shaking him didn't help. What was this wanker's name? Conley had attached himself to Patton like a leech; Declan had no idea who this kid was or why he was shaking him so hard. He looked over at Lang's bunk. It was empty. "Where is he?"

"In the mess tent, Sir. C'mon get up; we need to get going by 0500."

Declan looked at his watch; couldn't see a thing. He sat up. It was going to be a long day.

Two cups of black coffee and some greasy scrambled eggs later, Declan was in an armored half-track heading south. Lang sat next to him, smoking. He offered Declan a cigarette. "Feeling better?"

Declan nodded. "Last night; you said something about keeping Stalin out of London. Hitler couldn't get to London; why do you think Stalin could?"

"Hitler tried with the *Luftwaffe*. Bombs. Stalin's got a more powerful weapon."

Declan waited. Not for long, just enough time for Lang to take a drag on his cigarette.

"An idea. Comrade Marx's idea, actually: 'From each according to his ability, to each according to his need.' Powerful thought, huh? Lots of workers in England; lots of factories, lots of manufacturing. Awfully fertile soil for someone like Uncle Joe. Just wait and see. The Tories are riding Churchill like a rented mule but that won't last forever.

183

Ideas are like weeds; they're inevitable; they grow in anything, even shit, no matter what."

Declan let that sink in for a moment. The sun was just coming up. Looked like it was going to be a clear day, cool but clear. A good day for war. "What about here? What happens here?" He looked out at the barren, brown landscape. Lots of low hills, high ground.

"It's different here. A different idea for these folk to sort out. Colonialism is dead after this war. So what comes next? The problem here is that the French elites are entrenched, they hold all the cards. Ever been to a café and seen the good ol' boys playing *scopa*?" Declan looked at Lang blankly. "Italian card game. Tunisians love it. When someone plays a winning card, he bangs it down hard as he can, yells '*Scopa!*' sweeps up all the other cards. That's what the name means— 'broom' in Italian. Can get pretty heated sometimes. That's the first game to be played here: will the guy who yells '*Scopa!*' and sweeps up all the cards be French or Arab? Can't be both." Lang shook his head. "Once that game is finished, then maybe the other one, the big one. But *scopa* comes first."

The road was dusty, full of ruts and potholes. The half track kept swerving to miss them. Declan's headache was still there, just behind his eyeballs. Lang seemed oblivious. He lit another cigarette, blew the smoke out his nose. "Sure hope there aren't any mines."

CHAPTER FORTY ONE

Mareth

In military parlance, there are 'battles' and then there are 'demonstrations.' The latter were simply noisy distractions intended to shift the enemy's focus away from the former. To a soldier caught up in a demonstration, it felt for all the world like a battle and its consequences could be just as deadly. But farther up the chain of command, demonstrations of force were a sideshow; they drew enemy forces away from the main event—in this case, the Italo-German defensive line at Mareth.

The terrain in southern Tunisia is characterized by a series of high hills with rocky ridge lines, *chotts* (dry salt lakes), and ultimately the Great Oriental Erg, the first rolling sand dunes of the Sahara Desert. Options for military maneuvers are extremely limited. It had been almost exactly three months since Declan had viewed the Mareth Line with General Giovanni Messe. Since then, Messi had been appointed Commander of the Italo-German Tank Army, now organized as the 1st Italian Army in recognition of the fact that it was comprised of one German and three Italian corps. During their visit to Mareth in December, Messi had impressed Declan with both his broad vision and his attention to detail; he saw the forest and the trees. He also understood his role. Even then, he knew he would likely be pitted against a superior force, the British Eighth Army, under General Montgomery's command; his role was to tactically delay its advance, thereby allowing Rommel's *Afrika Korps* to retreat to Tunis and withdraw to Europe intact. The situation had changed since then, but not the odds. They were still not in Messe's favor.

***

"So you've seen the Mareth Line?"

"Yes, Sir, I have."

"And you know General Messe?"

"No, Sir, I don't really know him, but I did spend a little time with him. I have to say, I liked him."

General Montgomery raised an eyebrow. "Lang here says you might be able to help us. Tell me what you saw."

Declan looked over at Lang who sat expressionless, waiting. "Well, Sir, I honestly didn't see much. There's a lot of barbed wire, concrete bunkers, casements; trenches and firing blinds. I didn't see the mine fields, but he told me they were there, both anti-tank and anti-personnel. He thinks he can't be flanked."

Montgomery had been looking away but at Declan's last observation, he turned to face him. "Can't be flanked? He told you that?"

"Yes, Sir. Said the *chott*'s too wet this time of year and mechanized vehicles would be of no use in the hills. He said the only way around him would be to work your way to the south, then head far west. I think he said it would stretch your supply lines too thin. It was almost like he wanted you to know this, like he was daring you to try that."

"How interesting. Anything else?"

"No, Sir."

"Thank you, Mr. Shaw. That will be all."

Declan turned to go, looked at Lang. He hadn't moved. He was staying.

***

"Learn anything?" Lang was his usual informal self, but Montgomery didn't seem to mind.

"General Catroux—chap that built the line for the French—told me much the same thing when I saw him in Algiers. But there was one new interesting tidbit from your man. The part about 'motorized vehicles' being of no use at *Djebel Dahar*. Maybe so in 1938, but ours perform better these days. I think he's underestimating us there. Even Rommel thought Mareth could be flanked. He wanted the line further back at

Wadi Akarit, but *Comando Supremo* disagreed, so here it is. And here we are."

"So what's your plan?"

"Off the record. Understood?" Lang nodded. "We'll establish a bridgehead somewhere near their center, then make a wide left hook around the inland end of the line through Djebel Dahar, march north, then turn back east through the Tebaga Gap. Long range reconnaissance says it can be done. If your man is right, Messe won't be expecting that. He thinks there's no viable way through the Matmata Hills. He's wrong."

"I hope you're right."

Montgomery was fussing with his pipe. "If the LRDG says they found a gap, then they did. Even gave it a name: Wilder's Gap. Have no idea who Wilder is and frankly don't care. Thinking of sending the New Zealanders through. Conceal them in daylight, march them at night. Tough bunch. They'll do well."

Lang stood up. It had been a long day; he wanted his bedroll. "Good night," pause, "Sir."

Montgomery lit his pipe. "Good night, Mr. Lang. Pleasant dreams."

***

"Might be a commendation for you, even an OBE, if this works." Lang winked.

"What are you talking about?"

Lang poured a few drops of water from his canteen into his cup, swirled the liquid. "Seems your time with Messe was well spent. Montgomery liked what you said about mechanized vehicles."

"He shouldn't put too much stock in what I said. Sometimes, I had the feeling Messe was feeding me information he wanted to see in print. That's not always the same as telling me the truth."

"Did you feel that way at the time or later? It's easy to doubt yourself after the fact. Or maybe he just didn't take you seriously; wrote you off as just another Fleet Street hack with a cockamamy story to sell."

Declan thought for a moment. "No. He's too smart for that. I think he knows he's in a tough spot but he'll put up a good fight. He has a good reputation and he wants to keep it. I wonder if he knows about Rommel."

"I'm sure he does, but he won't say anything. Rommel is worth a lot even as a phantom general, to his own troops as much as to ours. They'll still fight hard for him—even if they don't see him at the front."

"So why don't we broadcast the news that he's gone?"

"And compromise the source of our information? What's the first rule of our trade? Protect your sources, boy! You may need them again someday."

Declan waited for the second rule, but heard Lang start to snore instead.

CHAPTER FORTY TWO

Left Hook

From the journal of Declan Shaw, entry dated, *17 March, 1943: Once... we used to write about battles as if they existed on one day, in one place. A cavalry charge was a cavalry charge; men lived or died on the same day. In the Great War, men swarmed out of the trenches, advanced, retreated; some even survived to do it all over again the next day. And the day after that...*

This war seems different. Its great battles are fought on multiple fronts, along miles of lines, and for weeks at a time. The one here at Mareth appears to be but a part of a larger theatre of war in southern Tunisia, involving almost a quarter million men fighting on unconnected fronts under multiple commands. There are plots and subplots, countless acts of heroism and probably cowardice, too; in the background, there's a lamenting Greek chorus, trying to make sense out of senselessness. But this is no play with actors declaiming on a stage. This is real. History will give us a better perspective, but right now, one tries to fit the pieces together like a blind man with a monstrous jigsaw puzzle. Sometimes the pieces fit, but more often, they don't.

Yesterday, Montgomery ordered XXX Corps (under General Leese) forward against the Italo-German line in an old-fashioned frontal assault, codename Operation Pugilist. This morning, it appears that XXX Corps has broken through the initial defenses and has established a bridgehead in the center of the enemy lines, but the rough terrain and more bad weather has made it impossible to deploy supporting tanks, artillery, or anti-tank weapons. Nor has there been any opportunity for aircraft to support the bridgehead, leaving our infantry exposed and isolated. It's unlikely they'll be able to hold out for long. It may prove to be a costly opening gambit.

***

"I thought you said it was going to be warmer down here." Declan pulled his wool cap down around his ears and turned up the collar on his flack jacket. It didn't help much.

"It gets cold in the desert at night. Nothing to trap the heat. Better get used to it." Lang always seemed oblivious to the cold; maybe it was all the alcohol in his blood—except he always seemed oblivious to that, too.

Declan didn't know how he had done it, but somehow Lang had talked Montgomery into allowing the two journalists to accompany a corps of New Zealanders on a two-hundred mile flanking maneuver around the Djebel Dahar and the Matmata Hills. Now it was well past midnight and the column was dead-reckoning toward a narrow defile near the southern extremity of a rock formation—Lang said it was called Wilder's Gap—which by morning would bring them around to the western side of the range, out of sight of Axis reconnaissance. The plan called for the corps to march through the night, then to conceal themselves during the day before resuming their march north the next night. Their ultimate objective was a place called the Tebaga Gap, a wide defile at the northern end of the hills that would enable the force to spill into the fertile coastal plain just south of Gabés. More importantly, if they could make it through the gap intact, they would be in a position to attack Messe's right flank and draw his attention away from the Eighth Army's planned frontal assault on the Mareth Line, still days away. It was an ambitious plan; timing and surprise would be the keys to its success.

An hour before dawn, the column halted and dug in to rest. There was a warm wind blowing out of the desert from the southwest and as the sun rose, a black cloud appeared on the horizon. As the New Zealanders watched nervously, the swirling cloud made its way closer and closer until the sky above was filled with the sound of millions of angry engines. In an instant, the column was enveloped by a swarm of locust of Biblical proportion. There was nothing to do but cover up and endure.

***

"Now you know how Pharaoh must have felt." Shaw shoved Declan into the cab of a lorry and slammed the door. It was almost black inside; locusts covered both windows and the windscreen, tiny red eyes glaring in at them. "It's a good thing we're here."

Declan stared at Lang. "What? Why?"

"Because if we were back in Missouri, the corn crop would be gone by the end of the day."

All Declan could say was "Jesus."

Lang laughed. "Try Moses; it was his plague. Let's just hope the bastards keep going. Here." He handed Declan a lit cigarette to share. Even with the windows closed, the noise was deafening; giant hailstones pelting on a tin roof. Plus, it was getting hot in the truck. Declan took a deep breath in an attempt to quell his growing sense of panic. As usual, Lang seemed genuinely unconcerned.

"This doesn't bother you? Does anything ever bother you?"

The driver's side door flew open; a body came flying in, squeezing Declan against Lang. The door slammed shut again, but too late. A locust whirred against Declan's face; he swatted at it like a madman.

"Tiny! Good of you drop in!"

"Shite! If I knew you were in here, Lang, I would've stayed outside with the bloody locusts. Who's your mate?"

"Mr. Declan Shaw, Correspondent for The Guardian. Declan, let me introduce you to Lieutenant-General Bernard C. Freyberg, Commander of this fine New Zealand Corps. Former dentist. Genuine war hero, Battle of the Somme. Swam the English Channel. Lovingly Known as 'Tiny' to his men—just look at that bulbous head, that thick torso, those stumpy legs! Also known as 'The Salamander' to no less a personage than Prime Minister Winston Churchill. Shown him your shrapnel scars, Tiny."

Freyberg stared at Lang, then laughed. "Heard about that, did you?"

"Oh, I heard, alright. Heard Winston stopped counting at twenty-seven."

"That's because I didn't show him my ass. Want to see it? Got a cigarette?"

Lang handed him the pack. "Keep it. I've got plenty. So, General Tiny, Sir, what's the news?"

Freyberg lit a cigarette, inhaled deeply and held it a moment. When he finally exhaled a blue cloud of smoke, Declan fought not to cough.

"Monty's made a bollocks of it again. Thinking too much about his victory parade in Tunis or maybe leading the invasion of Sicily, I imagine. XXX Corps got the shite knocked out of them; men had to crawl away. Over 600 casualties." Freyberg shook his head. "I don't know how the bastard keeps getting away with it. Wonder what Rommel thinks of him." Declan peeked over at Lang, saw him give a slight shake of the head. Freyberg fumbled in his shirt pocket, withdrew a piece of paper, started to hand it over to Lang, then stopped. "We're off the record in here. Right?"

Lang took the message. "Absolutely." Read it. Now it was his turn to say, "Jesus."

Lang started to hand the message to Declan. "OK with you?"

Freyberg looked at Declan. "Off the record to you, too."

"Yes, Sir. Off the record."

It was a message was from Eighth Army Command Post. It informed Freyberg of a complete change of plan: the 'left hook,' initially intended to divert some of Messe's forces away from the Mareth Line, was now going to be the primary assault on the Axis forces. General Leese would remain on the coast to make a limited frontal assault on the the Italo-German lines, but now Freyberg's New Zealanders, reinforced with Indian troops, would strike the main blow after coming through the Tebaga Gap. The name for the new plan was Operation Supercharge II. There was a final line in the message. "Sending Horrocks to take charge. Am sure you understand." It was signed 'Montgomery.'

Freyberg took another long drag on his cigarette, almost swallowed the smoke. "Horrocks. Younger by six years; lower rank. Bloody hell! Know what Montgomery did to soften the blow? Sent me a bloody bottle of brandy. Bollocks!"

Except for the last of the locust still banging against the windshield, it was quiet for a long time.

Finally, Lang said more to himself than to anyone else, "So the sideshow has become the main event."

Almost at the same time, Freyberg said to no one in particular, "It's too small a war for this many generals."

Declan shook his head and just whispered: "Jesus."

CHAPTER FORTY THREE

Tebaga Gap

Freyberg's column—now officially Horrocks' column—reached the western opening of the Tebaga Gap two days later. They had moved quickly and carefully, but had nevertheless been spotted by a Luftwaffe reconnaissance plane. The pilot radioed Messe's Command Post alerting him to the threat to his flank. Messe responded quickly, rushing seasoned German troops from the Mareth Line to the eastern end of the defile where it opened up onto the coastal plain, fifty miles away. But once again, the boys back at Bletchley Park outside London were paying attention. They intercepted the radio signals, decoded them with Ultra, and immediately advised Montgomery about what to expect. Game on.

Montgomery put aside his plans for a victory parade in Tunis and rose to the challenge. He formulated a curiously simple plan: a surprise late afternoon attack, the New Zealand Corps spilling out of the Gap with the sun directly at their back. Air and tank support. The Germans would be firing blind from an exposed position, unable to see their targets.

***

From Declan Shaw's journal, entry dated *27/28 March*: *War is choreography. Choreography and timing. Yesterday afternoon, the assault—Montgomery's 'left hook'—began right on time. The men had been waiting, hiding all day, playing chess to kill time. Then, precisely at 1530 hours, Allied planes flew out of the sun to attack the German line. The Gods decided to help, sending up a dusty sandstorm, making it impossible for the Germans to see what was coming at them and where to direct their fire.*

First, a thunderous artillery barrage, followed at 1615 hours by a cavalry charge of more than 250 tanks with Maori infantry, faces all tattooed, in their wake. What a sight! Our men poured into the gap, a giant wave crashing into a German wall, sending them running. Tank commanders threw grenades at point blank range. When the Maoris ran out of ammo, they threw rocks at the fleeing Nazis. Gurkhas from the 4th Indian Divisions ran the enemy down, their bayonets wet and bright red with blood. By nightfall, we were halfway through the gap, pushing the enemy in front of us toward El Hamma, a small oasis town at the head of the gap, only thirty miles west of Gabès.

Then the assault just seemed to stall. A last-ditch defense by a few German anti-tank guns stopped our boys cold for several hours—as it turns out, critical hours that let General Messe's army make an orderly withdrawal from Mareth and escape northward. By the time we finally broke through, all we could see was the the dust from their retreating column. Intelligence reports that Messe has organized a new defensive line sixty miles to our north at Wadi Akarit, but with Patton's army pressing them from the west, it seems only a matter of time until Messe and von Arnim will be forced to pull back again to form a tight defensive ring around Tunis. The men think the end is in sight.

Initial reports indicate that enemy casualties are heavy and that we have taken more than 7,000 prisoners, Italian and German. Allied losses are also substantial: roughly 4,000 men, killed or wounded but Montgomery is nevertheless ecstatic; he called Mareth the "most enjoyable battle I ever fought."

And yet: at the very moment when we have the initiative, the machine has ground to a halt. Instead of seizing the momentum and pursuing or even harassing the enemy, we're idling in Gabès. Tomorrow, the mayor of Gabès is presenting Montgomery with the ceremonial keys to his city while the 51st Highland Division is going on parade in full Scottish regalia, kilts and pipers! I wonder what the locals will think, let alone the enemy.

***

Declan and Lang were bivouacked in a small hotel near the center of Gafsa. There was a shower with a trickle of reasonably warm water, reasonably clean sheets on unreasonably lumpy beds. The beer in the bar downstairs was reasonably cold.

"This could have been a decisive battle, maybe *the* decisive battle, but it wasn't. Monty let them get away. He'll paint a rosy little picture—he'll say he intended to use the left hook as his primary assault all along—but that's bullshit. He's the one who swears by the doctrine of concentration of forces so either he's changed his tune or Leese's first frontal assault on the line taught him a hard lesson. He won't admit that. He'll crow like a...crow."

Declan laughed. "Put that line in your story. The editors will love it!"

Lang took a sip of beer. He seemed more thoughtful than usual. "You said you heard some of the boys talking about how the end was near. Maybe it is, maybe not. I'll say this: it will be different from here on in. The Americans are coming out of the mountains. The desert is behind Monty. Everything is moving toward Tunis now: the Germans in retreat and us in pursuit when we get around to it. Rivers and hills now, all the way home. Rivers and hills."

Declan nodded. "Which raises an interesting question for you and me. How are we going to get to Tunis? Punch left a message; he says he misses me. Knows I'm with you, too. Probably worried about that."

Lang shook his head. "Don't think that's going to happen for a while. We're out in the field for the duration. No left hooks around the line for us." He motioned to the barman, pointed at the two empty bottles in front of them, held up two fingers. "My kind of left hook."

CHAPTER FORTY FOUR

Gallant But Green

The problem for General Alexander had always been what to do with Patton's Second Corps. The memory of American soldiers fleeing in retreat after the debacle at Kasserine Pass haunted him. Patton's arrival may have altered the picture, but the fact remained: the American army had yet to prove it could be an effective fighting force. Now that Montgomery had seized the momentum following his victory at Mareth, Alexander couldn't afford another setback.

While Montgomery and the Eighth Army were engaged at Mareth, General Patton, at his headquarters near Feriana, was chomping at the bit. He wanted a piece of the action. Alexander had ordered him to retake the oasis town of Gafsa, but when his men attacked the town, they found the place deserted and all but destroyed, the Italian defenders already gone. Patton was furious. There was no glory in taking an undefended town.

***

In Declan's dream, it sounded like an artillery barrage, but now that he was awake, he realized someone was pounding on his door. He staggered over and opened it. Lang.

"Get up. Get your kit. The general wants to see you."

"What time is it?"

"Doesn't matter. Get ready. Car's here; we're leaving in fifteen minutes."

"Montgomery's sending a car? He's right here."

"Who said anything about Monty? Patton wants to see me. You, too. Seems to think he needs some good press in the British papers. Somehow, he heard Monty and Alexander don't think much of his American soldiers. Monty even told Ike to keep Patton out of his way. You can imagine how old Blood and Guts reacted to that. Needs you to paint a pretty picture. C'mon. Move! And if I were you, I'd shave."

Fifteen minutes later, Patton's armored car roared out of Gafsa, heading for the general's CP in an old school house in Feriana, a small town sixty miles to the north. The sergeant who was driving had taped red cellophane over his headlights; Declan had no idea how he could see the road. Normally, it would be at least a one hour drive. The sergeant made it in forty-five minutes.

Patton was waiting. It wasn't yet dawn, but the CP was fully awake, bristling with either energy or fright or both. Patton was in the middle of the maelstrom, dictating to an aide, smoking a cigar. "Lang! Good man! Is that your friend?"

"Morning, General. This is Declan Shaw, correspondent from The Guardian. The guy from The Times wasn't feeling well. This guy's better anyway."

Patton came over, stood inches away from Declan, looked him straight in the eye. Didn't say a word for at least thirty seconds. Then he nodded, said. "OK." He jabbed his finger at a map pinned to the wall. "There. If I were you, I'd get going. You're safer while it's still dark. TR is waiting for you on his little hill. He's got quite a show planned. 10th Panzers. If you're going to fight, you might as well fight the champ. If you lose, everybody will say they expected it. But if you win, well, then, you're the new champ. Am I right, Lang?"

"You're always right, General. Let's go go, Declan. Can't keep General Roosevelt or the Germans waiting."

"Teddy's too old but he's good, heart's in the right place. Darby's good, too. But some of those other officers aren't worth shit. Need to get off their asses. They're too complacent, need more drive. Some of them need to get killed. Would help the men's morale if one or two officers got shot. If you see Pinky, tell him I said so. That's all."

Back in the car, with the same sergeant driving, Declan and Lang raced out toward a place on a map designated as Hill 336, but better known to the soldiers of Second Corps as Wop Hill. "Who's Pinky?" Declan asked.

"Pinky Ward. Major General Orlando Ward. Commander of the First Armored Division; they've had some problems. Patton's convinced Ward's overly cautious, too reluctant to incur casualties. Patton thinks he's a bit of a whiner. Was a protege of Marshall's and sometimes still pulls that string. Ike told me he's not too sure about him either, but right now, he's our man at Maknassy."

"And Roosevelt?"

"FDR's nephew. Teddy Roosevelt's eldest son. Talk about a line of communication to the top. But word is he's a front-line guy. Patton keeps an eye on him because Roosevelt's a buddy of Terry Allen's and because he dresses down. He's not regulation enough. But his men like him. Brad said something interesting—that TR loves his division too much. Patton was serious about officers getting shot. He wants to see more bodies. Thinks the men will fight harder if they see some dead bodies, especially officers' dead bodies."

"I don't understand Patton. Is it because he's American?"

"Understanding Patton's simple. He's a warrior. As far as he's concerned, the more war, the more blood, the better."

"So why am I here?"

"That's simple, too. The Yanks love Patton. He's practically a god at home. But he wants you Brits to love him, too. He's very savvy when it gets to PR. For all his reincarnation bullshit and crazy beliefs, he's no fool."

"What if I don't give him what he wants?"

"You will. Trust me; you will."

***

Notes from Declan Shaw's journal, undated entry: *The sergeant driving us pointed up the hill. "It's getting light. When you get near he top, stay low," he said. "If somebody says 'Three' to you, you say 'Strikes' right back; that's the password. Give the young rough rider my regards." He made a quick three-point turn and headed back to the CP.*

We scrambled and clawed our way to the top. Just at the ridge line, we came to a slit trench; there were three men in it, prone positions, looking down on the plain below through field glasses. The one in the middle turned and waved an old hickory cane in our direction. "That you, Lang? And you must be the chap from The Guardian. Welcome to the Wop Hill penthouse, gentlemen," he said. "Did Rawley drop you off on the lower level and make your walk all the way up here? Lazy cracker. Call me Teddy. Come have a look, but keep your head down. Snipers love a good target at first light. Oh, and by the way, watch out for scorpions." He moved over, made a hole for us, handed me his glasses. "Zeiss. You can thank a dead German for these babies." He pointed to the valley floor, several hundred feet below. "Isn't that a magnificent sight? You're never gonna see anything like this again!"

"Teddy" was right. We had an eagle's eye view of a wide, circular plain, several miles in diameter. A highway bisected the plain running east-to-west from the town of El Guettar to our rear to Gabès, just over the horizon. Patton's orders were to move down the highway, pinching the flank of the Italian forces retreating from Mareth.

I heard someone say, "Here they come!" Out of the sun came an advancing fleet of more than thirty German Panzers in rectangular formation, hundreds of Wehrmacht infantrymen trotting behind. It was almost medieval, foot soldiers behind knights on armored steeds, advancing steadily toward the enemy. There was little cover in the valley, nothing more than a few tufts of sisal grass, an olive tree or two.

Artillery was blasting away but on they came, a steady human wave. Roosevelt, watching through his field glasses, whispered, "It's the 10th Panzer Division, their very best." We watched, mesmerized by the peril below. The American line was retreating, forming a new line at a wadi. The fighting became hand-to-hand; bayonets, knives, grenades. "Allen's down there. The line will hold. Just watch."

The line buckled and bulged but did not break. Tank destroyers were firing at almost pointblank range. The noise was deafening; smoke began to obscure the battlefield. It didn't seem possible, but somehow, more shells whistled through the air. The German tanks veered left and began to bog down in a minefield. "Welcome to Death Valley, boys," Roosevelt whispered. The tanks were taking a shellacking; they stalled, turned, began to retreat. All down the hill, men began to cheer. It was nearly noon. A voice behind us roared, "That's right! Run, you Hun bastards!" Patton had arrived on the scene.

***

"Good job, Teddy, but you know they'll be back. Once is never enough for those bastards."

"Yes, Sir. In fact, they said they'd be back in time for tea at 1640. Terry intercepted a radio transmission. Even told 'em not to be late, to come on in. We'll be ready. I've got a little surprise for them. You might want to stay and watch."

Patton raised an eyebrow. "Terry taunted them? Jesus, I wish that S.O.B. would take this war seriously. What's your plan?"

"Ricochet fire from our guns, then scissors and search pattern. If their tanks hang back—they will because they can't afford to lose more—we'll mow their infantry down like hay."

Patton's jaw jutted. "Those are brave men down there, Teddy. They won't run. You'll have to crucify them. It seems like a crime to murder such good infantry. Too bad it was such a defensive battle for our boys. God, how I would have loved to see them charge!"

"Still, General. We beat their very best. We adapted to the situation and we showed them some stunning firepower. They'll remember this day. Our boys may still be a little green, but they're gallant as hell."

Patton was thoughtful for a moment. "I like that, Teddy. 'Green but gallant.' I like that very much. Mr. Shaw? Did you hear what General Roosevelt said? You might want to remember that quote. I'd write that down if I were you."

"I already did, Sir. I already did."

"Just change one thing."

"What's that, Sir?"

"Tell your readers I said it."

CHAPTER FORTY FIVE

Stalemate

Patton spent the following day with Terry Allen's troops, shaking hands, pounding backs, passing out cigars. He had Lang and Shaw with him, Lang shooting dozens of rolls of film, Declan interviewing officers and men, all under Patton's watchful gaze. By evening, he was tired but still elated. Before returning to his headquarters at Feriana, he said to General Allen, "Terry, I feel washed in the blood!"

The good feelings didn't last. With the fight at El-Guettar behind him for the moment, Patton could turn his full attention to Pinky Ward's predicament only forty miles away to the north. General Alexander had ordered Ward to take the village of Sened along with its railroad depot, then push on to occupy the town of Maknassy. Sened was low-hanging fruit; its garrison of Italian defenders surrendered after Ward's first artillery shell flew overhead. Emboldened, Ward pushed east to Maknassy, only to find it had already been abandoned. There, his objectives achieved, Ward stopped. A French liaison officer suggested he continue eastward another few miles and take two hills that overlooked a small German airfield at Mezzouna and the highway to Sfax, but Ward hesitated. When Patton heard about it, he picked up the field radio and exploded.

"Goddamnit, Pink, this is your moment. Seize it! It's every commander's dream. Every minute you sit there is a minute the enemy can use to reinforce his position. Get off your ass and take those hills. Let me know when you do!" Patton slammed down the handle on his radio.

"Lord God in heaven, give me patience," he said, just loud enough for Declan and Lang to hear. "Pinky's too timid. Hugs the rear. Wouldn't know an opportunity if it bit him in the ass. I'm going to send Jenson over there to assess the situation and see what the hell is going on." He looked over at the correspondents. "Want to ride along?"

Lang shrugged. Declan knew there was only one acceptable answer to that question. "Yes, Sir."

General Ward was in his command post in Maknassay, pacing. "Captain, my orders from General Alexander were explicit: take Maknassy and assemble more forces before moving into the hills. I'm not going to incur unnecessary casualties just to please General Patton." Declan looked at Captain Jenson, Patton's favorite aide. He didn't envy the man who would relay that message.

"Tell George this, too," Ward said. "I don't trust Robinett anymore. He's able enough in the field, but he has no respect for the chain of command. Keeps going behind my back. Even Ike knows it. Told me to use the iron in my glove if I had to, but I believe in catching my flies with honey. General Patton may not believe in honey, but he's not here. I am." It sounded more defiant than Ward intended; he softened his tone."Tell George that if he wants me to move into the hills, I'll do it. I await his orders."

Jenson, with Declan and Lang in tow, headed back to Feriana to report to Patton. The 'go' order arrived at Ward's CP within an hour. Patton would get exactly half of what he wanted: plenty of death but little glory.

***

Entry in Declan Shaw's journal, dated *April 1: It has been an utterly horrific ten days. Erratic leadership, too many changes of plan from the top, and poor staff decisions in the field have resulted in the gory, senseless slaughter of men. Ward's division is totally exhausted. General Patton blames General Ward, says he has "no driving force," but in fairness to the man, he was given a poor hand to play. Alexander wanted to use Ward and his men to draw Axis troops away from Montgomery's Eighth Army. Patton was more critical than helpful; he never even offered Ward infantry reinforcements. Omar Bradley, who told me he thinks Ward is "a fundamentally kind and decent man," simply thinks he's "unlucky."*

Ten days ago, when this all began, it seemed it would be easy enough for Ward. Things were going well. Send and Maknassay fell almost without a shot. Then, when Patton orders him to push on, a single battalion took the first of the two hills east of Maknassy without any significant opposition. But another battalion sent to take the second hill, Djebel Naemia, met fierce resistance from the Begleitkompanie— Rommel's former personal bodyguards—who were dug in like badgers at the top. Raking machine gun fire, land mines, even stones and cascades of boulders, kept the Americans pinned down for three days and nights, unable to advance or retreat. Patton was furious. He ordered Ward to personally lead an attack up the hill, then fretted about ordering a fellow general officer to his death.

But a grim and determined Ward rose to the occasion. He took command from the front, seemingly oblivious to his own safety, encouraging his men forward, but the enemy fire was just too intense. One sergeant told me it was like "a shooting gallery with us as the ducks." Casualties mounted; stretcher bearers couldn't reach the wounded. Ward, still under intense fire, tried again to rally his men but they were too exposed, their will to fight was gone, ground into the blood-soaked dust. I saw a machine gun bullet trace an angry line down the back of Ward's field jacket; a shell fragment caught him between his right eye and the the bridge of his nose. Bleeding profusely, he continued to direct fire at German positions. But it was no use: the Germans held the high ground. An hour later, his forces depleted and exhausted, Ward called off the attack. More than 300 of his men had been killed, another 1,400 were wounded or missing in action; 40 tanks had been destroyed. By the time he got back to his CP, Ward was in shock. Two days later, Patton made a show of awarding him a silver star for gallantry but excoriated him in private for his initial delay. Even Eisenhower thinks Ward lacks what is most needed for battlefield command: a "veneer of callousness." Ward's days in Tunisia are surely numbered.

This morning, a corporal brought a package to my tent. Inside, I found a pair of high-optic Nazi field glasses—Zeiss—with a note: "With my compliments along with those of Herr Hitler." It was signed "TR."

They arrived in the morning. But then at noon, we received word that Captain Richard Jenson—Patton's favorite aide, the same officer who drove Lang and me to Ward's headquarters last week—was killed in an air raid four miles east of here. Eight Stukas attacked his convoy; Jenson and two others were killed when a bomb exploded nearby. The concussion broke every bone in Jenson's body without breaking the skin. Patton was devastated. He received Jenson's body in tears, snipped a lock of the dead man's hair to send to his mother. That's General Patton: the same man who ordered General Ward to "take that damn hill or don't come back" is a complex, mercurial man, the sum total of many strange and conflicting moods.

***

It was getting late; Declan and Lang were on their third and final game. Rubber match: Lang had won the first game; Declan had rallied to win the second. Neither had much patience so they were playing speed chess: no more than thirty seconds were permitted between moves.

They were sitting in the officers' mess tent. Lang had refilled his canteen with more Cutty Sark, but he wasn't fooling anyone. "Everyone's exhausted. We'll never break through to the sea now. Can't trap the bastards, can't cut them off. We're stuck here in these damn foothills. Messe's ready and waiting for Monty at Wadi Akarit; it's the defensive line Rommel—bless his dear, departed soul—wanted all along. If Monty gets pushed back or even delayed, the Germans will throw everything they've got at the First Army up north. If they're successful there, then von Arnim will bring his down here and reinforce Messe. But if the First Army can hold off von Arnim and if Monty can break through at Wadi Akarit, then it's on to Sfax and one long continuous Allied front advancing toward Tunis and Bizerte. That's a fight the Germans can't win; they just don't have enough fuel or supplies. Best they can hope for is to hold out long enough to escape…live to fight another day. It's just a chess game, only on a bigger board. You ok?"

Declan shrugged. "Just tired. This is getting to me."

"This game?"

"No; this war." Almost all the pawns were off the board. Declan picked one of his captives up, seemed to study it. "You should have seen the body bags today. Mattress covers. Crosses and Stars of David stacked up like firewood."

Lang moved his bishop. "I know. It gets to me, too. But what are you going to do? Your move."

Declan hesitated. "So many…" His voice trailed away.

"But just as many of theirs are dead, probably more. We can stay in the fight longer than they can."

"Maybe." Declan studied the board, moved his knight forward. Check."

Lang studied the board for a moment, then moved his bishop back to block his king. Declan could capture it, but it would expose his queen. The choices of war.

"How do you Americans do it? How do you stay so bloody optimistic?"

"We're a naïve people, Dec. Maybe it's just our nature, or maybe we just don't know any other way. We always think we'll win. This stuff helps, too. Here." Lang raised his canteen, tipped some liquid into Declan's tin coffee mug. "Now all you need is a little whipped cream. Irish coffee for my Irish friend." He winked. "Know what?"

Declan looked up, nodded. "Shite. This game's a bloody stalemate."

Lang stood up and stretched, tipped over both kings. "Let's hit the sack. Tomorrow's another day."

CHAPTER FORTY SIX

The Worm's Eye View

In Declan's experience, Lang never deferred to anyone with the possible exception of General Eisenhower. But he definitely deferred to Ernie Pyle, the Scripps-Howards correspondent assigned to cover the war in North Africa. Their paths had crossed a few times, but Lang almost seemed to go out of his way to avoid extended contact. Declan had asked Lang about it once and all Lang said was, "It's never a good idea to bother the gods."

But tonight, when Declan walked in to the officer's mess, Lang and Pyle were sitting there, sharing a bottle of something that looked vaguely like wine. He sat down to a look from Lang that seemed to say, "Sit down, shut up, and listen." So that's what he did.

"You realize, it's been only been five months since these boys landed on the beaches of Morocco and Algeria. Some haven't even been over here that long. But those five months have been awfully cruel: rain-soaked, freezing cold, muddy, and lately, increasingly bloody. Ike's Operation Torch adventure has turned into a grisly war. Remember when Rommel called his time in the desert *'Krieg ohne Hass'*—war without hate? Well, it's not like that anymore, my friend. This has become a sanctioned scientific experiment in human sacrifice on a massive scale. Five months ago, most of these boys were right off the farm or just out of high school, hardly ready to shave. Now, we've transformed them into primal killing machines. In just five short months, they've learned how to hate. They've seen their brothers and friends die horrible deaths, and now they intend to exact more of the same or worse on their foes. War does that to men: it dehumanizes them."

Pyle took a sip. "Even these poor innocent Tunisians are paying the price. Two days ago, I heard about a couple of privates who were having what they called a 'wog shooting contest.' Their target was an old man on a donkey. They thought it was like shooting at gophers, funny as hell until a sergeant showed up and busted their asses. But it's not just those two idiots. Sentries are authorized to shoot anyone wearing white, whether they know the password or not and just yesterday, I heard about incidents of gang rape, murder, and mayhem you don't even want to know about in some little village just across the border in Algeria.

"Le Tarf," said Declan. Lang shot him a look but Pyle said, "Yep; that's the place: Le Tarf."

Pyle kept going. "People back at home hear all these stories coming out of Europe—like about Jews being murdered in Nazi death camps—and think we're over here fighting on the side of the angels. Ain't no angels in this war, Will." Declan had to think for a moment—he had never heard anyone else use Lang's first name before. Lang was always just Lang—except apparently to Ernie Pyle.

"They will never be the same, these boys. Their happy, old lives are gone forever. Most of them are good boys, good men, but every barrel has a few rotten apples. It's sad, but you need hate to win a war these days. It's standard issue, hate is."

Later, when they were alone, Lang said to Declan, "He's more than a correspondent. He's a storyteller. He doesn't write about generals or troop movements, he writes about the men. Not so much the officers, but the enlisted men. He calls it his "worm's-eye view." That's why the dog-face soldiers love him so much, and that's why people back home read every damn word he writes. He makes war personal. He knows how to connect with soldiers and he know how to connect with his readers. He's a friend to both, the bridge between army and civilian life. He's got an in with these men neither you nor I will ever have. Mauldin's good, too, everybody loves his Willie and Joe cartoons, everybody except Patton, that is. Patton thinks he's insubordinate, called him 'an unpatriotic anarchist,' wanted to throw his ass in jail. But he loves Ernie Pyle. Ernie Pyle is Babe Ruth, and you and I are just watching from the cheap seats.

Learn whatever you can from that man, Dec. Someday, if you're half as good a writer as Ernie Pyle, maybe a few more people will pay attention to your copy, too. What's wrong? You looked puzzled."

"Who's Babe Ruth?"

Lang stared at him for a long moment. "Jesus, Declan. You've got a lot to learn about your American cousins. Babe Ruth's our patron saint. Kind of like your St. Patrick, except he's hit more home runs."

CHAPTER FORTY SEVEN

Together and Apart

General Giovanni Messe's line of steel at Wadi Akarit melted away during the night. No matter; it would not have been a fair fight anyway. Montgomery's Eighth Army had 462 tanks: Messe's Italo-German force had 25. Montgomery's army took more than 5,000 prisoners, but only one in ten was German; the rest were Italian. Messe was uncharacteristically succinct: *Non è stata una bella battaglia*. This was not a good battle.

With the retreat of the Axis army from Wadi Akarit, the American Second Corps was finally able to push through the western mountains onto the coastal plain. But just like Montgomery's left hook at Tebaga Gap, they were too late to do any real damage. They took a thousand more prisoners, but the bulk of the enemy was already over the horizon. Patton, perhaps channeling one of his many former lives, was equally succinct. "*Sic Transit Gloria Mundi*," he wrote in his diary. Thus passeth the glory of the world.

As the Axis forces retreated toward Tunis, for the first time the American and English cousins could unite. The Americans who had landed on the beaches of Morocco and Algeria five months earlier had finally crossed the mountains in Tunisia and reached the Eastern Dorsal. Montgomery's army which had chased Rommel across the top of Africa for a year and a half had now broken through at Wadi Akarit and were finally flowing north toward Tunis. The two armies converged on the coastal plain south of Sfax. They were hesitantly glad to see each other—long-lost cousins at a family reunion—but the initial encounter was underwhelming, to say the least. A British sergeant said it was "a pleasant surprise" to encounter the Americans. An American private responded by saying in a southern drawl that it was "sure nice to see someone besides a damn Nazi."

But for Ike, back at his headquarters in Algiers, it was the culmination of more than a year's hard work. It had been a costly effort but now the armies of the west and the east were together at last. Now there were not two separate fronts, just one long, continuous Allied line pushing the Axis inexorably back toward Tunis in what looked like a last stand. Perhaps the end was finally in sight.

But first, there were wounds that needed healing. British and American commanders didn't trust each other. They got on each other's nerves. Montgomery thought Eisenhower was shrill, more a politician than a fighting general, and that American forces were undisciplined and impulsive. "They are not like us," he wrote to a fellow officer. Eisenhower thought Montgomery was too slow and methodical, that he wouldn't move until he was sure he could win. His personal assessment of Montgomery was more blunt: "Goddamn it, I can deal with anybody except that son of a bitch. He is a thorn in my side!"

Despite the animus that lay just beneath the surface, there was still a campaign to win. For his part, Patton was suspicious of British intentions. He had come to the conclusion that the British were planning a coup: Anderson's First Army would take Bizerte while Montgomery's Eighth Army would seize Tunis. The Americans would be sidelined, mere bystanders. Patton wanted to be in on the kill. He dispatched General Bradley to enlist Ike's support. Ike's response to Patton was cautiously optimistic: "General Alexander assures me that your corps will not be pinched out of the coming campaign." It looked good on paper, but paper often doesn't fare well in war.

***

From the front page of 'The Guardian,' by Declan Shaw, Sunday, *April 11, 1943*: *Fondouk is not a pretty place. It can scarcely be called a village—there's nothing but a few mud huts and a small adobe mosque. Prickly pear cactus and an occasional ancient olive tree are the only ornaments on the otherwise dreary landscape. Nearby, the Marguellil River has sliced a narrow pass through the Eastern Dorsal of Tunisia about twenty miles southwest of the central city of Kairouan. At this time of year, the river's flow is shrinking fast, only a few shallow, muddy channels running between steep banks. Bunches of wildflowers and some bright red poppies somehow have managed to find a foothold among the rocks. They will be gone in a few weeks, burned to a crisp by the Tunisian sun.*

The Fondouk Pass is barely a thousand yards wide. On either side, two rocky escarpments overlook the narrow defile that leads onto the coastal plain. For some months now, German soldiers have been burrowing into these hills, creating fortress-like redoubts complete with kitchens and sleeping quarters in the high ground that commands the plain below. According to intelligence reports, one of the entrenched battalions was composed entirely of court-marshaled soldiers who hoped to be rehabilitated through combat. These "Schwarzschlächters" (Black Butchers) wore no military or national insignias; they were dangerous men who had nothing to lose.

Fighting—real combat—is done by enlisted men led by junior officers. They are only following orders that come down from on high, in this case from British Lieutenant General John Crocker, only recently arrived in North Africa, and American Major General Charles Ryder who skirmished here only weeks ago. Ryder wanted to encircle the hills overlooking the pass, attack them from the north and south; Crocker overruled him, insisting on a frontal infantry assault that would clear the way for armor. The goal was to push through the pass to liberate German-held Kairouan and to intercept and destroy Messe's retreating Italo-German army before it could merge with von Arnim's northern army to form a strong defensive ring around Tunis.

The combat was brutal, the cost heavy. American infantry were pinned down for two days: to twitch was to die. Even at night, green tracers from German machine guns on the heights lit the exposed ridges with a deadly daylight. "We were peas on a plate," one American sergeant told this reporter. There was no way to retrieve the dead and wounded; men died quickly or they died slowly, their anguish echoing off the rocky hillside. Chaplains wept.

On the second day, British armor was devastated. Anti-tank guns and minefields claimed more than thirty Shermans. Crews trying to escape were cut down by machine gun fire. Men were burning. The smell of singed flesh clings to the nostrils for days.

Nevertheless, thirty-four hours after the battle began, the Allies finally broke through the pass. Kairouan fell the next day. When the city was liberated, its Jewish population wept with joy, tore off the yellow stars they had been forced to wear. But the second objective—the annihilation of the Italo-German Army—was not achieved. The Germans held out just long enough to let Messe escape. Once again, the Allies were moments too late. Although we took more than a hundred prisoners, just as many of the German defenders escaped to join the thick cloud of dust that was Messe's army retreating north toward Tunis. Another opportunity to bring this long campaign to a close has gone lost.

After Waterloo, Wellington mused that "nothing except a battle lost can be half so melancholy as a battle won." Today, the melancholy of the battle of Fondouk Pass is compounded by the deep rifts it exposed within the Allied ranks. General Crocker was caustic about our American cousins: "American commanders were too far to the rear... leadership by junior officers was very weak." He even went so far as to opine that the American infantry should be removed from the field for retraining. His opinion has filtered down to the ranks. This reporter witnessed an exchange between groups of soldiers: one of our men made an obscene gesture to a passing American convoy. "Going to 'f...' up another front, are you?" Even dispatches by American correspondents decry the Yanks ability to fight. No less a distinguished publication than 'Time' magazine called Fondouk "a downright embarrassment for our men" and that "it afforded a sharp comparison between British and U.S. forces." The Tommies were described as "efficient" while the Yanks were "tentative."

For their part, Americans commanders feel their British counterparts to be "too methodical, inflexible, even quixotic." There is also the troubling belief that British commanders are callously using American men and material to win the war. They likened General Crocker's frontal assault to the charge of the Light Brigade in Crimea in 1854. "Forward, the Light Brigade! Charge for the guns!" he said. Into the valley of death rode the six hundred. They do not believe that British tactics have evolved much, if at all, in almost a hundred years.

As for the men themselves, the ones who survived the butchery of Fondouk, there is only way to think and that is not to think. Best not to talk about or even remember the dead. They no longer exist. Yesterday is over and done. The task is to live until tomorrow, then the next day and all the days thereafter.

***

Declan's head was down over his coffee cup. Lang was smoking, unusually empathetic. "I'm not saying you're wrong, only that Patton didn't get what he wanted out of you. You're officially on his shit list along with those other American correspondents, but he blames the military censors as much as he blames you. We've all been there at one time or another. Trust me: he'll get over it. He knows there's always another story to report. By the way, EP liked your piece, especially, the 'peas on a plate' line."

Declan lifted his head just enough to look Lang in the eye, to see if he was kidding; concluded he wasn't. "But you know it's all true. There are bad feelings on both sides. It's hard to fight a war when you don't respect your ally. I thought the Germans and the Italians were lousy partners. We may be worse."

"No; not worse. We're just different. We're still together, just a little apart." Lang gave a shrug. "It's sour now, but it won't last. Keeping us all on the same side long enough to win a war just might be Ike's greatest challenge."

CHAPTER FORTY EIGHT

Behind the Line

The ever-tightening German cinch around Tunis and Bizerte changed life in those two cities. Food became increasingly scarce; fresh meat was almost impossible to find. People were lucky to eat one meal a day, usually a couscous with an oily fish head or a lamb bone, a carrot or two, or just some *harissa* for flavor. There was a strict evening curfew and heavily armed German patrols, fearing fifth column support for the Allies, kept people off the streets much of the day as well. The colonial French police were nowhere to be seen. Shops were looted, shopkeepers beaten for no reason other than the Germans felt like it. Fear—fear and desperation—does that to men.

Disease and contagion were rampant; hospital wards were overflowing, and mosques and the few French churches in the city tended to the sick and weak as best they could. Every road leading out of Tunis was choked with refugees, a few in cars but most of them on foot, carrying whatever they could, everyone desperate to escape the gathering storm. Those who remained behind were either unable to travel or prevented from leaving by German overlords who required their services.

La famille Fabron—Paul, his mother, and father—had been trying to get to France for several weeks but civilian transport was almost non-existent. Once there—that is, if they could ever get there—they planned to move on to the Levant and start again, perhaps in the Bekaa valley. It would not be easy. Banks were barely functioning and personal capital and assets routinely and mysteriously got lost in transit.

M.Fabron had sold all his real properties and wine-making equipment to a wealthy Tunisian for *sou* on the franc. His wealth, such as it was, was vastly diminished, but there was nothing he could do. He was alive. He and his family would survive, that is if they could ever leave this madness once and for all.

Once, in a moment of near panic, Paul had attempted to see General Kesserling or someone else in the high command who knew about the cases of wine Paul had delivered to win the general's favor. But the sergeant who sat outside Kesserling's office in the Hôtel de Ville simply stared at him before rudely sending him away, telling him in unmistakable German not to come back or he would be shot. He laid his Luger on the desk for emphasis. Paul left as quickly as his dignity would allow.

Leila Ben Zayed had not left her home in nearly a month. She filled her days with books and writing wistful poetry. When she left her room, she would watch her despondent mother try to manage a home and kitchen without help or supplies, but the sad scene only made her feel worse. It was like watching a human being crumble away like one of the sand castles she used to make on the beach at Gammarth when she was a child.

Her father was a different story. He seemed strangely energized and purposeful, almost as though he had awakened from a long nap, refreshed, ready to explore a new world. At first, Leila had discounted his change of spirit, telling herself that he was only putting on a brave face for her benefit or trying to cheer up mother. But as the weeks wore on, it became apparent it was more than that. During the day, he remained in his study, reading and writing lengthy letters; once or twice a week, in the late afternoon before curfew, he would leave the house, not returning home until the following morning. The only explanation she could summon was the painfully obvious one, and that was unthinkable; she adored her father, and the thought that he was not the good and faithful man she believed him to be was devastating. She could not bring herself to confront him about his new routine and talking to her mother would surely only make matters worse.

Finally one afternoon, unwilling to let her family disintegrate any further, she went to see her father in his study. He kept it as a traditional *majlis,* a traditional council room with a lovely Berber *kilim* covering the floor, plush cushions and pillows strewn against the walls instead of chairs, a writing tablet instead of a desk. There was a small window high in one wall fitted with four colored panes of glass that cast a cool glow of afternoon light on the far wall. Si Kamel sat cross-legged on the floor leaning on a large cushion. He was wearing a pale grey *djellaba* and leather slippers. He had draped a white scarf loosely around his shoulders; his head was bare.

"*Messelkhir, ya binti. Tfathali.*" Good afternoon, my daughter. Please. He motioned her to a cushion covered with tasseled silk. She had given it to him as a gift when she was twelve or thirteen in hopes she would be allowed to sit quietly with him, reading or watching him work but like most young girls, she had quickly lost interest in the notion of sitting quietly with her father. He had kept it near his favorite spot in hopes she would one day return. Today was that day.

Leila didn't know how or where to begin. The pleasant small talk ran dry soon enough. She decided to ask her father about his work. He hesitated.

"My daughter. I have new work but for now, it must remain a secret. I will tell you because it is important, and someday, God willing, you may choose to carry on the work we have begun."

"What work, father? Who are you working with?" Leila tucked her knees under her, listened intently. Her father's voice was wonderfully soothing; she had loved hearing it tell her stories when she was a child. Now, she was a young woman, and somehow she understood this story was different. She closed her eyes and drifted on the tide of that same voice.

"Moncef Bey, God's blessings upon him!"

Muhammed VII, commonly known as Moncef Bey, was the reigning monarch of the Husainid Dynasty, an old Ottoman family that had ruled in Tunisia since the 18th Century. He had only recently ascended the throne on the death of his father, Ahmed Bey. Although the French protectorate had held the real reins of political power in Tunisia since it was established in 1881, to the Tunisian people, Moncef Bey was their legitimate sovereign, his power undiminished by any foreign protectorate. Needless to say, the French colonial authority did not agree.

Kamel's voice was soft but intent. "Moncef Bey has courageously advanced many progressive new ideas: a consultative legislative assembly composed of a majority of Tunisians; access to civil service positions for our people; measures combating poverty and unemployment; the nationalization of some important businesses; even compulsory schooling in Arabic…thanks be to God!" Leila was thrilled to hear the fervor in her father's voice. She had never thought of him as being overly political, certainly not an activist.

Kamel continued. "You heard about what he did at the Eid-al-Fitr ceremony a few months ago?" Leila shook her head. "Moncef Bey had the audacity to remark that not a single Tunisian was among all the senior government officials who had been invited to an event at the home of the French Resident General, Admiral Estiva. Estiva told him—actually scolded him—saying that only Frenchmen were suited to positions of authority. Naturally, Moncef Bey was insulted and sent a telegram to Marshall Pétain, head of the Vichy government in France, demanding that Estiva be recalled. Of course, that didn't happen, but it established a tone, the first of many difficult confrontations.

"Now the war has turned our country into a battlefield. The Vichy demanded Moncef Bey remain loyal to the collaborative government of France, but President Roosevelt asked him to allow free passage in Tunisia for the Allied forces. Publicly, the Bey has proclaimed Tunisia's neutrality in this fighting, but—and I tell you this in secret, my daughter—he has privately informed the American President that we will support the Allies. He sees this as the pathway to our eventual independence. I have been honored to help him in this endeavor.

"There is one other element to this work you should know about. We used to refer to Moncef Bey's father, Ahmed Bey, as 'The Bey of the French.' Too often, he sided with the Vichy regime, even signed several decrees that the Germans wanted in place, decrees that were detrimental to the Jews of Tunisia. But since his ascension, Moncef Bey has ensured these decrees either have not been put into effect or will be rescinded.. He has been a protector of our Jews. He is against them wearing yellow stars or doing forced labor or prevented from owning businesses. Why? Because they are like us, they are Tunisians and he—Moncef Bey—is the protector of all of us, thanks be to God!"

There were tears in Leila's eyes, tears of concern and worry and and love and pride. All she could think to say to her father was, "Yes; thanks be to God!"

***

The University had been closed for nearly a month. The German military authorities did not want students to congregate, and the travel restrictions, fuel shortages, and official and unofficial curfews in effect made it difficult for professors and staff to come to work. An eerie silence hung over the streets surrounding Zaitouna, a forlorn emptiness in a neighborhood that usually sparkled with the laughter and energy of young men who had few cares and plenty of good connections that would ensure bright futures.

But Ali was not one of them. His life would be shaped by his own thoughtful choices, native intelligence, and industry rather than his father's name or the influence of family friends. He would have to earn his place in the world, not be gifted it. That simple truth might have fostered resentment in Ali but instead, he used it to motivate him to learn more and to work harder. The effort would either take him far or lead him nowhere. He believed that what is written—*mahktoub*—was in God's hand, and that God's hand favored those who believed and did good.

Since the university closed, Ali had spent many days at the Sidi BouBakr mosque, tending to the ill and serving the needy. He discovered the satisfaction of service, so much so that he had come to the conclusion to give up engineering and study medicine instead. It would be a longer, harder road, but Ali felt it was the direction in which God pointed him. He could still participate in building an independent country someday, but for now, this was where he was needed and where he wanted to be.

***

Three years ago, on a trip back to London, Punch had gone to see a new called movie "The Wizard of Oz." It was a technicolor marvel, but what really struck him was its subtle political message. Here was a land—Oz—ruled by a benign omnipotent leader who manipulated all the levers of power behind a screen of secrecy, lulling his child-like people into a happy, but false, sense of security. The main thoroughfare of Oz was its yellow brick road—gold; greedy capitalism. But change comes to Oz in the form of Dorothy—innocence personified, the inherent goodness of mankind—and her three friends. The scarecrow representing farmers and all those who produce our food. The tin man: a symbol for labor and the industrial workers of the world. And the lion? All the lion needed was courage. A mind, a heart, and courage—all that was ever needed to remake the world. It seemed to Punch that the film was part fairytale, part allegory. The beauty of its message lay in its subtlety. It was all Hollywood glitz and glitter on the surface; no one would really discern its true meaning until the day when, like Dorothy, people awoke from their slumbers and found themselves part of a brave new world.

Unlike almost everyone else in Tunis, Punch felt buoyed by recent events. The barbarian horde had been defeated at the gates of Stalingrad. The Soviet Union was no longer on the defensive, but was beginning to push into Eastern Europe, a golden opportunity ripe for the taking. And then there was this: Punch's young war correspondent was filing good copy from the front almost every day, a rising journalistic star that reflected brightly on his bureau chief. If that kept up, it could mean a promotion for Punch, one step closer to a more influential posting somewhere in Europe, perhaps an exciting capital far away from this dreary little African backwater, a place with access to all kinds of people, people who controlled the levers of power, not like Baum's Hollywood wizard, but real wizards with real power, wizards who could change the course of history.

CHAPTER FORTY NINE

The Wager

There were a few reasons to like General Montgomery, but many more not to like him. He was a skilled soldier, efficient, strong-willed and incisive. But he was an unbearable person. He didn't care what anyone thought of him; he had neither tact nor diplomatic skills. His own men didn't like him very much, and his fellow officers found him insufferable, probably because unlike many of them, he had no social pedigree. Middle class: his father was a cleric from Tasmania. Churchill put it this way: "In defeat, Montgomery was unbeatable; in victory, unbearable."

Eisenhower was cordial enough with Montgomery in public, but privately, he railed. He thought Montgomery's ego boundless, that he was abrasive, meddlesome, and pedantic. Moreover, Ike suspected—with some justification—that Montgomery didn't think very much of American troops; he was aware of Montgomery's disparaging comments to General Alexander about sloppy American soldiery and resentful that Montgomery didn't have the courage to say it directly to his face.

For his part, Montgomery seemed to enjoy poking the bear. In a taunt to Ike's Chief-of-Staff, General Walter Bedell Smith, Montgomery had boasted he would take the city of Sfax by mid-April. Smith thought it nothing more than a joke and said as much to Montgomery, then went on to say that if Monty indeed captured Sfax by mid-April, Smith would give him a B-17 of his own—a "Flying Fortress"—and a crew to fly it. The bait was set.

Weeks and months passed; Smith forgot about the joke. But not Montgomery. Now he was chasing General Messe's Italo-German army and the remnants of Rommel's *Afrika Korps* north toward Tunis. Patton and the Americans had not been of much help; they never seemed to get through the Eastern Dorsal in time to flank the retreating German army. Montgomery saw it this way: he was winning, the Americans weren't, or if they were, not winning fast enough.

Montgomery's Eighth Army entered Sfax on the tenth of April, five days ahead of schedule. Once in control of the city, his first action was to send a message to General Smith saying that he was "ready to claim his winnings." At first, Smith didn't know what Montgomery was talking about, but Montgomery didn't hesitate to remind him. Smith told him the bet was only a joke, but Montgomery didn't find it funny in the least. He wanted his plane.

When a red-faced Smith brought the news to Ike, the Supreme Commander was furious. B-17s were in short supply, and Ike saw no reason to give one to Montgomery just to fuel his ego. Ike went so far as to meet with General Alan Brooke, Montgomery's mentor, and insisted that Brooke convince Montgomery to "just let go." Brooke tried: he admonished Montgomery and berated his "crass stupidity." Bombers were for bombing, not for personal use. Monty didn't give a damn. He had won the bet, and he wanted his plane.

Ike was the diplomat that Montgomery was not. He knew there was a war to win and he needed Montgomery to help win it. In the end, he gave Montgomery a B-17 and a crew to fly it. But the plane came with a high political cost: Ike and Monty would never work effectively together again. The joke, the bet, whatever it was, left a sour taste in each man's mouth. To make matters worse, General Patton fumed that Montgomery traveled in a personal plane while he, Patton, had to cadge a ride in a Jeep or travel by lorry convoy.

In the end, it was all for nought. Less than a month after Montgomery had taken possession of his airplane, it experienced a crash landing. Damaged beyond repair, it never flew again.

CHAPTER FIFTY

Vulcan

Generals and senior officers get to smoke cigars and sleep under clean covers in comfortable beds. If they're lucky, junior officers might get an occasional few hours of sleep on a cot in a field tent. But enlisted men have to sleep on the ground in pup tents, or worse—rough. That life gets old fast, and the men had been doing it now for more than five months. They lived on C-rations, hadn't had a decent hot meal in weeks. They were foot-sore and bone weary; their bodies sagged with exhaustion. And still they fought on.

It was becoming painfully clear to everyone—Allied and Axis armies alike—that the Tunisia campaign was coming closer and closer to Armageddon. The Allied landings on the beaches of Morocco and Algeria; the long road from Tobruk through Libya and into Tunisia; the freezing slough through the mountain passes of the Western Dorsal; everything now pointed to a final confrontation along a line that stretched from Cap Bon on the east, around Tunis, and up to Bizerte. The Axis armies would be outnumbered and outgunned, but they would be desperate and desperate men fight desperate battles.

Declan could barely remember the last time he felt rested or clean or well-fed. His flat in the *medina* was less than two hour's drive away, but it might as well have been on another planet. All the little things he had once taken for granted—a café au lait and butter croissant for breakfast, a cool bottle of beer before supper, a Sunday lie-in with his *petite amie*—what was her name?—they all seemed like fragments from some strange dream. Two days ago, he had visited a field hospital and interviewed a wounded captain from Western Australia, a high school teacher from Perth. "That was another life," the man said. "Now I know what the Abos mean when they warble on about their 'dream time.' Christ, I miss my wife and kids!"

But nothing seemed to bother Lang. Flies buzzing around a corpse; the whimpering agony of a horribly maimed soldier in hospital; Lang would just fiddle with the settings on his camera, take a few snaps, scribble in his notebook and move on. If anything touched him on the inside, he never let it show. Declan had asked him about his detachment once and Lang just said, "Sherman was right. War is hell. I just want to live through this one and go home."

Montgomery's Eighth Army was advancing north up the coast, rolling it up like a giant rug. First Gabès, then Sfax, Sousse a few days later. All "liberated." The British First Army and American Second Corps were closing in from the west, Second Corps now under the command of General Bradley. After all Patton's grousing about his British allies, Ike thought he would be of greater use and less of a problem if he were back in Casablanca planning Operation Husky, the eventual invasion of Sicily. Not surprisingly, relations between the Allies had improved considerably since Patton's departure. He seemed happier back there, too. He had secured Ike's promise that Second Corps would have a say in the final stages of the Tunisian campaign, while the Sultan of Morocco had honored him with a medal and the Order of *Ouissam Alaouite*; the accompanying citation said "even the lions in their dens tremble at his approach."

***

"The fact of the matter," Lang was saying, "is that Rommel never thought the German position here was tenable. He wanted all German troops evacuated to Italy a year ago, but Hitler said 'No.' Now the Air Force's Operation Flax has cut off all their supply lines and the Navy's Operation Retribution has denied them any means of evacuation. They're isolated, cut off, no supplies. They'll make us pay for a while, but in the end, they have no choice but to surrender. Or be killed."

Declan knew when Lang got on a roll, he was a runaway train. He waited for the next bit of track. He didn't have to wait long. "But there's a subtext to all this. We—Americans—seem to have something of an inferiority complex when it comes to war. Your British friends seem to think our little Revolution never happened; they're always looking down their smug noses at us. Makes Patton screaming mad. Anderson's the worst. He thinks our plan to take Bizerte is a 'childish fantasy.' Patton's ready to wring his stiff little British neck. Patton actually told me—and you can't quote me on this—that he'd rather be commanded by an Arab!"

Declan went over to the coffee urn and poured two more mugs of luke-warm coffee. He took a sip, made a face. "Mary and Joseph! What I wouldn't give for a hot cup of real coffee!"

"Good luck with that. Maybe you should go over to Monty's mess. I bet you his tea's hot." Lang took a sip from his own mug, grimaced. "Maybe I'll go with you. Listen to this: Ernie stood by the road last night. He clocked our convoys going by: one truck every thirty-seven seconds, hour after hour. I figure that when all's said and done, we'll have thrown at least 300,000 men at those bastards. Montgomery's coming from the south; he wants to smash through their line at Enfidaville, but that won't be easy. He's used to fighting in the desert and those hills are going to give him a mess of trouble. The Bosch are dug in deep and they know they've got nothing behind them but the ocean. They'll fight like the little schnauzers they are. Anderson's moving in from the southwest, straight toward Tunis. He may have more luck; the terrain is smoother that way. And then there's Bradley's 'childish fantasy' moving on their left flank through Mateur to Bizerte. Wouldn't it be fucking delicious if he was the one to deliver the *coup de grâce?* That would shove it up Anderson's tight English arse. No offense."

"None taken. Remember: I'm Irish."

***

Vulcan's Forge
(Special to The Guardian by Correspondent Declan Shaw. Enfidaville, Tunisia, 23 April, 1943.)

Vulcan, often depicted as a blacksmith, was the Roman God of fire. He was also the god of the forge, of volcanos, and, perhaps to the liking of General Bernard Montgomery, commander of the British Eighth Army, of deserts. Monty loved fighting in the desert; he had built his reputation in the deserts of Egypt and Libya, had finally defeated German General Erwin Rommel, the Desert Fox, in the sands of southern Tunisian. The problem was Montgomery was no longer in the desert. Now he was going to fight in rugged hill country, among mighty pinnacles of rock, pleasing enough to the eye but certainly not to the eyes of the men ordered to storm up their slopes and to root out a deeply entrenched enemy.

At this time of year here, the days are warming fast. The hills of northern Tunisia overlook lush valleys, green with olive groves and spring wheat. Wildflowers bloom on the slopes, small explosions of bright color among great grey boulders. But as every infantryman knows deep within his bones, the hills belong to those who hold the highest ground. To fight uphill is agony. It is knowing that someone above you will do whatever it takes to kill you. He will never relinquish his advantage; you must wrest it from him.

Among all these hills, Takrouna is noteworthy because it rises abruptly from the coastal plain, almost like a stalagmite. The formation is more than 600 feet high, and atop it, there is an ancient Berber village carved from the pinnacle rock. Italian and German forces were dug in there, a rabbit warren of rock-walled tunnels with hidden entrances and natural bunkers with embrasures that overlook the slopes, perfect for laying down fields of murderous machine gun fire.

The deadly duty to take Takrouna fell to Lance-sergeant Hanne Te Rauawa Manahi and his platoon of New Zealand Maoris, the same men who had performed superbly at Tebaga Gap. Three days ago, at dawn, Manahi led his men up Takrouna's rocky path and overran the Italian defenses at the summit. It was hand-to-hand combat with grenades, knives, rocks, fists, bayonets. Men were thrown from the sheer precipice, drifting down like leaves in the wind onto the plain below. On the following day, a Nazi counterattack retook the hilltop but with murderous artillery support, Manahi's men reclaimed the hill's first ledge and then, after several more hours of brutal hand-to-hand fighting, finally occupied the summit village. The Maoris took 300 prisoners but at the exorbitant cost of over 550 souls who valiantly lost their lives on a rocky hill in Tunisia, as far away from their ancient ancestral home in the Pacific as can ever be imagined.

A forest fire destroys but it also has the power to cleanse. New growth follows devastation. But not in war when Vulcan's fire burns hot and deadly, and the fallen do not sprout from the soil to repopulate the forest. Montgomery has learned this lesson, but, sadly, too late for many of his men. He has, for now, halted his 'Operation Vulcan.' He needs a better strategy. The Eighth Army continues to hammer and peck away at the eastern end of the Axis defensive line, but the monstrous crack in that line that he so desperately wanted to pry open—his doorway to Tunis—has so far eluded him.

***

On an unusually cool spring evening, Declan, Lang, and Ernie Pyle were bivouacked in a small hut, a few safe miles from the front. The place had apparently once been used as a storeroom for harvested olives; a redolent, earthy aroma infused the small room. A kerosene lamp cast flickering shadows on the mud walls, but the place was quiet and oddly peaceful. For the first time in weeks, Declan felt relaxed; he sat on the dirt floor, his back leaning against a stack of bags filled with hard green olives, sipping something supplied by Pyle that tasted reasonably like brandy. Maybe grappa.

Lang was talking quietly. "Monty's not a hill general. He needs wide open spaces, tank terrain. His Maoris and Gurkhas are hellacious fighters in close quarters, but it's slow going in these damn hills where progress is measured in meters, not miles. Yesterday, I heard that the ratio was one dead soldier for every three meters of ground gained. Monty's not used to that. He chased Rommel across a thousand miles of desert, but here, in the hills, the real estate is too damn expensive. Plus, he's now involved up to his eyeballs in planning the invasion of Sicily. He figures sooner or later we'll win here, that the Germans don't have the men or the ammunition or the fuel to hold out much longer so we might as well just send another batch of men up another hill and get this show over. Eventually, we'll kill all the bad guys—even if a lot of our guys get killed in the process. We just have more of everything. It's a sad calculus but he's not wrong."

"So what happens next?" Declan asked.

Lang looked over at Ernie, but Ernie was happy just to listen. "I'm not much of a betting man, but I think Alexander and Ike have decided to move the show over toward Anderson's First Army; if he can take Longstop Hill, there's nothing to stop him from marching into Tunis. So Monty will stay on this end of the line while Bradley's Second Corps hits Bizerte at the northern end of the bridgehead. If he's lucky, Anderson will get the glory of taking Tunis. Look: the end is inevitable; it's just a matter of time. The men know that, too. All each guy is doing now is trying to stay alive for another week, two at the most. What a shame it would be to be the last man killed here. What a fucking waste that would be!"

It was quiet in the hut for a few moments, then Pyle said, "I'll drink to that." They all did.

***

Less than fifty miles to the northwest of Montgomery's position near Enfidaville, Lieutenant-General Kenneth Anderson's British First Army was attempting to drive toward Tunis through the Medjerda River Valley. The hill fighting had been just as murderous as it had been for Montgomery's Eighth Army; incremental progress came at an outrageously bloody Allied cost. Operation Vulcan, planned as a concentrated and unified Allied assault on the defensive Axis ring around Tunis and Bizerte, had failed to deliver the fatal blow that would crack and sever the enemy's bridgehead. Instead, Vulcan had played out as a series of multiple limited engagements along a line that stretched for more than forty miles against a desperate and entrenched enemy with its back to the sea. Anderson's assault, like Montgomery's, had stalled.

Ironically, the heaviest fighting occurred over Easter weekend. By April 26, Easter Monday, Anderson had had enough; he called off his attack. Search parties were sent out to comb fields ripe with spring wheat and retrieve the dead only to discover that German sappers had mined the fields, then planted more wheat to cover their work. The bodies they were able to find were marked with upturned rifles stuck in the ground with their bayonets, the helmet of the fallen balanced on top. Wheat fields all through the valley looked more like forests of rifles.

But by the end of the month, Longstop Hill, the deadly ridge that had been the scene of such fury back in December and now again in April, was finally in Allied hands. It was the high ground that controlled the Medjerda Valley and thereby held the keys to Tunis. But Anderson's forces were seriously depleted; his men were too exhausted to push on.

Von Arnim's divisions were just as depleted. They were dangerously low on supplies: fuel and ammunition were almost non-existent. To the east, Messe's Italo-German army was also seriously reduced in force and bogged down trying to keep Montgomery from breaking through from the southeast. The long North African campaign—seven long months of rain and mud and blood—had turned into a war of attrition. The end was near, but it would not come easily. War is fickle. It would fall to General Omar Bradley and his once-reviled American troops pushing against the German line around Bizerte to initiate the action that would bring down the final curtain.

CHAPTER FIFTY ONE

Hill 609

"Nope. He's happy enough. He may not be vain, but he sure-as-hell is self-conscious about his crooked teeth. You'll never see him grinning for the photographers like Patton."

Declan and Lang were in a jeep, driving north to find General Omar Bradley's command post. "He's a plain-spoken Missouri boy, kinda like Truman. No bullshit. Loves to hunt. Pretty good at it, too. I hear he has his aides throw rocks in the air for him to shoot. They say he never misses. But here's the thing: he was born to be a general. Sees terrain like an infantry man. He won't make the same mistakes the others did; he knows the hills up here aren't tank friendly. That's why his men trust him, and that counts for a hell of a lot more than a whole lot of jut-jawed magazine photographs or good press. Just don't be fooled: Brad's a born leader. They called his class at West Point 'the class the stars fell on' because almost 40% of those guys made general. But Bradley's star was the one that fell first, even before Ike's. Never heard anyone say a bad word about him; the worst I ever heard was 'competent.' We should all be so lucky!"

Declan was taking this all in. People in England read daily about men like Eisenhower and Patton, Alexander and Anderson and Montgomery. But Omar Bradley? Who was he?

***

Special to The Guardian by Correspondent Declan Shaw,
somewhere near *Béja, Tunisia, 3 May 1943:*
Hill 609

*To the people who live here, the hills have names, but to General
Bradley and his staff, they are designated on their maps only by a
number, their height in meters: Hill 350 or 469 or 444. The highest of
these hills is the one the Arabs called Djebel Tahent, but otherwise, it is
known to the Americans only as Hill 609. A flattop mesa, it is the highest
of all the surrounding hills and as such, it is the lynchpin to the Axis
defense of Bizerte. It dominates the countryside and looks down on the
road that leads from the town of Béja to Mateur and just twenty miles
beyond, to the port of Bizerte.*

*It's axiomatic that the second highest hill in a battle is a graveyard.
Be that as it may, it took five days for the Americans to reach the summit
of Hill 609, five relentless, bloody days of deadly uphill fighting. For
General Bradley and the gallant men of Second Corps, the battle for
609 began, as it must, by clawing their way up many of the surrounding
lesser hills and rooting out the elite German troops—maybe the best in
Africa—who were dug in like fierce badgers to create murderous fields
of fire that served to protect the flanks of 609. The price in blood was as
steep as the slopes, but it had to be paid.*

*The southern and eastern faces of 609 are sheer limestone cliffs,
fifty feet high and exposed to intertwined fire from lesser neighboring
hills with numbers for names: 461, 490, 523, 531, and 455. Not only
are these rock walls almost impossible to scale, but they are also easy to
defend. General Anderson, commander of the British First Army, would
have preferred to bypass 609, but General Bradley knew the awful truth:
609 was the ultimate prize: whoever controlled its heights controlled the
way to Bizerte and to victory in Africa. Without 609, the entire North
African campaign might wither and die on the vine.*

*If endless artillery rounds and angry machine guns were not enough
of a deterrent, sickness and disease were rampant in the American ranks.
Malaria was raging, and there was no quinine available so the men were
given a synthetic drug called Atabrine. Reaction to the drug was swift*

and devastating: many of the men suffered uncontrollable vomiting and diarrhea. When the order to attack came, many men stumbled forward covered in foulness.

But still they did their duty. American artillery rounds pounded the top of 609; to the observers below, it looked like a volcano. At dawn on the last day of April, General Bradley, against all reason, sent seventeen Sherman tanks crawling up the west slope of 609, infantry trailing behind, firing, firing as they climbed. By mid-afternoon, American soldiers reached the summit, killing the last defenders and taking few prisoners.

Atop Hill 609, the carnage was almost beyond description: it resembled hell. There were bodies everywhere, spent shell casings reeked of powder, family photographs, torn from tunics, were stained with blood. Shell craters pockmarked the mesa, most only a few inches deep owing to the hardness of the surface rock. The flying debris must have rained down on the men like a deadly torrent.

But once the summit was won, the tide of war in the north finally began to turn. From the heights of 609, one looks out on a broad, flat valley to the town of Mateur, and beyond, to the port of Bizerte and the shining Mediterranean Sea. In the first days of May, the way to Bizerte and eventually Tunis seems finally clear, for having finally broken through the Axis defensive ring, nothing now stands in the way of the ultimate prize: Tunis. Our enemy is in full retreat. The fox has nowhere to run or hide; the hounds are in hot pursuit, and will either run him to ground or tear him to pieces.

The greatest burden of the taking of Hill 609 fell on the men of the 34th Division of the American Second Corps, the very division that had performed so poorly at Fondouk three weeks earlier. Since then, and with General Omar Bradley now in command, they have endured intense remedial training, practicing night attacks, tank-infantry tactics, and assault procedures tight on the heels of rolling artillery barrages. The stuff of war. This time, the 34th performed admirably in combat, moving forward bravely and relentlessly under the most difficult conditions. Many died, many were wounded, but they never quit. On Hill 609, they proved their mettle. The American fighting men have come of age; our courageous allies have redeemed themselves in courage and blood, and on Hill 609 and all the other hills they captured here over the last few days, their battle honor has been fairly won.

***

There wasn't much left of the old farmhouse and almost nothing left of the door to their room, just the frame and a piece of canvas for a curtain. There was a knock on the frame and a captain stuck his head into the dimly lit room. Pyle and Declan were sharing a table and a kerosene lantern, writing in their journals; Lang was on a cot, his eyes closed. "They're in here, Sir."

The man who entered made almost no impression. He was shabbily dressed in dirty combat fatigues, balding, spectacled; "meek" was the word that came to Declan's mind. But Pyle, who was not one to observe much protocol, was immediately on his feet. "Hi ya, Ernie. Good to see you again."

"Evening, General. Congratulations. Hell of a win."

"Sure was. The boys finally did it, didn't they? I guess they don't need more training now." He grinned. "Hi, Will. How ya feeling?"

"Been better, Brad. Must have been that chateaubriand I had for dinner last night. Tell the chef it was underdone again. "

"Yeah, I heard. Brought you something for that. Not the usual, but under the circumstances…" He grinned again but this time, wrinkled his nose.

"Paregoric. How thoughtful, Brad. Cheers!" Lang took a swig, grimaced. "Jesus. Not a great vintage."

The man turned to Declan. "And you, by process of elimination, must be Mr. Shaw. Be careful, son. A man is often judged by the company he keeps. You sure about these fellas?"

Declan had figured it all out. "Yes, sir, General Bradley. I'm always learning something from one or the other."

"Well, Mr. Shaw, they must be pretty good teachers. I really just stopped by to say 'thank you' to you. Read your dispatch, liked it a lot. You gave credit where credit was due. Those men of the 34th did a good job on 609. I'm proud of them. Some people didn't think they could fight, but I guess you think they can."

"Yes, sir, I certainly do. They proved it."

Bradley looked pleased; offered Declan his hand. "Well I just hope some of my dear British colleagues read your piece today. Maybe they'll think better of us now. Keep up the good work. Boys, I'm going to bed. Tomorrow's another day. Still gotta kill a few more Germans. Will, let me know if you need more of that good hootch." Gone.

There was quiet again in the room. Pyle said, "He's a piece of work, that man. One hell of a good piece. A few more like him and the war would be over next week. How's that taste, Will?"

"It's a chalky white with light notes of opium, aniseed, and camphor. Now both of you go to hell. Let me go back to sleep."

CHAPTER FIFTY TWO

Waiting

Punch had been able to watch the distant battle for Hill 609 from the rooftop of his flat in Tunis. At first, he thought it was just a gathering summer storm coming out of the mountains to the west of the city; the rumble and flash of artillery in the night sky recalled the thunder and lightening squalls he had so loved to watch roll in from the North Sea. But once he had scanned Declan's story, he knew what he had heard and seen was no meteorological event. This was a man-made storm, coming closer and closer, sounding more and more like the crescendo of Armageddon.

That pleased Punch. He had seen enough of war to know the look of both victory and defeat. Von Arnim's army and the remnants of Rommel's *Afrika Korps* were now in full flight; Messe was hanging on by a fingernail at Enfidaville. This would be the second great defeat of one of Herr Hitler's vaunted armies in just a few months. Stalingrad had been a crushing blow and now North Africa would soon be lost. That meant an Allied invasion of Western Europe, through Italy or France, was inevitable. Fascism was doomed; the dawn of a new Socialist era would soon be rising in Eastern Europe and then spreading across the world.

***

Paul was staring at the papers in his father's hand. "Where did you get these? How much did they cost?"

"It doesn't matter where I got them, and as for the price, it had to be paid. We have to get out of here and we can't leave from La Goulette.

Have you seen it recently? So many boats are sunk, the masts sticking out of the water make it look more like a forest than a port. The only way for us to escape is to get to Tabarka and find someone with a boat willing to take us to France. "These," he waved the safe-conduct papers he held in his hand, "will get us as far as Tabarka."

"And how do we get there? It's at least four hours away. There are armies killing each other between us and Tabarka!"

"Mohammed says he'll take us. I've promised to give him the truck in payment. These will get us through the German lines; the Americans won't care about us. We'll just look like all the other refugees fleeing the city. Or maybe we'll get lucky and meet Free French troops. The important thing is to get to Tabarka and get the hell out of here. Once we're in France, we'll figure out the next part."

Madame Fabron looked distraught; her hair was undone and she constantly twisted the rings on her fingers. "What can we take with us?"

Her husband softened his tone. "We can't take much, *ma chère*. Some clothes, maybe a little of the silver, a few photographs. If anyone asks, we'll say we just want to get out of the city until this is over. We don't want to raise any more suspicions than we have to. I will make sure that what is left of our money is well hidden in our baggage. It's not much, but enough to convince someone to take us to France and start over."

***

Leila had been secretly watching her father for the past two days. The fire that had been burning so brightly seemed suddenly extinguished as if it had been doused by a bucket of sea water. The house was quiet as a tomb, and just as sad.

Finally, she summoned the courage to speak to her father. *"Shpeek, Baba?"* What's wrong?

Si Kamel held a glass of tea in his hand. It was almost colorless, the reused leaves long since spent. Only the sprig of mint in the glass gave it any flavor or aroma. Staring out the window that looked out on the empty beach and the sea beyond, Kamel sighed. *"Moncef Bey. Hala yessir."* Bad; very bad. Leila waited quietly.

"The end is near. The Germans will be defeated and the French smell their blood. They will do everything they can to weaken Moncef Bey.

They are afraid of him and what he stands for. Already, they are accusing him of collaboration. Of collaboration! The same Vichy generals who have done nothing but collaborate with the Nazis…now they accuse Moncef Bey of collaboration! Esteva, our Resident General who has done nothing but collaborate with the Germans, has fled the country. Juin will surely replace him, but he is Giraud's puppet. Giraud wants Moncef Bey gone; he is too great a threat to French rule. They only want to restore the Protectorate, and Moncef Bey stands in their way. It is only a matter of time before Giraud orders his arrest. Can you imagine: ordering the arrest of our legitimate sovereign? It is beyond shameful and we are powerless to stop it!"

Leila had never seen her father like this. Just a few weeks ago, he had seemed energized and hopeful. The Germans would be gone, the French would soon follow. Tunisia would finally be free again, ready to take her rightful place among nations, a modern leader in a new Arab world. Now, he seemed defeated, lost in events beyond his control. His future, along with the fate of his family, was in danger—not from a foreign war fought on Tunisian soil, but by a system built by men who were bent on retaining their pre-war colonial power. The age of colonialism should be finished, but instead, it was consolidating its demeaning power. The cherished prize of independence seemed farther away than ever.

***

Each day, Ali went to the Sidi BouBakr mosque, now more a hospital than a house of prayer. For many of the sick and wounded, comfort was all he could offer; there were almost no medical supplies available, and doctors, almost all French, remained in their hospitals, unable and unwilling to aid those suffering in the makeshift *cliniques* that were sprouting up in the poorer residential neighborhoods all over the city. They shrugged their shoulders; what could they possibly do? Maybe once the Germans were finally gone…

It was late in the day and the interior of the mosque was uncomfortably warm. Two tired ceiling fans rattled away, trying their best to move the fetid air. Ali had long since become accustomed to the fulsome smells of the place; he wore a sprig of jasmine behind his left ear to remind him that somewhere, life was sweeter.

He looked up to see a woman wearing a *safsar*i standing in the doorway. The light from the street was dim, and he couldn't make out her face. Probably another one of the suffering sick, or maybe just someone coming to bring a morsel of food to one of the patients. He walked over and greeted her politely.

When Leila removed the covering from her face, Ali was too surprised to speak. Or maybe he was too moved by the lovely green eyes looking up at him. All she said to him was "*"urid 'an asaed."* I want to help.

CHAPTER FIFTY THREE

Strike

Ernie Pyle woke Declan and Lang after just a few hours of sleep, early on the morning of Thursday, May 6. "Here we go, boys."

Lang grunted, rolled over and farted. Declan sat up, rubbed his eyes. He wished someone would come and hand him a hot cup of tea and to his amazement, Ernie did just that. The steam felt good on his stubbled face. "Get him up." He pointed at Lang. "Better hurry. You won't want to miss this." Gone.

There was not even a hint of light in the eastern sky, but Declan could still feel a pulsating tension in the pre-dawn stillness. Something big was about to happen; there was too much fear, too much excitement in the cool night air. It didn't take long to know what that something was.

Precisely at 0300 hours—by now, Declan had grown accustomed to thinking in military time—the inky stillness was shattered by what sounded like a thousand guns. An artillery barrage, unlike anything he or Lang or even Ernie had ever seen, erupted, sending shells shrieking across the sky like deadly comets, five or six hundred rounds a minute, pounding the German positions to the east under a blanket of steel. Gunners plotted one shell for every six feet along the enemy line, marching the shells eastward by a hundred yards every three minutes, destroying every living thing in their wake.

Ernie had given them all cotton balls to stuff in their ears, but even so, the noise was deafening. The men watched, mesmerized, as the muzzle flashes of the great guns turned night into a hellish new day. Even Ernie, who had watched giant battleships slug it out in the Pacific, seemed transfixed by the fearsome display of firepower unleashed by the Allied artillery. It was an irresistible force; no army could possibly withstand such an onslaught. It was finally the beginning of the end.

After more than two hours of this torrent of steel, the Allied air force took over, unleashing a bombardment unlike anything seen in the campaign. Fighters and bombers concentrated on German targets along Highway 5, the main road leading to Tunis. By the time the sun rose, the entire Medjerda valley was in flames. Billowing smoke darkened the morning sky; the smell of cordite and burning spring wheat left both the retreating German army and the advancing Allied forces gasping for air.

In the center of the Allied attack, Anderson's First Army, reinforced with 30,000 of Montgomery's Desert Rats, surged forward. It was not a marriage made in heaven; far from it. Monty's seasoned desert fighters and Anderson's mountain troops were as different as chalk from cheese, but no matter: they all smelled blood. By noon, they had broken through the German lines and begun to push toward Tunis. There was nothing von Arnim could do to stop them. Out of fuel and low on ammunition, the Germans broke and ran. The British troops streamed forward using a prearranged code word—"Butter"—and by early afternoon, every radio along the front chirped a "Butter!" message. By nightfall, Anderson's First Army could see the white walls of Tunis less than a day's march away.

At the northern end of the Allied line, General Bradley's Second Corps had Bizerte squarely in its sights. They were in a hurry: it was essential to take the city's deepwater port before the enemy had a chance to sabotage it. On Friday, May 7, they rolled forward against light opposition and by afternoon, a little more than a day after Operation Strike began, the Americans passed through the gates of the city.

Bizerte was a ghost town. Wrecked by bombs and plagued by disease, Bizerte was empty. Ernie jotted in his diary that the town was "the most completely wrecked place I've ever seen." He made one other observation on Friday evening: an out-of-place bit of graffiti scrawled across the walls of the town—"Kilroy was here."

"Who's Kilroy?" a perplexed Declan asked him.

"No fucking clue," Erine responded, scratching his back against a wall of rubble while he surveyed the destruction, "but he sure as hell was here."

***

Ike decided to visit the front on Friday afternoon. He had just signed off on the plans for the invasion of Sicily, and was awaiting concurrence from Washington and London. But first, Tunis had to fall, and Ike wanted to be there when it did.

Declan, Lang, and Ernie, along with a few other correspondents, met with Ike and General Bradley at First Division headquarters just west of the Tine River. Neither Ike nor Bradley were in a good mood. Terry Allen, commander of First Division, had gone on a fool's errand the day before and attempted to take Hill 232, one of the last German-held positions east of the river. It was a costly mistake, as unnecessary as it was foolish. Nearly 300 men had died as a result of Allen's vainglorious blunder.

Despite the mood in the field headquarters, Ike was surprisingly sanguine. He talked to the correspondents about the lessons the Allies had learned in planning and executing a large-scale invasion of enemy territory, and about not making the same mistakes twice. He noted the difficulty in rooting out enemy troops from defensive positions in mountainous terrain, something the Allies would surely face as they sloughed through Italy in the months to come. At the end of the interview, Ike grew philosophical, allowing the journalists a rare glimpse into his usually taciturn Kansan soul. He felt the weight of command, the sad duty of having ordered brave men to their death, and the surety that he would have to do it over and over again. This time, it was Declan who took down the Supreme Commander's somber words: "Far above my hatred of war is the determination to smash every enemy of my country, especially Hitler and the Japs."

Declan looked at Ernie who seemed lost in thought, then at Lang who was busy taking photographs of Ike and Bradley. The irony of what he had just said was not lost on any of the three. War might well be worthy of hate, but it could only be won through absolute and total victory, no matter its horrific human cost.

***

Tunis fell later that afternoon. It was more chaos than a pitched battle. The end came so quickly that German officers were still getting shaved by Arab barbers or drinking schnapps in the bar of the Majestic Hotel. There were a few snipers firing from rooftops, but many more deliriously happy French citizens who emerged from their homes with open arms, full of bouquets of flowers or bottles of wine, often both. Someone sang *La Marseillaise* at the top of his lungs. Some houses were ransacked by loyalists looking for suspected collaborators, while other buildings that had housed German operatives were targeted for destruction.

Unconditional surrender was the order of the day. Any German soldier who tried to escape was killed. More than 41,000 prisoners were taken on May 7 alone; in the next few days, the number of captured soldiers swelled to more than 225,000. General Kesselring at his headquarters in Rome made a half-hearted effort to evacuate the few remaining holdouts by U-boat, but an armada of Allied ships controlled the Sicilian Straits and only one submarine made it to shore before it, too, was sunk. When he heard of Kesselring's effort, a British intelligence officers was heard to paraphrase Churchill's remark in 1940 when a German invasion invasion of Britain seemed imminent: "We are waiting and so are the fishes." By the end of the month, there were so many German and Italian prisoners of war under guardian and around Tunis that the Allies were barely able to transport or feed them. Conditions in detention centers or POW camps—most under French control—were subhuman at best.

Almost as an afterthought, British forces surrounded the royal palace in Hammam-Lif, a seaside town only a few miles southeast of Tunis. Inside was Moncef Bey and his entire Tunisian Cabinet. Acting on a tip from the commander of the Free French forces, General Henri Giraud, the Bey was arrested for collaboration, and summarily sent into exile. In a matter of only a few hours, French colonial control of Tunisia was firmly reestablished.

CHAPTER FIFTY FOUR

Surrender

On May 8, the day following the liberation of Tunis, Declan, Lang, and Ernie Pyle rode into the city on the back of a Sherman tank. Tunis had been spared much of the devastation that had reduced Bizerte to bare bones of rubble and dust. Once inside the gates, Lang and Ernie hopped down from the tank and headed off to the Majestic Hotel to get good and drunk, but Declan went in the opposite direction. He made a quick stop at the office to drop off his latest copy—"Hail the conquering hero!" Punch declaimed when Declan walked in—but he wasn't in the mood to debrief or chat up his editor quite yet. All he wanted to do was go home, close the door to his flat in the *medina,* and sleep for a week. He hurried through the crowded streets; when he opened the door, the place smelled a bit musty but his mattress was softer than anything he had seen in three months and even the noise from the street below didn't keep Declan from dropping into a deep and dreamless slumber.

Seventeen hours later, Declan awoke to the sound of heavy artillery. No; not artillery. Someone was pounding on the metal gate that gave onto the stairway leading up to his flat. He stumbled down to find Punch standing in the street, hammering away on his door. "Get dressed. Something decent. We leave in an hour."

"Who's 'we' and where are we going?"

"Lang, Pyle, you and me. We're going to witness the bastards surrender. Get going! We leave in an hour." Still dazed with sleep, Declan stumbled back up the stairs and heated two pans of water on the gas burner—one for tea, the other for shaving. While waiting for the water to boil, he rummaged through drawers trying to find something fresh to wear. He settled on a pair of khakis and an olive drab shirt he found hanging in a corner of his closet. With his sleeves rolled up to his elbows and his face reddened by the sun, he looked more like a tourist on holiday than a war correspondent, but it was the best he could do on short notice. At least nobody would be shooting at him for a change. He soaked a stale biscuit in a mug of scalding tea sweetened with some condensed milk—better than nothing—then headed down the street to meet his mates.

***

It was a little more than a hundred kilometers from Tunis to Enfidaville. Normally, the trip by car would have only taken a couple of hours, but on this day, the pace slowed to a crawl. Hundreds, then thousands, of German and Italian prisoners were being herded north, clogging the road. Some had the haunted look of men who were starving, utterly exhausted, and had seen unspeakable horrors. A few others, proud Italian paratroop units, seemed oblivious to humiliation or defeat, let alone to the building heat of the day; with their polished boots and their tunics slung over their shoulders, they looked like friends out for a casual Sunday stroll. Some smoked and even sang. But this was no walk in the park; these were prison-bound soldiers for whom the war was now over, all being closely watched by British and American guards who had shoot-to-kill orders for anyone who broke ranks and tried to escape.

As they slowly weaved their way through the throng, Declan and Ernie jotted in their notebooks, alone with their thoughts. Punch, at the wheel of an American Jeep, was uncharacteristically silent. Lang took hundreds of photographs: the hollow eyes of a defeated army, the fresh faces of the wary young guards who herded them along like sheep, the jeering civilians out to watch the passing show. There was dust everywhere, settling on the hair and the gaunt faces of the prisoners, making them look even more ghost-like. The sound of tramping feet; the soaring voice of Uum Kalthoum singing *Raq el Habib* blaring from the radio of a roadside café; flies, vermin, lice; the stench of feces, vomit, and crusted blood—an endless and overwhelming spectacle of abject human misery moving ever northward like a greasy slack tide.

Messe Surrenders

Special to The Guardian by Correspondent Declan Shaw, Enfidaville,
Tunisia, 12 May 1943:

It was only five months ago—but five months can be a lifetime in war—that I spent a day with General Giovanni Messe near a place called Mareth in southern Tunisia. On that day, he seemed a confidant commander, a worthy adversary for General Bernard Montgomery who had chased Rommel's Afrika Korps across Libya, and was closing in for the kill. General Messe and his Italo-German Army would face Montgomery along an old defensive line built a decade ago by the French to protect their colony in Tunisia from an Italian invasion from Libya. But war is full of ironies, and now the Mareth Line would protect a retreating German army from the British. On the day of battle, Messe's forces would fight bravely but they would lose. Even then, the writing was already on the wall: greater battles were raging on the Eastern Front and as a result, German forces in North Africa lacked sufficient supplies of ammunition, fuel, and, most importantly, reinforcements.

For the last two months, Messe and his diminishing army have fought a gallant defensive campaign. At Enfidaville, they made a last stand, hoping against hope to protect Tunis or at least to buy sufficient time to allow an evacuation of Axis forces. But once the British First Army broke through the center of the German bridgehead and the Americans took Bizerte, there was no place for Messe to go. Surrounded, he would either have to surrender or be slaughtered.

Messe's orders were to stand and fight to the last man. But in another of war's remarkable ironies, yesterday, Mussolini gave his greatest general permission to surrender. "As the aims of your resistance have been achieved, your Excellency is free to accept an Honorable surrender." Il Duce even promoted Messe to the rank of Maresciallo d'Italia, Field Marshall. The Allies were not so generous. Messe was given a deadline: unconditional surrender by midnight or be annihilated. With only minutes to spare, Field Marshall Giovanni Messe struck his colors.

And now Giovanni Messe sits in a staff car guarded by hardened British soldiers, reviewing his army as they march away to POW camps in England or America. He tries to stand and salute his men, but he is too exhausted. He slumps forward, all gaunt cheeks and hollow eyes, his charm and confident swagger evaporating in the hot Tunisian sun. Such is war: glorious in victory, cruel in defeat.

***

There were times when Lang had an almost childlike buoyancy. "Just one big fish left in the river. C'mon; let's go watch him get caught." Declan thought to refuse—he was tired of this drawn-out end game—but he was a journalist, and he had a duty to play out his hand. He was living through history and had a responsibility to help record it. "Who? Where?"

"Von Arnim. He scavenged enough gas to get him and Hans Cramer to Ste. Marie-du-Zit, twenty miles north of here. You get Punch; I'll find Ernie. Should be a good show. C'mon!"

By the time the four journalists arrived on a hill overlooking von Arnim's encampment, white flags had sprouted like mushrooms after a spring rain. Smoke was rising from a burned-out vehicle. Ernie, surveying the scene through his field glasses, pointed and said, "That was Rommel's personal trailer. I was in it once. I guess von Arnim didn't want it to go to the British Museum alongside the Elgin Marbles."

A British staff car sped by. Declan caught a glimpse of the passengers. "General Allfrey and General Tucker, commanders of the British Fifth and Fourth Indian. I wonder why they got this job."

Punch had a thought. "It's a message from Alexander. He's sending in the second string so von Arnim doesn't get a swelled head." He put the Jeep in gear and followed the staff car down the hill.

The German generals—Hans Cramer and Hans-Jurgën von Arnim—were standing at attention, resplendent in spotless uniforms and polished riding boots. By contrast, Allfrey looked like he had just come in from a training exercise, threadbare and covered in dust. Declan thought he could discern a sneer on von Arnim's Prussian countenance, but the German was in no position to bargain. Allfrey got straight to the point: "Either surrender or be blown off the map." He gave the German fifteen minutes to pack for prison, and demanded they surrender all their personal weapons.

Von Arnim was clearly angry. He pulled his Luger out of its holster and threw it on the table.

"Your pocket knife, too, General."

Von Arnim glared, slammed his knife down next to his gun and stared at Tucker. Then he turned and walked down the ranks of his officers who had formed up outside the caravan, saluting and shaking hands. He got into his Daimler and with a final "*Heil Hitler!*" was driven out of the war under British escort.

"Where do you think they'll take him?" Declan asked Ernie.

"I hear he's headed to a camp in Algiers. Ike has already let it be known that he has no intention of meeting with him. Or with any other German general, for that matter."

***

A little after ten o'clock on the morning of the following day, May 13, Prime Minister Winston Churchill was in the bathtub, reading his correspondence and dictating responses to one of his private secretaries who was sitting on the loo, lid closed. A military aide knocked on the door. "Come!"

The man entered, eyes averted, and handed Churchill a sheet of paper. "Sorry to disturb, Sir. This just arrived. Thought you would want to see it right away." He handed the paper over, took a quick pitying look at the young lady sitting on the toilet and left.

Churchill glanced at the message, then read it again, his cigar clenched in his teeth. He read it a third time, banged his hand on the side of the tub and let out a mighty "Huzzah!" Then he bowed his head, and, lips moving silently, prayed. When he was finished, he handed the note to his secretary and said, "Take this down: To the President of the United States: "My dear Mr. President, I am forwarding to you this message which just this minute has arrived from General Alexander with great joy in my heart and my deepest gratitude to all who have made this day possible. Victory is ours! (From Alexander): *Sir: it is my duty to report that the Tunisian campaign is over. All enemy resistance has ceased. We are masters of the North African shores.* Sign it: Your humble ally, Winston."

"Oh…and, dear girl, would you mind terribly fetching me another glass of champagne? Pour one for yourself, too. This deserves a celebration!"

CHAPTER FIFTY FIVE

Parade

By eight o'clock on the morning of Thursday, May 23, it was already steaming hot. There was not a breath of moving air. But neither the African sun nor the crushing humidity seemed to bother the thousands of people who poured into Tunis, lining the Avenue Maréchal Gallieni and the Avenue Jules Ferry to watch the Allied victory parade that would celebrate the end of the Tunisia campaign and the war in Africa.

The French tricolor hung from every window and rooftop along the parade route. Flowers fell like rain. Over and over again, the stirring chorus of *La Marseilles* resounded from on high while Arab men on the street banged *darbukas* and the women joyfully danced and ululated. It would be a day to remember forever.

But not for everyone; Leila could feel the conflict going on within her father. Foreign armies had come and gone for centuries in Tunisia, and she imagined he was happy enough to know the Germans, British, and Americans forces would be departing soon. But the French; they would be staying. French General Alphonse Juin would be given the honor of leading the victory parade, an intentionally ominous message to any nationalists in the crowd who might harbor hope for an independent Tunisia. The arrest and exile of Moncef Bey had been the first salvo in this new phase of the colonial war, and Si Kamel had told Leila that Henri Giraud—the presumptive head of the new Free French colonial government—would be watching him and their family closely for any sign of dissent. That the French had already installed Lamine Bey as the titular head of the royal Tunisian family did not bode well for the nationalist movement. Most nationalists considered Lamine Bey a usurper and a French toady, certainly not someone capable of leading their country to post-war independence.

Nor would it be a day to remember for the Fabron family. They had sold off their vineyards in Medjerda and their home in La Marsa, desperate to avoid the conflict that had engulfed them. But in the process, they had earned a reputation as collaborationists with the defeated Nazi administration. Their days in Tunisia were numbered; they would be shunned by their neighbors and highly suspect by the newly installed Free French regime. Paul and his father knew their future lay elsewhere, most likely in another French colony—Greater Syria or perhaps Indo China. They were already making plans to leave Tunisia as soon as it were possible, but for now, the family's destination, along with its future, was a mystery.

Even Ali Abbas, waiting for the parade to start, had mixed emotions that morning. The end of the fighting would surely bring some relief to the sick or wounded patients he tended at the mosque, but it might also spell the end of his days with Leila. She had been tireless and caring, and he had come to admire her courage and her commitment to the sick and the poor. She came from another world, but she crossed over easily into his world, and the thought that he might not stand close to her again filled him with deep sadness.

Ernie Pyle had hopped a military flight to Casablanca; he wanted to be the first to file about the invasion of Sicily that was being planned there. Lang was close to the reviewing stand, busy shooting photographs of Ike and the other bigwigs who had arrived in Tunis last night to review the parade. Punch and Declan were sitting at a crowded café near the parade route. They each had a *café au lait* and were sharing a plate of honey almond samsas sprinkled with rose water. The parade wasn't scheduled to begin for another hour, and there was just enough shade under the café's awning to keep them from roasting as the sun climbed higher in the sky. Punch had something on his mind.

"I'm leaving," he said. Declan waited; there was no use in hurrying Punch who was taking a long sip of his coffee. "There's an opening in Budapest. Bureau chief. I'm going to take it."

Declan waited to see if there was something else, but apparently there wasn't. "Congratulations. It will be cooler there."

Punch shrugged his shoulders. "Maybe. But it will be more interesting. The war's finished here but a new war is just beginning there. A different war. East versus West. Hungary will be one of the new front lines. Want another?" He held out the plate of samsas to Declan. "Do you want to take over here?"

Declan looked at the plate of samsas; said, "No thanks. *Yizzi.* Enough."

"More for me." Punch surveyed the platter, took another.

"No; I mean the job here. The war's over here. It'll be all politics here now, independence. That's not likely to happen quickly. I guess I got used to more action."

Now it was Punch's turn to wait.

"I talked to Lang about it; Ernie, too. The AP needs someone in Palestine. I accepted yesterday."

Punch ate another samsa. "Palestine. You think you'll see more action in Palestine?"

Declan leaned forward. "We're riding the tiger there. The Zionists want a Jewish state; the Arabs want their own country. The Mandate is finished; everyone is bracing for trouble. Britain is in the middle, enemies on both sides. It's a bloody mess in the making. Just what I want. I know that now."

Punch looked away, then back at Declan. Nodded. "I get it, but be careful what you wish for. When are you going?"

Declan picked up the last samsa and popped it in his mouth. "As soon as I can get out of here. They want me in Haifa by the end of next month."

***

Victory in Africa
Special to The Guardian by War Correspondent Declan Shaw. Tunis, May 24, 1943.

It was just a little more that a week ago that the last deadly shots of the North African campaign were fired. Today, the Allies celebrated their hard-won victory over the combined forces of Germany and Italy, the first giant step in the long march to liberate Europe, with a magnificent victory parade.

The torrid African sun beat down on the reviewing stand but General Eisenhower, Supreme Allied Commander, looked relaxed and confident in creased riding breeches, polished knee boots, and a swagger stick tucked under his right arm. To his right, General Henri Giraud, commander of the Free French forces, stood ready to receive the salutes of the brave men—British, American, and Free French—who had fought so gallantly over the last seven months to free North Africa from Axis control.

Shortly before noon, with the scorching sun almost at its apogee, the massed pipes and drums of the Highland regiments marched to the reviewing stand and wheeled right. Grenadier Guards in tall bearskin bonnets took up their positions, a few wilting, then one or two fainting from the intense heat. Then precisely at noon, the brass band of the French Foreign Legion, struck up "La Marseilles" while General Alphonse Juin and his Free French troops in capes and kèpis strutted past the reviewing stand, a not-so-subtle reminder to any Tunisian nationalists who might be watching that Tunisia was—and still will be—a French colony.

The Free French and their allies—Moroccans, Algerians, and Senegalese troops—were followed by the American infantrymen who had displayed such valor in the fight for Hill 609. Dressed in drab olive-green wool and sweating profusely, they delighted in the crowd's joyful cheers of "Vive l'Amerique" as they passed the reviewing stand in ragged step under a disapproving glare from General George Patton, who, along with General Omar Bradley and a few other minor French and British dignitaries, had been relegated to an unshaded bleacher off to the right of the main reviewing stand.

And then, resplendent in new uniforms—khaki shorts and knee socks, polished brass buttons and buckles—came His Majesty's forces from every corner of the Commonwealth. Canadians, Aussies, South Africans, Indians, Maori, Sikhs, and Gurkhas marched proudly, hobnail boots ringing on the pavement, arms swinging high in unison, eyes snapping right as they took the salutes of the assembled Generals while British Spitfires and great American Flying Fortresses streaked overhead, wings wagging proudly.

The parade lasted more than two hours. When it finally ended and the last notes of martial music faded away, we were left to contemplate *the immense cost of this victory. The dead and wounded—the ghosts of the parade—will be remembered for their courage, heroism, and devotion to duty. While it may be true that to the victors belong the spoils, war is never as glorious as a parade would have us believe. War is a cruel and indifferent beast, and no amount of spit and polish or marching in review or military bands or flying flags can bring back the dead or heal the wounded. More than seventy thousand young men are now gone forever. They march silently by in our memories; they have earned their eternal rest.*

***

It was late in the evening, the air close and still as a tomb. There was a clutter of beer bottles and an ashtray full of cigarette ends lying on the table in front of Punch, Lang, and Declan as they talked quietly, rehashing the events of the day while they watched heat lightening illuminate the clouds that hung over the hills to the west of the city.

Lang spoke quietly: "Shakespeare; the Scottish play. Act one, scene one: In a desert place. '*When shall we three meet again/ in thunder, lightening, or in rain?*"

Declan, with a faint laugh: "*When the hurlyburly's done/ When the battle's lost and won.*

Punch: "*Fair is foul and foul is fair.* Aren't we the literate ones!" He paused. "I'll miss this place."

Declan: "Me, too. Pity me. In a few months, I'll be sitting next to Bismuth, drinking a coffee, watching the strumpets parading along the strand in Tel Aviv. What about you, Will?"

"We'll be deep into Act Two by then. Imagine I'll be somewhere in Sicily drinking chianti with Ernie. He wouldn't miss this next bit for all the beer in Milwaukee. This," Lang waved his hand over the city, "was only preamble to what's coming next in Italy, maybe even to an invasion of France someday. But this will be nothing compared to what's coming in Europe. That's their homeland. The fighting will be fiercer, much more deadly. Difficult terrain. It'll make North Africa look like child's play, nothing more than a training maneuver."

There was a heartbeat of silence, then Declan asked, "What do you think we learned here?"

"How to fight. How to take a punch and get back up. How to make an amphibious assault; how to attack with massed armor; how to use terrain. How to hate. How to kill. Maybe that's the biggest lesson of all. Before this place, this war was just theory and planning, but now we know; now we really know. It takes hate—death and hate—to win a war."

There was another heartbeat of silence, then Lang gave a soft little laugh.

Declan looked at him. "What's so funny?"

"After we're gone, that's what it'll be like here." Lang pointed to the sky. "There will be some thunder and lightening, but no rain—no independence—for quite a while. France is already digging back in. But someday...someday, it will rain here. It's inevitable. Empires died after the Great War: the Ottomans, the Austro-Hungarians, Czarist Russia. The colonial system will be the next to go. It's already started. Here in Africa, Asia; a hundred new countries, all struggling to get by, to feed their people, educate their children, grow their wealth."

Punch, animated: "And that's when the real battle will begin. All those new nations; everybody will have to choose, to line up with an ideology. East or West; Marxist or capitalist. Mark my words: that will be the next bloody great conflict, and it will swallow us all up like the bloody giant whale that swallowed Jonah."

Cigarette smoke and beer and silent thoughts, while to the west, great flashes of lightning continued to gild the darkening sky.

POSTLUDE

Gide

A few weeks later, on a softer summer evening, André Gide got up from his writing desk, stretched his tired back, and leaned out a window that opened out onto the sea that shimmered below the cliff. Across the Bay of Tunis, the twin peaks of *Bou Kornine* were lit by the setting sun. He was pleased that here, in the charming little town of Sidi Bou Said, life was finally returning to normal. He could hear men's laughter and the slap of cards coming from the terrace of the Café des Nattes. He could smell the oil frying in the great pan of the old man who sold powder-sugar *bombolone* from a small cubicle on the far side of the square.

The girl was there. He was sure it was the same one who had inhabited his dreams for months: the golden Botticelli curls; the café au lait skin, the flashing green eyes. But now she was with a young Tunisian man, dressed in a summer white jellaba, a spring of jasmine behind one ear. Something about them spoke of contentment, a sentiment Gide had almost dismissed a few months ago. But now, maybe contentment— even outright happiness—was possible again. The war had moved on. In its wake, there was sorrow, bitterness, and still some residue of fear, but there was also something else: hope. Maybe, as he watched, there was even love, although love was never on public display here. But it was there, hovering, flitting through the air like the bats that came out at dusk to feed on insects.

Gide understood restraint. He had been raised in a puritanical tradition but he was not immune to the sensuous culture that lay just below the surface of Tunisia's Muslim tradition. Perhaps this was why he had chosen to ride out the storm of war here. Let Europeans kill each other; here, in the aftermath of battle, there was an almost child-like innocence and sense of wonder. He was sure there would still be battles to come—he was an anti-colonialist to the core—but tonight, all that seemed as far away as the moon that was rising over the peaks of the mountain across the bay. Maybe someday, when the war in Europe was finally over, he would return to France, but tonight, this place was his home, these people were his people. They were far from perfect, they struggled to exist between two conflicting cultures, but nevertheless, there was a serenity here that suited his soul. Perhaps it was the memory of happiness that had settled over this place; he could see it in the sugar that coated the beautiful girl's lips and in the eyes of the young man who strolled beside her, longing to touch her, but daring not.

A long-lost thought seeped into his mind: the color of truth is grey.

HISTORICAL NOTES

There are 2,841 American soldiers lying in eternal repose at the American military cemetery in Carthage. Many of them are known only to God. At a nearby war memorial, the sun sets on the names of more than 2,903 Commonwealth soldiers—British, Canadian, New Zealanders, Australian, South African, Indian, and Nepalese. At a cemetery in Bordj Cedria, about twenty miles south of Tunis, 8,562 German soldiers are memorialized. There are 1,241 Italian graves at the war cemetery in Tripoli, Libya. The Free French Forces suffered 2,156 casualties. The number of men wounded, missing in action exceeds 60,000 and over 240,000 prisoners of war were taken, Allied and Axis. No one really knows how many civilians died in the fighting in Tunisia. While there may be ways or measures to calculate the cost of war, its impact on human lives is not one of them.

All the historical characters who appear in my story survived the Tunisia campaign. Now, all are gone, their names engraved in history books. Some of their stories are familiar, others less so.

Dwight D. Eisenhower, Supreme Commander of the Allied Forces in North Africa, went on to military and political greatness. General of the Army, he was in command of Operation Overlord, the invasion of Europe at Normandy, and oversaw the ultimate defeat of Nazi Germany. In 1953, he became the 34th President of the United States and served for eight years. He died on March 28, 1969 and is buried at the Eisenhower Presidential Library in Abilene, Kansas.

Field Marshall The Right Honorable Sir Harold Alexander, The Earl Alexander of Tunis, fought with great distinction in the Italian campaign and was named Supreme Allied Commander Mediterranean. After the war, in 1946, King George VI appointed him Governor General of Canada where he was a popular and enthusiastic proponent of the Canadian Wilderness. In 1952, he returned to London as Prime Minister Churchill's Minister of Defense. He died in 1969.

General George S. Patton's career has become the stuff of Hollywood legend. Following the Tunisia campaign, he commanded the U.S. Seventh Army in the Mediterranean theater (where he was temporarily relieved of command for slapping two shell-shocked soldiers) and the U.S. Third Army in France and Germany after the Normandy invasion. Following the war, Patton served as military governor of Bavaria in occupied Germany but was relieved for making overly aggressive comments about the Soviet Union and for trivializing thyme denazification of Germany. He was severely injured in an automobile accident in Germany and died twelve days later on December 21, 1945. His last words were, "This is a hell of a way to die." In accordance with his wishes, he was buried at the Luxembourg Military Cemetery to be near his men.

Field Marshall Bernard Law Montgomery, 1st Viscount Montgomery of Alamein, was given command of all Allied ground forces in the Battle of Normandy following the D-Day invasion of France. Given temporary command of the U.S. First and Ninth Armies, he was instrumental in defeating the German army at the Battle of the Bulge in 1944. After the war, he became Commander-in-Chief of the British Army of the Rhine and then Chief of the Imperial General Staff. In 1951, he became Deputy Supreme Allied Commander Europe. Monty was a teetotaler and a vegetarian and was never one to be overly tactful or diplomatic. He died in 1976.

Following his departure from Tunisia in Match, 1943, Field Marshall Erwin Marshall, the Desert Fox, spent a day in Greece in anticipation of a British invasion there before being recalled to Italy upon the overthrow of Mussolini. In November, Rommel became Inspector General of Western Defenses; he had a staff and could make suggestions, but he did not command a single soldier. In July of 1944, Rommel was seriously injured when a British fighter pilot strafed his car in France. By then, he was implicated in a plot to overthrow Hitler—a charge Rommel vehemently denied. However, in November, Rommel agreed to commit suicide in exchange for military honors at his funeral and his family's receipt of his full pension. He died after taking cyanide capsules and was given a state funeral. The official cause of death only referred to the wounds he suffered when his car was strafed.

General Albert Kesselring, Generalfeldmarschall of the Luftwaffe, fought in Italy until he was injured in an accident in October 1944. He recovered in time to lead German forces on the Western Front in the final months of the war. Although respected by his Allied opponents, he was convicted of war crimes and sentenced to death for ordering the massacre of 335 Italian civilians and for inciting his troops to kill civilians in reprisals for supporting the Italian resistance movement. The sentence was later commuted to life imprisonment. He died in a West German sanitarium in 1960.

General Hans-Jürgen von Arnim, commander of the 5th Panzer Army and Rommel's eventual replacement as Commander of the Afrika Korps, surrendered to British forces in Tunisia in May, 1943. He was interned at Camp Clinton in Mississippi and released in July 1947. He died in West Germany in 1962.

General Omar Bradley, who replaced General Patton as Commander of Second Corps, went on to win four stars in World War II. Overshadowed by his more colorful counterpart General Patton, Bradley was known as "the honest mechanic" for his understated competence. After the war, he became the first Chairman of the Joint Chiefs of Staff and was largely responsible for military policy during the Korean War. He received a fifth star and attended Ronald Regan's first inaugural in a wheelchair. He died a few months later at the age of 88, the last of the army's five-star generals.

After his service in the Tunisia Campaign, Brigadier General Theodore Roosevelt, Jr., although nearly crippled with arthritis and plagued with arrhythmia, led the first wave of troops ashore at Utah Beach during the Normandy invasion. He died of a heart attack a month later in France. For his heroism, he was recommended for the Distinguished Service Cross, but that recommendation was upgraded and Roosevelt posthumously received the Congressional Medal of Honor. Generals Patton and Bradley were among the pallbearers at his funeral.

Lieutenant-General Bernard Freyberg, raised to 1st Baron Freyberg, whom Churchill called "The Salamander" because of his regenerative powers, won the Victoria Cross and became the seventh Governor-General of New Zealand. He died in 1963 when one of his many old war wounds ruptured.

Major General Orlando "Pinky" Ward was relieved of command of the First Armored Division by General Patton after the fight at Maknassay. He returned to the United States to command the army's Tank Destroyer School. He returned to Europe in February of 1945 and was present at the capture of the city of Munich. He died in 1972 at his home in Denver, Colorado.

Following his defeat at Kasserine Pass, Lieutenant General Lloyd Fredendall returned to the United States. Never formally reprimanded by Eisenhower, he spent the rest of the war in training assignments. Described by one historian as "a man of bombast and bravado" and by another as "one of the most inept senior officers to hold a high command during World War II," Fredendall retired from the army in March 1946. He died in California in 1963 and is buried at the Fort Rosecrans National Cemetery.

William John Lang, Jr. was born in Chicago. Before heading off to North Africa, he was based in Washington and covered the Presidential campaigns of 1936 and 1940 for Time-Life. During that time, he dated a former classmate named Kay Meyer, later to become Katherine Graham, owner of The Washington Post and Newsweek magazine. After Tunisia, Lang went on to cover Patton's campaign in Italy and was nearly killed in the explosion of the post office in Naples. After D-Day, he filed reports from Europe and covered the Battle of the Bulge. He died of a heart attack on a family skiing trip to Austria in 1968.

Bill Mauldin won two Pulitzer Prizes for his cartoon work. He died in 2003 from complications of Alzheimer's Disease and a bathtub scalding. He is buried in Arlington National Cemetery. In 2010, the Post Office honored with a stamp depicting him with his two most popular dogface heroes, Willie and Joe.

Ernie Pyle was an Indiana farm boy before becoming the most popular war correspondent of World War II. He loved aviation. In 1940, Scripps-Howard sent him to London to report on the Blitz and the Battle of Britain. He covered the war in North Africa, Italy, and at Normandy Beach. He won the Pulitzer Prize for journalism in 1944 but in September of that year, he returned to the United States to recuperate from combat stress, but a few months later, he was off to the Pacific theater to cover the war there. He was killed by a machine gun bullet in April, 1945 on the island of Ie Shima near Okinawa. He was buried wearing his helmet and posthumously awarded a Purple Heart, a rare honor for a civilian.

Habib Bourguiba continued to lead the fight for Tunisia's independence. After the war, he went to live in Egypt but he found the Arab world more inclined to become involved in events taking place in Palestine rather than to support independence movements for the French colonies in North Africa. Bourguiba continued the struggle and In 1956, he became Prime Minister of a newly independent Tunisia; a year later, when he declared Tunisia a republic, he became its first President. He was eventually named President for Life but in 1987, but personal health problems coupled with ongoing financial and economic crises and concerns about human rights violations brought about a bloodless coup led by Prime Minister Zine El-Abidine Ben Ali. Bourguiba was placed under house arrest at his home in Monastir where he lived until he died in 2000. He is interred in a mausoleum on the grounds of his home. The cry *Yahia Bourguiba!*—Long Live Bourguiba!—still echos in parts of Tunisia to this day.

Thank You

Marian Haley Bell and John Coyne, lynchpins of Peace Corps Writers and keepers of the flame.

Jane DeHart Albritton who read an early draft and helped me steer a better course.

Christian Landskroenner, *mon vrai ami* and a close reader *extraordinaire*.

And, finally, to my wife Kat Conley who encourages and supports me.

www.ingramcontent.com/pod-product-compliance
Lightning Source LLC
Chambersburg PA
CBHW030650020726
47493CB00006B/1961